TAKE ME WITH YOU NEXT TIME

TAKE ME WITH YOU NEXT TIME

Stories

Janis Hubschman

Betty

SANTA ROSA, CALIFORNIA

Edited by Peg Alford Pursell
Designed by Mike Corrao
Cover Design by Mike Corrao

Library of Congress Control Number: 2024932148
Take me with you next time / Janis Hubschman.
ISBN 979-8-9877197-3-2 (pbk) | 979-8-9877197-4-9 (epub)

Published by Betty
WTAW Press
PO Box 2825
Santa Rosa, CA 95405

Betty is an imprint of WTAW Press, a not-for-profit literary press.

Lines from "Kathe Kollwitz," by Muriel Rukeyser. Reprinted by the permission of International Creative Management as agent for the author. Copyright © 2005 by Muriel Rukeyser with permission of John Ingold.

For Michael, Caroline, and Sarah

CONTENTS

ALAMO

THE BRIDAL SHOWER GUESTS were due to arrive in ten minutes, but Nina was still assembling the cardboard wishing well, forcing unwilling tab A into too small slot B. Her husband had been texting from his weeklong meditation retreat up in Woodstock. She'd encouraged him to go, but the word *retreat* held new significance now. No word for five days and then Remo texted *Sick of engineering. Let's buy B & B @ NJ shore.* Phones were forbidden in the Zendo, but he'd found a way to shoot this message to her. She imagined her lean, newly shorn husband hiding under a yoga mat in a Zen garden. *We'll talk when u r home 2 morrow,* she'd texted back. Whatever he was going through, she hoped it would pass like a fever.

She'd made the trip to Party City only a few hours ago. Clock ticking, she'd been forced to buy whatever the young bearded salesman deemed essential. When she wondered about the symbolism of the wishing well and the pink parasol, the clerk appeared as flustered as one of her clueless students. "Good luck and protection?" he tried. "I'll buy that," she said, and tossed them into her cart.

She gave up on the wishing well now and went to the kitchen. From the refrigerator, she pulled out the finger sandwiches, deviled eggs, and pâtés the local caterer HausFrau delivered earlier. She removed the cellophane from the platters and arranged them on the center island along with her old wedding loot. The Wedgwood cuckoo tea plates, the Waterford double old-fashioned glasses, and the Reed & Barton silver had charmed her a quarter of a century ago and continued to entice her with the promise of the perfect dinner party.

All her parties ended the same way, with her guests, mostly Remo's friends—he'd never left his hometown—staggering out of their house an hour or two past their longed-for departure. At least one of them, usually Dunkin' Donuts cop Dick Sharkey, would need to stay the night. She'd grumble, but Remo, loyal friend, would mount his standard defense: any one of his friends would come to her rescue at three a.m. His theory would never be tested. They were the last people she'd call.

This afternoon's guests, four middle-aged college composition teachers like herself, were bringing the buttercream sheet cake and the bride-to-be. Lee-Anna Hill, a thirty-two-year-old recent Georgia transplant, knew what she was walking into. All agreed: they were done with surprises.

The phone rang. Nina checked the caller ID, then let the machine pick up.

"Listen, whoever has my goddamned car has to bring it back today, or I'm taking action. Do you hear me?" Her mother-in-law had the kind of accent you didn't hear anymore except on TV shows about New Jersey mobsters. Roberta paused, as though waiting for a response. "I'll go after you sons of bitches. I don't know what I did to deserve such horrible sons."

Remo, the youngest of the three sons, had driven off with her car last week, after the home health aide had taken her to the doctor's. For months, Roberta had refused to comply with the State of New Jersey's verdict that she was unfit to drive. Remo had told his mother about the carjacking over the phone, using the same patient tone he'd use with Nina when he tried to jolly her out of a dark mood. At the time, Roberta seemed to accept the situation with uncharacteristic grace. Twenty-four hours later, the calls started, coming twenty, thirty times a day.

The bell rang. Nina opened the door to Joy, holding an enormous boxed sheet cake. "They're still in the car," Joy said. "Lee-Anna's making them listen to her wedding song. I got to put this thing down. It weighs a ton." She brushed past Nina and headed for the kitchen.

Nina had met Joy seven years ago at Ramapo College's orientation meeting for new hires. They were in the same group of jittery older women returning to teaching after a long hiatus. Some, like Nina, had stayed home with children—her Brooke had entered high school that year. Joy, childless by choice, had left an advertising copywriter's job. Later, Nina would learn she'd had a mini nervous breakdown at a client meeting. That day in the seminar room, Joy's corny jokes had kept the anxious teachers laughing. "I knew a cross-eyed teacher once," she said. *Oh?* Everyone smiled uneasily. "She couldn't control her pupils." Impeccable Borscht-Belt timing.

Nina knew all about it. Her own family deployed puns and one-liners like antimissile lasers to defuse tense situations and deflect intimacy. It had taken time to break through this defense, but she and Joy had become good friends.

Though Nina was at least a half-foot taller than Joy, they otherwise looked similar with dark cropped hair and fashionable chunky black-framed glasses. A few colleagues called them Frick and Frack after the two Swiss comedian skaters who came to the U.S. in the thirties. Neither skated, but they shared a love of documentaries, particularly ones featuring underdogs overcoming oppressive systems. Once they were asked to leave a Manhattan theater after Joy climbed up on her chair to cheer on a female union worker.

"You look frazzled," Joy said after dropping the cake on the table. "Are you sorry you're doing this?"

"I'm overwhelmed." Her eyes filled. She was stoical until anyone showed her the least bit of empathy.

"Whoa, get a grip on yourself, little lady," Joy said. She got busy deconstructing the cake box, flattening it out on the table, so she could slide the cake out. "It'll be over in a few hours." She avoided Nina's eyes as she worked. "Then we'll have a good laugh."

"It's not the party. Remo's meditating up in Woodstock, and his mother—"

"*Meditating?*" Joy made a face of disbelief.

"Doctor's recommendation. He's got high blood pressure. You wouldn't recognize him. He's lost fifteen pounds. He's got this weird buzz cut. It's because of his mother—" The phone rang. "There she is again."

Roberta's voice blasted into the kitchen. "If I don't get my goddamned car back in the next hour, I'm walking over there and taking it. I don't need anyone's permission. You won't get away with this. I'm pressing charges."

"Holy moly. Is she really coming?" Joy said. "How far is it?"

"A little over a mile, but that won't stop her. Nothing does. She's not supposed to drive, but we saw her on the road again a couple of weeks ago. She rolled through a stop sign and almost hit us! I made Remo tail her all the way to Harrison Drugs, her home away from home."

They'd pulled to the curb and waited for her to come out of the drugstore. Earlier, on that same day, Roberta had shown up in Remo's office, limping, her arm in a sling, asking if he had any "extra" money. "That's where your fifty went," Nina said when his mother came bounding, sling-less, out of the drugstore, swinging her little white bag. Roberta loved her drugs, oxycontin in particular. "My mother's a con woman," Remo said with wounded incredulity. He tended to believe in the best version of the people he loved.

The phone rang again. "How are you not losing your mind?" Joy said.

"Who says I haven't?"

Charlotte came into the kitchen, dragging a black leaf bag. Nina caught Joy's eye and sent her a warning: *we'll talk later*.

"Hello, ladies. Isn't this fun?" Charlotte said. Tall and thin with a blond bob, Charlotte had two faces. In repose, she appeared sour and disapproving. Smiling, she was angelic. "Where's the wishing well?"

Nina steered Charlotte toward the family room, an extension of the kitchen, leaving Joy hovering over the answering machine. Before Nina could tell her not to, Charlotte dumped the leaf bag's contents into the listing well. Filled with presents, the well stood erect. Charlotte had a similar effect on people. She inspired the right balance of love and fear in her students. In an emergency, Nina would not hesitate to call her.

Lee-Anna, the striking guest of honor, came into the kitchen, unwrapping a jewel-toned cashmere shawl. Her smile showed off deep dimples. "Y'all didn't have to go through so much trouble for me."

"Of course we did," Nina said. "Anyway, we needed a party. Midterm blues."

"Oh, lordy, I know what you mean," Lee-Anna said. "Every semester I think my syllabus is failsafe, with every contingency covered, but those kids are like viruses, changing and adapting, finding new ways to weasel out of assignments."

"The forgotten email attachment," Joy said, dryly, turning away from the ringing phone. "Hey prof, here's my paper on the due date. No attachment. No reply to my emails asking where it is."

"Technology's a game changer," Nina said.

"No, honey," Lee-Anna said. "The game has always been rigged against us. We should just give up."

Over Lee-Anna's shoulder, she saw Rona and Cindy waiting to greet her. They were partners, together for ten years. No one knew what Rona, a fit, intense forty-year-old, was doing with overweight Cindy who was at least a decade older and a rabid gossip.

"Your home is lovely," Rona said. "Georgian Colonial?"

"More like Remo Colonial," she said, then seeing Rona's frown, added, "My husband, Remo, designed it."

"He's an architect?"

"Civil engineer, actually." Her face heated up as though she were caught in a lie. If he had his way, they'd be changing soiled B & B bed sheets in Ocean Grove next summer.

"I don't want to alarm you," Cindy said. Her lazy eye made it hard to tell where she was looking, so Nina focused on her mouth, her rubbery lips and white veneered teeth. "Some lady's screaming on your answering machine."

Nina snatched up the cordless phone and whisked it into the garage. "Who do you think you're threatening?" she said. "Mister Softy isn't here. You want your car? You'll have to deal with *me*. Come and get it, you witch. I'll be waiting." She listened for a moment to Roberta's heavy breathing before hanging up.

In the kitchen, she muted the machine, feeling angry enough to smash the phone against the wall. She smiled at her guests. That did the trick: she began to feel calmer.

Seeing each other outside the college had made everyone giddy, it seemed. The world expanded a little. Maybe Remo's world had expanded, too, up in Woodstock.

Poor Mister Softy. Even the astronauts returned to earth eventually, and Remo would return to her. "I was happy," he'd told her a few weeks ago, "until you pointed out how miserable my life is." She'd merely stated the obvious: his father had abandoned him to an abusive mother, his brothers were always sponging money off him, his friends were fuckups who never reciprocated their hospitality, and his engineering business was killing him.

"Okay, my life sucks," he'd said. "What can I do about it?"

"Sell the house and your business and hit the road," she'd told him. "See the country. The Grand Canyon. Yosemite. The Alamo. Remember the Alamo?" It was a joke. She never thought he'd take her up on it. He was the patient martyr who managed his mother and made sure the mortgage and Brooke's college tuition were paid on time.

"Are we playing games?" Charlotte sidled up to Nina.

"Games?"

"Get everyone together," Charlotte said, with a pitying smile. "I'll do the rest."

Nina tried to usher the women into the family room, but they all wanted cake. After cake, Rona insisted on gathering and rinsing the plates, and Joy loaded them into the dishwasher. Cindy had found the three-year-old bottle of Veuve Clicquot Nina had been saving at the back of her refrigerator for a special occasion that had never arrived.

At last, Charlotte herded the women into the family room, nipping at their heels. Everyone took seats. Joy settled on the couch beside Nina. "The phone stopped ringing," Joy said. "All's quiet on the demented front."

"I gave the witch a piece of my mind," she said. "Now I want it back." Her voice rang out in the hushed room. She glanced around. But everyone was focused on Charlotte who stood next to the wishing well, twirling the opened parasol.

"Let's play a game, ladies," Charlotte said.

Nina felt dazed. The twirling parasol was hypnotic.

"Since no one has met the lucky groom," Charlotte said, "we can't play wedding jeopardy, my favorite, but I've got another game I think you'll like. You'll need your purses." No one moved. "Run and get your purses, ladies."

The women rose and headed for the kitchen. Nina snatched up her leather hobo bag from the desk in the corner, uncovering the throbbing red light on the answering machine. She regretted losing her temper with Roberta. How did Remo manage it? His boundless patience seemed like a virtue now. On her way back to the family room, she jostled Cindy, who was leaving the table with another slab of cake. Nina bent to pick up the smashed cake from the floor, then went to the sink for the sponge. There, the bride-to-be had opened her mouth under the running faucet.

Lee-Anna straightened, wiping her lips. "Xanax," she said. "Ajay's mother's driving me nuts. She hates me. I can't do anything right."

Run, she wanted to say. *Get away while you still can.* "Don't make the same mistake I made," she said. "Stand up to your mother-in-law from the start. Set the ground rules."

"I'm terrified of her. She's scary. Where are my manners? Would you like one?" Lee-Anna held out the pill vial.

Nina had never taken Xanax before, but Remo seemed more like himself after he did. "Yeah, sure, what the hell, give me one."

Lee-Anna tipped out two pills into Nina's open palm. "Oops," she said. "Take them both. Think I'll have another one, too."

"Lip gloss!" Charlotte called out, and the women dug inside their purses like terriers. Nina's head grew heavier the longer she stared into the dark interior of her hobo bag. If only she could crawl inside and lie down next to her wallet for a nap. What was she looking for? She never wore lip gloss or any other kind of makeup. It made her face feel dirty. "Put on a little blush; wear some lipstick," her mother and sister were always telling her. The makeup police, Remo called them.

"Got it! Got it!" Cindy waved something. "I win!"

Charlotte recorded her point in a notepad. For all they knew it could have been a bottle cap she'd waved. No one bothered to check. I don't care, Nina told herself. Stupid game. No prizes.

"All righty. On to the next item." Charlotte paused. "Rona? Where's *your* purse?"

"Don't have one," Rona said. "If purses are such a great idea, why don't men carry them?"

"Damn straight," Nina said, wiping her mouth with her sleeve. She'd lost control of her saliva. "Why *don't* they carry 'em? Is it because it's a stand-in for the vagina?"

Everyone laughed, except Charlotte. "I don't know about you, Nina," Charlotte said, suppressing a smile. "But I don't keep lip gloss in *my* vagina."

The room fell silent. Did their Charlotte make a naughty joke?

"It *is* handy for carrying a couple of kilos of heroin," Joy said. "Or so I'm told." Her pocketbook was a canvas PBS tote, a new one every year.

"I lost a mascara wand up there once," Cindy said. "*Don't ask.*"

Rona doubled over, appeared to be choking. Joy jumped up, crossed the room, and slapped her once, hard, on the back. Rona sat up and glared at her.

"I carried a baby in there once," Nina said. How would she tell Brooke they wouldn't have the money for her last year of college, because her father bought a B & B at the beach?

"The Things They Carried in Their Vaginas," Joy said. "Great story. Loved the climax."

Hysterical laughter erupted. *Hysteric.* From the Greek, hysterikos: suffering in the womb. A century ago, they'd all be locked up in a room with yellow wallpaper. Nina imagined her mother-in-law there now, scratching at the walls.

"Can we get back to our game?" Charlotte rapped the coffee table with the closed parasol. We are looking for things in *our purses*."

Joy started back to the couch but froze. "Um, a cop?"

"Joke's over," Rona said, sharply. "Let Charlotte get on with the game."

But Joy didn't seem to hear. Nina followed her gaze to the kitchen, where a policeman stood with his legs planted widely, arms crossed over his chest. A voice squawked from the radio on his hip. He looked at them as though waiting for instructions.

"Y'all are too much!" Lee-Anna said, slapping her knees. "*Really?* I mean, *really?*" She climbed unsteadily to her feet as the officer came forward into the room.

Joy shot Nina a questioning look. Nina shrugged.

"Nice of you to come to my party, Officer," Lee-Anna said. "As the bride-to-be, I'd like to welcome—*what?*" She took a step back as though affronted. Sarah Bernhardt had nothing on her. "You don't believe me? I'm the bride. Want to see my hope chest?"

Before he could answer, Lee-Anna yanked off her sweater and unhooked her red lace bra. "Here's my chest! *Hope* you like it!" She scooped up her large breasts and presented them like prize piglets to the stunned cop.

Nina recognized that dumb open-mouthed stare now. It was Dick Sharkey. She rarely saw Remo's friend in uniform. Lee-Anna wriggled around him, shaking her breasts, as Cindy cheered her on. How anyone could mistake the fifty-four-year-old cop for a stripper was beyond Nina. Some women might go for that dumb lumberjack type, but not too many, if you listened to Sharkey. Twice divorced, he hadn't gotten laid in over a year.

Nina needed to warn Lee-Anna, but when she tried to stand, her knees buckled, and she fell back onto the couch. *C'mere*, she gestured to Joy.

Joy came over and sat on the arm of the couch. "She on something?" Joy said, glancing at Lee-Anna.

"It's—" she squeezed her eyes shut. "Can't say it. Took sumpin'. It's Dick Shark—"

"Dick Shark? Oh, that's good," Joy said. "Where'd you find him?"

"No, he's real." Nina turned for help to Cindy who was seated on her other side. But Cindy was fumbling with her phone. She selected a bluesy tune from her playlist, top volume, set the phone on the coffee table, and joined Lee-Anna. Sharkey grinned down at the gyrating ladies like he'd hit the Atlantic City jackpot.

"If Cindy takes her shirt off, I'm leaving," Joy said.

Charlotte, grim-faced, held Lee-Anna's sweater out to her. Lee-Anna pulled it on, looking chastened.

Sharkey pouted. He held up a finger. Lee-Anna and Cindy froze, watching him. He removed his hat and tossed it on the kitchen table.

"Take it all off, Mr. Policeman!" Lee-Anna clapped her hands.

Sharkey unbuckled his belt. It looked heavy, Nina thought, weighed down with the gun, tommy stick, radio, and flashlight. Cindy made a grab for it. He gracefully swung the belt out of her reach and set it on the table next to his hat. His load lightened, he joined the women in dance, swiveling his hips and punching the air with beefy fists.

"This is why I drink," Rona said, draining her champagne flute.

Charlotte came to sit beside Nina, her lips pursed with displeasure. "How do we make it stop?"

As the hostess, Nina was supposed to restore order, but time felt slippery and loose. Someone had turned on the lamp. When had the sun set? "He's real," she managed to say again.

"Remember Chekhov's rule about the gun?" Rona said.

"Remind me," Charlotte said.

"If there's a gun in the first act," Rona said, "it has to go off by the third."

"But it's fake," Joy said. "Probably a starter gun or something, right? Poor Dick Shark shoots blanks."

"He's real," Nina repeated, louder this time. Charlotte, Rona, and Joy gaped at her. "All of it." Nina clumsily swept her arm through the air. "All real." Why did they look at her like she had two heads? Wasn't she making sense?

"Who's the old lady?" Charlotte said.

Nina's mother-in-law had slipped into the kitchen without anyone noticing. She wore an old red Christmas sweatshirt, dirty denim slacks, white orthopedic sneakers. She was fumbling with something on the table.

"She's got the gun," Rona screamed. She leapt up and hid behind the wishing well. Charlotte followed.

Sharkey shoved Lee-Anna and Cindy behind him and held up a hand as though Roberta were a truck bearing down on him.

"Hey, take it easy there, Mrs. Calare," he said. "Didn't I tell you to stay in the car? *I* was gonna do the talking. We had a deal." He sounded more peeved than alarmed. A surge of adrenalin had cleared her head, but she felt close to losing control of her bowels.

"Don't you talk down to me, little Dickie Sharkey," Roberta said, pointing the gun at him. Lee-Anna and Cindy shrank back farther into the corner.

"Nina," he said, "I found Remo's mom walking on County Road. She says you took her car. Think you could help us out here?"

"Nina?" Roberta swung the gun in Joy's direction. "Go get my keys."

"Don't shoot. Don't shoot." Joy clambered up onto the back of the couch. Her eyeglasses clattered to the floor.

"Here I am." Nina got up, feebly shielding her face with her hands. "*It's me*, Nina, your daughter-in-law." She doubted Roberta would pull the trigger, but an accident with a twitchy arthritic finger fatigued from repeated dialing was not out of the realm of possibility. She asked Sharkey, "What should I do?"

"Go ahead and get the keys for Remo's mom," he said genially, as though he were suggesting she get the old woman a piece of cake.

"Really? Just because she has the gun, she wins?"

"Yeah," Sharkey said. "That's how it works."

"Please, please, please, get the keys," Joy said in a tiny voice.

Nina started for the kitchen, keeping one eye on her mother-in-law. Roberta followed her movement with the gun, her arm drooping so that she now aimed for her daughter-in-law's shins. Nina pulled out the desk drawer and stared into the mess. She shook her head to clear the Xanax fog, and pushed aside bills, take-out menus, and old birthday cards, searching for the Snoopy key ring.

If Roberta *did* fire the gun, they'd have to lock her up. No more drama. A strange peace came over her with this realization. She'd been thinking about Remo's seaside B & B: they could convert it into an artists' retreat part of the year. She'd preside over stimulating dinner conversations, nurture budding artists' careers. What could be better than a new start with Remo? Maybe she'd have to take one for the team. She could play the martyr role, too, if she had to. "I can't give you the keys," she said. "You're not supposed to drive."

Joy moaned.

Roberta lurched. Before Nina could scream, Sharkey had one arm around the old woman's waist and one hand on her forearm. An explosion sent Nina ducking for cover behind the center island. The acrid odor of gunpowder filled the room. *Stupid, stupid, stupid*, Nina whispered. She'd never forgive herself if Roberta had shot one of her colleagues. Feet rushed past her hiding spot, white dust covered all the shoes. Doors slammed behind her.

"*Nina!* Help me," Roberta cried.

"Come on out now, Nina," Sharkey said. "It's okay. Everyone's fine."

She stood, holding onto the granite countertop for support. Sharkey restrained Roberta from behind. Both were covered in white dust. A hole gaped in the ceiling over their heads. Roberta twisted and grimaced in Sharkey's grip. To come so close to getting her car, Nina thought, only to be foiled by little Dickie Sharkey. She almost felt sorry for the old witch. Sharkey nudged something black with his toe. The gun slid across the floor like a hot chunk of guilt and came to rest at her feet.

BY SUNDAY EVENING, SHARKEY's brother-in-law had patched over the hole in the ceiling. Roberta was undergoing a forty-eight-hour psych evaluation in Bergen Pines. Her next stop would most likely be a nursing home where they would have to visit her every single weekend and holiday for the rest of Roberta's life. Nina hung up the phone with Lee-Anna. The wedding would go forward, despite Lee-Anna's misgivings about Ajay's mother. Nina waited in the dark family room for her husband, who knew nothing about what had transpired in his absence.

When he came into the bright kitchen from the garage, she saw him before he saw her. His hair had started to grow back. Thank god. Gray fuzz covered his cheeks. He entered the family room, apprehension in his eyes. She could see him thinking: what's her newest grievance? What hard truth will she make me see now? Or maybe he was thinking about something else. Can you really ever know another person, she wondered? She got up to meet him halfway. His mother was in the psychiatric hospital, and Nina was partly to blame. She'd have to tell him soon, but the truth could wait: he looked so rested, so serene. She felt left behind. She stopped short, her arms at her sides.

"No hug?" He reached for her, pulled her in tight. "It's your fault I couldn't meditate. Every time I closed my eyes, I heard *your* voice, saying open your eyes, open your eyes."

"Wasn't me," she said, touching his stubbly cheek. What she wanted to say was: Take me with you next time. *Every time.*

WILD QUAKER PARROT

"**S**OMEONE CAME IN WITH you," the psychic says when Astrid enters the small, windowless office.

"Anyone I know?" Astrid takes the seat opposite the roly-poly redhead at the wide desk. A skeptic about everything woo-woo, she wills herself to keep an open mind. She found the psychic on the internet. Lorna Devine is her name. Yelp gave her three and a half stars and according to her *HarperCollins* author's page, Ms. Devine has solved real-life murder cases. She's been a guest on *Good Morning America* three times.

But Astrid's not interested in celebrity or crime. She needs a direct line to one particular dead man. She smiles without showing her teeth, signaling her eagerness to begin. Lorna does not begin. Instead, she stares with unblinking milky-blue eyes. Astrid squirms, imagining how she must look to the other woman. Her paint-splattered jeans and Oxford shirt, her grubby Converse sneakers must appear eccentric outside of the Rockridge Art Center where she teaches painting.

"This person," Lorna says, eyelids fluttering, "his name starts with a J." She inclines her head as though listening to something far away. A spirit? The receptionist in the next room, whispering information through the heating vent?

"James," Lorna says. "Is it James?"

Close enough. "Yes."

"It's a recent death. A few months ago." The psychic reaches, without looking, for a worn deck of tarot cards on her desk and shuffles overhand, head shaking back and forth. "Something's not quite right," she mutters.

Nothing about that day was "quite right." If Astrid hadn't lured Jaime to her studio, he would still be alive. His last day he'd bounded across the lawn, hoodie unzipped, sneaker laces flapping: unraveling before her eyes.

"I'm sensing music," Lorna says, laying down the cards in an overlapping column. "Did James have something to do with music?"

"He teaches...*taught* guitar to my son," she hears herself saying. The shock on Keith's face when he walked in on them kissing. He's clammed up, her eleven-year-old son. Not that she's made any real effort to talk to him. Whenever she approaches, he recoils.

The psychic inhales deeply. "It's an old relationship," she says. "There's history." She taps a card with her index finger. Astrid leans forward for a better view. A jester in a multi-colored hat. "I'm sensing trouble. Was he in some kind of trouble?" Lorna asks.

Astrid doesn't respond. The psychic's questions feel like prying—a cross examination, not a foretelling. She stares at the card. Did she really expect to find some alternative truths, as though death were merely a misunderstanding?

Lorna sweeps up the cards and taps the deck sharply on the desk. Astrid blinks, sits back. Voices sound in the waiting room, and she notices the crumpled Coke can in the waste-basket, the real world fighting its way in.

"What is it you want to know?" Lorna asks, not unkindly but like someone on a time clock.

"I don't know," she says, rising and backing away. "I'm sorry, I have to go."

"James is near." Lorna waves her hands as though to clear cigarette smoke. Her voice follows Astrid out of the room. "Watch for signs."

ASTRID DRIVES DOWN RIVER ROAD in her Outback feeling panicky. She hasn't been able to paint for months, not since Jaime's death, and when she can't paint, she's not herself. Memories of their last kiss distract her. She wants what happens in that Jim Carrey movie where the heartbroken man pays to have selected memories erased. When they were fifteen, she and Jaime broke into their swim coach's house to have sex. It was a story she told through the years to new friends and lovers to make herself sound brave. Only Jaime was caught after the coach found his beach towel on his bachelor's bed. How young they were then, young enough to have their belongings labeled with a laundry marker. His parents sent him to a military school. After she finished high school and entered art school in Philadelphia, she heard rumors: he was abused at the military school, he'd sold a kidney to pay his rent, he played backup guitar on Springsteen's last album. Every incarnation seemed both illogical and true.

Was she the siren who lured Jaime to shipwreck his life? Or simply a high-spirited girl, testing the sensual waters? How can she move on when she doesn't know the answer?

She opens the car window, letting in the brackish scent of the Hudson River, the dusty odor of mulching leaves. The Edgewater roads are quiet. Her windshield frames a view of the gleaming apartment buildings on the river side of the road and the derelict buildings on the other. The disproportion gives her vertigo; she makes a wrong turn, and gets lost in the narrow streets where the old wood-framed houses are tall and set close together like top hats on a sloping shelf. She climbs a steep road, sunk in the shadows of the Palisades. A harsh sound like squeaky pulleys grows louder as she ascends. She slows, then brakes the car. Dozens of small lime-green birds swarm the branches of a Callery pear tree. She yanks the emergency brake, and mesmerized, watches the green frenzy, the take-offs and the landings, the fluttering, bobbing, and flapping. The tree is a complicated engine of moving green parts.

A rusted yellow VW Beetle rattles downhill, slows, and stops across the street. Behind the wheel, a clown: red nose, bald cap, white face paint. He beckons her. She leaves her car and crosses the road in a daze, a Fellini dream.

"I'm looking for Daibes Court." A sandpapery voice like Jaime's. *The jester.* Look for signs, the psychic said. Astrid studies his face, erasing the makeup, searching for the man inside the clown. She raises her hand and the clown raises his hand in a mirroring gesture. Before she can stop herself, she touches his cheek. He jerks back. "Hey, watch the makeup, lady. It takes hours to get this shit on."

"Sorry." She glances at the white makeup on her fingertips. "I can't help you. I'm lost, too." A green bird swoops overhead, and she flinches, though she's in no danger of being struck.

"Wild Quaker parrots, from South America," the clown tells her. "We got them in Brooklyn, too. A couple got loose from a crate at JFK years ago. Harry *fucking* Houdinis. They can escape any cage you put them in."

A horn sounds behind her. The birds dart from the tree singly and in pairs, flying east to the Hudson River, west to the Palisades. She dashes to her car. When she looks back, the clown is gone. She peers down the sloping road. No sign of clown or car.

THE MUSIC LESSONS WERE Lee's idea after their son showed promise with the recorder last year in the fifth grade. The recorder! Ha! A glorified tin whistle. Her husband's enthusiasm rankled her, as though he were taking genetic credit. When they first met, he was a session musician. She loved watching him play bass onstage; his total absorption in bluesy improvisations or those boogie jams made her hot for him. But then five years ago, not long after Keith's sixth birthday, Lee quit playing backup, and joined his father's financial services firm. The money helped, of course, but her husband became someone else. Instead of late nights in Bowery dive bars, he attended evening classes at Columbia Business School. His bewildering shift from "Gimme Shelter" to tax shelter felt like a betrayal. She'd married a musician, not a suit. "*You* find the music teacher," she told him. "I'm not qualified."

Six months later, on a damp April afternoon, she opened the door to a panting man holding a guitar case. He wore a black hoodie zipped to his chin, and one leg of his cargo pants was rolled to expose a muscular calf tattooed with chain grease. Behind him on the wet spring grass was a mountain bike, the tire spinning like a roulette wheel.

"Keith's mother?" He had the kind of voice that made her want to clear her throat. "I'm the guitar teacher."

"I know you!" His face was fuller, his body burlier, and his coarse blond hair receding. The boy from Indian Lake. Their childhood town lay twenty miles west on Route 80, but it seemed as though he'd traveled a greater distance to reach her. Her chest tightened. The same feeling she'd get before the fifty-meter freestyle race seconds before exploding off the starting block. "You're my first...You remember me, don't you?"

"It's you." He took a step back on the porch, looking alarmed and pained.

Driving home from the psychic under a canopy of gold and scarlet leaves, she remembers Keith's first lesson. Jaime kept up a nervous chatter while she wrote out his check. "I bet you have no idea what a badass your mother used to be," he told Keith. "We played these epic water polo games after practice. Your mother, man." He jerked his head to look at Astrid. "One guy, Billy, a little punk, kept getting up in her face, and she just hauls off and *punches* him in the eye."

It wasn't the most flattering story. A "handful" they called her then. Today, they would medicate her, but at that time Billy's black eye meant she was the first girl chosen for teams. She stole a sideways glance at Keith. At eleven, he resembled her with his long Modigliani face, lanky frame, and dark hair. He leaned against the countertop, arms crossed, shoulders rounded in that I-don't-give-a shit slouch he was perfecting, but his eyes were dilated with curiosity.

"Ask her sometime how she always got away with stuff," Jaime said, widening his eyes at Keith. "Girls are like cats. Nine lives. Us guys? We're always stepping in the traps. Like this other time, she talked me into stealing a boat—"

"Go get started on your homework," she told Keith. He gave her a hard, measuring look before leaving. Clearly, Jaime did not have children. But he did teach music to middle school kids, so he should've known better. Of course, she'd Googled him; she'd Googled all the men she'd ever had sex with, all eleven of them. She held out the check. When he reached for it, she drew it back. "If I hire you—because I'm still not sure— you can't share any more of your stories with my son."

She slows for the turn into her driveway. Her house is braced with scaffolding; broken cedar shingles litter the grass. Find the worst house in the best neighborhood, the real estate agents advised back when she and Lee were younger and poorer. That was eight years ago, before Lee joined his father's financial firm and their bank account swelled. Now, the renovations are more ambitious, more expensive. The neighbors knock on her studio door at regular intervals to complain about the noise, the construction debris, the trucks blocking their driveways. The chaos mirrors her roiling emotions; it must be controlled and concealed at all costs.

As she rolls down the long, winding driveway, the neighbor's black cat darts from the hedge dividing the properties and shoots beneath the slowly lifting garage door. Astrid rolls on into the darkness, giving Roxie a chance to scram. She shuts the engine and reaches without looking into the back seat for her satchel. Screeching. A searing pain shoots through her hand. She snatches it back. Blood. What the hell? Green wings beating. She gropes for the door handle, leaps out, slams the car door.

The parrot flings itself against the windshield over and over again. She watches it, helplessly, until the green bird finally settles on the dashboard. She steps closer, yanks the door open, and then springs back out of the way.

"Go!" She flaps her hands. "Get out!"

The bird stares back at her, head cocked, as though sizing her up. Loud thumping rock music blasts from the house next door. The Broderick kid plays the same hard-driving, head-banging rock Jaime favored. His taste had struck her as immature, undisciplined, compared with her husband's meticulous study of the blues. The parrot drops to the passenger's seat, bobs its head in time with the heavy bass and—could it be?—taps its tiny claw.

She inches closer, stares into the bird's inscrutable poppy-seed eyes.

With a squawk, the bird soars from the car. She ducks, covering her head with her arms, and looks up to see the parrot has landed on the high shelf where Lee stores the poisons. Something brushes against Astrid's ankles. It's Roxie. The cat watches the bird with murder in her eyes.

Later, at the dinner table, Lee and Keith gorge on pasta with clam sauce. Their mouths are stained red; spaghetti dangles from their lips like entrails. She carries her plate to the sink and leans over the dirty pots to peer out the window at her studio. The converted garden shed sits behind the house in the shade of oak trees. The space is just large enough to hold an easel, a worktable, and a parrot trapped inside a recycling bin. It didn't take long to lure the dumb bird into the bin with a jar of peanut butter.

"Go paint," Lee says, watching her. "I'll clean up."

"Who said anything about painting?"

"It's obvious your head's in the studio."

"I wish."

"Look, you can blame me for a lot of things, but keeping you from painting isn't one of them." Lee pushes back from the table. "That's on you, Astrid."

"It's all me." The days after Jaime's return were feverishly productive. For months, she locked herself in her studio, channeling her desire and memory. "I really had something going this summer," she says, dreamily. "Something volcanic. I was on fire."

Her son snorts, and then masks it with coughing when she frowns at him. He picks up his glass and drinks, eyes cast downward. He's eleven, but the shadow of a mustache darkening his upper lip allows her to see him as a man, separate and secretive, hoarding his sorrows. She doesn't believe him when he says he's not grieving for his guitar teacher, but she's stopped asking.

"The dust is killing me, too, buddy." Lee stands with his empty plate. "How long does it take to replace crown molding?"

He kicks the dusty drop cloths, rolled and piled against the wall. "If that carpenter ever comes back, tell him he's fired." He carries his plate to the sink, and grabs the sponge.

She runs hot water over the dirty pots, keeping her eye on Lee as he moves to the table and wipes around Keith's plate. The saggy seat of his pants and the patch of thinning hair at the back of his head give her a cramp of sadness. It's not that he's lost the ability to surprise her, she suspects, but rather he chooses not to. Does he forget the nights they stayed up late in their Hunt's Point apartment with her painter friends, drinking wine and smoking cigarettes? Does he forget the rush of performing to a standing-room-only crowd? How they'd have hurried sex between sets in the back of the van atop the grubby moving blankets? They are thirty-seven years old, not so old, but they only have sex on Saturdays at one o'clock during Keith's soccer practice and sometimes late at night if they can both stay awake.

Keith pushes back from the table and starts for the door.

"Where do you think you're going?" Lee says. "Give us a hand here."

Keith slumps. "I got a shitload of homework."

"Hey, watch your mouth," Lee snaps, then adds more gently, "Want to play some guitar later?"

"I *said* I have homework." Keith's voice cracks. "You want me to fail Spanish? Okay, I'll fail. What do I care? It's all bullshit anyway."

"You're right about that, buddy," Lee says. "It's all bullshit."

Keith stares at his father, mouth open.

"But it's the *bullshit* that'll get you into college. It's the *bullshit* that'll put a roof over your head and food on your family's table someday." He lobs the sponge onto the countertop from across the room. "Go get started on that *bullshit*."

"Lee?" she says after their son flees the room. Her husband has grumbled about his workload, his difficult clients, but he's never expressed such anger or unhappiness before. Something hard rises up inside of her to deflect it.

He shakes his head and leaves the kitchen.

It's almost eight p.m. when she stuffs her pockets with Grape-Nuts—the closest thing to birdseed she can find—and heads for the back door. In his study, Lee strums his vintage Gibson. The expensive guitar materialized a month after Keith's first lesson. Neither of them has mentioned it, as though he'd smuggled something as wicked as a mistress into their home. It was Jaime who told her what it cost after she pulled him into Lee's study to see it. "Man's got good taste," Jaime said, and then blushed when she preened. She lifted the guitar from its stand and held it out to him, but he backed away. "No way," he told her. "You *never* mess with another dude's guitar."

She pauses in the doorway, watching Lee strum with eyes half closed. He doesn't look up, though he must sense her there. The room smells like him, a smell she likes—spicy deodorant and worn leather shoes. He appears content, self-contained. Why does she find this so appealing?

Their eyes meet. "What're you playing? It's nice."

"'Be Careful with a Fool,'" he says, still strumming. "B. B. King."

She listens for another moment then inclines her head toward the back door. "So, I'm just gonna..."

He nods, slowly, solemnly. Or maybe he's only keeping time.

Outside, the air is autumn cool. A small, dark animal, probably Roxie, slips through the hole in the hedge. The studio windows are awash in moonlight. She crosses the lawn and unlocks the door. Inside, the air is warm and close. Along with the faint odor of paint and thinner, a new smell, the stink of birdcage. She gropes for the light switch. A rush at her left: squawking and rumpling feathers. Something sharp strikes her hip. It feels like a tennis ball spiked with pins. She flings the Grape-Nuts into the air. The pattering sound of the cereal landing is followed by a squawk and a swoosh. Her eyes adjust, and she finds the light switch. At her feet, the bright green bird pecks at the cereal. The overturned recycling bin rests against the back wall. Houdini, indeed. She fills a palette cup with water from the utility sink and places it on the floor a little distance away. The bird hops over and dips its beak. It pauses, water dripping, to eye her.

"I don't trust you either," she says.

The bird stretches and swivels its neck like a man in a tight shirt collar.

"Okay, look, if you are Jaime, which is totally crazy, why did you come home with me? What do you want from me?"

With a squawk, the parrot flies up into the rafters. She staggers backward, bumping into the old canvases stacked against the wall. She recovers her balance and watches the parrot pace the narrow rafter above before turning to the painting on the easel. She has been staring at it for months. It was supposed to be included in her first solo gallery show in December. Without thinking, she picks up a tube of green paint and smears it on the palette, mixes it with titanium white.

Thirty by thirty-six, the painting is larger than her usual canvases. The colors are vibrant, the composition surreal: a girl and a boy on a four-poster bed floating on a green lake. A blur of purple hills in the background. She painted it with a nervous urgency, something like the rush of first love or lust.

Jaime snapped into focus the summer of 1997 when they were both fifteen. A few boys from his posse cornered her at the beach gate before swim team practice. "Cassidy likes you," Joe said. That summer, she developed what her mother called a "figure." The boys elbowed each other every morning when she arrived at the swim lanes in her green striped Speedo. During practice, she observed him from the adjacent lane, watched him get into a splash fight with Billy and Joe. Heard him make that obnoxious crow sound all the boys were making that summer. *Caw, caw, caw.* He flicked his wet hank of hair from his eyes over and over again. Hideous, she decided. His feet and hands were too big for his body, which made him an exceptional swimmer but also a freak.

It started the usual way: He circled her street on his bike. Next came a series of hang up calls before he worked up the nerve to speak. In a timid voice, he admitted he liked her. Oh yeah? She'd said it, as though it were a dare. Would he help her hijack a boat? After practice the next day, he stood guard while she clipped the lock with her father's bolt cutter wrapped inside her towel. They launched the aluminum boat into the water, and paddled with their hands, because—as they joked—the boat's owner wasn't considerate enough to leave the oars. A half-mile out from the shoreline, she let him kiss her. Not her first kiss, but nicer than she was used to. He flicked his hair, suggested they lie down. He caressed her breast, and his big mitt was startlingly tender. She touched him through his shorts, and when he moved to slip a finger inside her, she didn't stop him. In the frenzy of her desire, she had the clear, astonishing thought that he knew his way around a girl's body. She hated herself for wanting him, and hating herself, she threw a long leg over his hip and drew him closer. They ground against each other until they both came, then dozed in the afternoon sunlight, waking every now and then to kiss. The softness of his lips astonished her every single time.

The five o'clock siren startled them awake. Too dazed to paddle back, they abandoned the boat and swam to shore. A fisherman, one of Jaime's neighbors, recognized the blond Cassidy watermelon head bobbing on the water. Astrid changed course, heading for the beach, but Jaime kept swimming, his beautiful slicing stroke, carrying him toward disaster.

If his father hadn't grounded Jaime, if their weeklong separation hadn't made her crave him, she might not have devised her idiotic plan to break into Coach Eddie's house. During one of their furtive late-night phone calls, Jaime made the mistake of bragging he knew the code to Eddie's garage door from the time he'd fed the coach's snake. When he timidly asked if they'd ever have sex, Astrid told him that breaking and entering was the only way she'd do it. The test she set was intentionally unreasonable; she never expected him to agree to it, and when he did, she was convinced he'd back out at the last minute. On the night of the next home swim meet, a sticky humid August evening buzzing with cicadas, they slipped through the beach gate after their races. They hadn't touched since the afternoon in the boat, but now he took her hand. In grim silence, they walked the quarter-mile to Calistoga Road under the ghostly street lights.

The green parrot swoops down from the rafters and lands atop her painting. She drops her brush and backs away. It paces along the upper edge before presenting its tail feathers to her. Gray liquid dribbles down the face of her painting.

"You little fucker." She hurls the palette knife. The bird dives for her head, and she runs for the door. Outside, she turns in circles, swatting at her head, at the bird. A rumple of feathers, a whoosh. The bird takes off into the night sky.

She returns to her studio, head stinging, and looks at the gray shit sliding down her painting. She will never tell anyone about this, she decides. Who would believe her? She caps her paints, and cleans her brushes in the sink, talking to herself. "Jaime did *not* come back as a parrot to shit on my memories. I know that. Of course, I know that." She turns out the light and locks the studio door.

Lee is asleep when she climbs into bed. She kisses the back of his head, rests her cheek between his freckled shoulder blades. He turns to embrace her, rocking the mattress. "You were out there for a while. Did you get your mojo back?"

She sighs into his hairy chest. "I'm too old for a mojo."

"Okay, Grandma Moses. I thought you had enough paintings for your show."

"This last one doesn't fit. It's too much of a departure. Too strange."

"What does the gallery think?"

"I'm afraid to show them. They won't be happy. All summer, I kept telling them I was finishing up the perfect final piece. They trusted me."

"Maybe you need to trust you."

She lies in her husband's arms, thinking about trust. She has to tell him about the kiss. If Keith hadn't seen it, she'd keep quiet. The kiss meant nothing. But she can't expect her son to keep her secret forever. For weeks, she's been mulling over her confession: She'll say Jaime was confused, misread her friendliness. She remembers how eager she was to show Jaime her painting. After Keith's lesson, he loped across the lawn, his sweatshirt unzipped, shoelaces flapping. She watched him from the studio door, disappointed in the physical reality of him. Every Thursday, during the long hot summer, she expected to open the door to a different person—the compliant, up-for-adventure boy perhaps—and found this awkward, inarticulate, and timid man on her porch.

He blushed when he saw the canvas, shifted his oversized feet, avoided her eyes. Roxie leapt down from the shelf where she'd been napping, and Jaime jumped back with a terrified shriek. Astrid laughed. "It's a harmless cat." She came toward him, thinking she'd give his arm a maternal pat, but at the last minute she pressed herself against him. He stiffened.

"Don't," he said, pulling away, knocking into the workbench. "You're married." She tugged him back by the hem of his sweatshirt; she reached for his crotch. His body relaxed against hers as she'd known it would. She felt buoyant and light as he rocked against her. When they kissed, it was the same impossible softness she remembered from all those years ago. She was aroused, stirred by the memory of herself, her younger reckless, dangerous self.

Sunlight flooded the studio. They turned at the same time to see the open door and Keith running away. *Keith.* What must this look like to him? The end of his world, probably. All of her concern centered on her son. Jaime was only in the way.

"I can't believe I let you do this to me again," Jaime said, before clomping outside. She leaned against the studio doorway, watching him. He seemed fifteen again. Close to her son's age. Lost. Unsure of himself.

"Oh, *please*," she said.

"Should I talk to him?" The idea seemed to terrify him.

"That's my job," she said. She told him to go. Let Jaime worry until next week's lesson, she thought, as she watched him pedal out of her driveway, the soft guitar case strapped across his back. She'd have to fire him, but that could wait.

When he didn't show up the next Thursday, she left three messages on his cell phone, while her son practiced a Guns N' Roses song over and over again in the living room. "Don't be a fool," she whispered into her cell. "Nothing happened. I don't feel that way about you."

She learned about the accident a few days later when the carpenter asked for newspapers to protect the granite countertop. The local rag was spread out near the sink. *Man Killed on Bicycle.* Thursday afternoon, the driver couldn't stop in time. The cyclist ran the stop sign.

SHE DRIVES HER SULLEN SON to school. When he flings open the car door, she says, "We're going to talk later, Keith, whether you want to or not." He leaves the car with a grunt. She watches him approach his two best friends, sitting on their usual bench, reading comic books. She drives off, listening to the B. B. King CD Lee left for her on the dashboard.

Instead of driving home, she heads for Edgewater with her Leica on her lap. She makes a right turn off River Road, and drives in and out of the sleepy side streets, searching for the tree. She ejects the CD and lowers the window, listening for the parrots. At the top of a steep hill, she hears the screeching. She descends, pumping the brakes. The Callery pear tree's branches shudder with lime-green feathers. She stops the car and raises the Leica to her eye, focuses the lens, and snaps a half dozen shots. Then she taps the car horn, and takes a few more as the parrots burst from the branches like green confetti into the steel blue sky.

She steps on the gas, flies down the steep road. A left onto River Road brings her smack into the middle of rush hour traffic. She slows the car for one of the many traffic lights and groans at the thought of wasting her precious painting time idling behind a FedEx truck. She pops Johnny Winter into the stereo, and drums her thumbs on the steering wheel, visualizing a medium-sized canvas, maybe twelve by sixteen inches, taken up entirely by the pear tree. A commotion on the sidewalk breaks through her daydream. A block ahead, a redheaded woman, weaving back and forth, scatters the pedestrians. It's Lorna Devine, the psychic. Drunk at nine a.m.? Good god. Astrid feels vindicated as she watches Lorna narrowly miss a delivery woman pushing a handcart piled with boxes. Of course, Lorna Devine, the celebrity crime solver, is a charlatan! Jaime was never near; he is always and forever dead.

As Lorna zigzags closer, Astrid sees the red-tipped cane, tapping the sidewalk. She remembers the psychic's milky blue eyes. How had she missed something so obvious? All of her certainty flutters away.

When Astrid finally opens her studio door, she scans the rafters for errant animals before entering. She dampens a rag at the utility sink and then wipes the dried-up, powdery bird shit from her painting, from the girl and the boy in the bed on the lake. This is it, she thinks. This is the painting for her show, not the tree frozen inside her camera. She steps back from the easel to get some distance from the image and bumps into her old landscapes stacked against the wall, knocking one over. She bends to right the canvas and a spot of iridescent green catches her eye. She jerks back, heart thudding, before inching closer. Son of a bitch. It's her French cigarettes, the pack she hid five years ago. Hello! Her long-ago self was thoughtful enough, no—*prescient* enough—to slip a matchbook inside the cellophane.

In the open doorway she takes the first intoxicating drag. Her head swims. The green grass ripples and sways. She closes her eyes to steady herself. Nothing feels solid or certain or real.

That's okay, she decides. In fact, it's an auspicious place to begin. She puts out the cigarette on her rubber sole, then flicks the butt into the yard. Roxie creeps along the hedge. Astrid makes a clicking sound with her tongue, inviting the cat into her studio, but the animal darts away and squeezes through the scribble of branches.

ESCAPE ARTIST

I was in my front hallway, stretching a tight Achilles tendon, delaying my run. I'd passed the morning drafting a student's college recommendation letter and furiously packing up my daughter's old bedroom: in other words, delaying my run. I never enjoyed running until the first mile was behind me. Before each run, I'd remind myself: all that stands between you and bliss is one uncomfortable mile. It made no sense. I loved running. Still, I put it off until the eleventh hour. At 1:40 p.m., it was now or never, and never was out of the question, since yesterday I'd missed my run, waiting for my daughter's text.

The doorbell rang. My first impulse was to hide, but the woman had seen me through the bubbled pane of the sidelight window. She was bent forward at the waist as though she'd been shot in the gut. If Frank were here, he'd open the door and say: "Not interested," without giving her a chance to speak. He wasn't curious. "People are predictable," he'd say. "They all want something from me." I *was* curious. Or, maybe I wanted someone to want something from me, but if I spent even three minutes on whatever this was, I'd have to forget my six-mile run. Four miles allowed for a shower before my three o'clock tutoring appointment, but a shorter run wasn't worth the effort. Just as I got warmed up, the run would be over, but four miles was better than no miles—

The woman rapped hard on the glass. I opened the door.

"It was running loose." Her tone was indignant. Ash-blond with bulky shoulders, she had two fingers hooked through the collar of a gray terrier. She wore a navy serge pantsuit and leather pumps, like a detective or a nun, like someone who meant business.

"Not mine," I told her. "I don't recognize it." At the sound of my voice, the terrier looked up; I wanted to pet it but held back in case that signaled a willingness to get involved. My cell phone rang in my office. On the slim chance it might be my daughter—Jennifer only texted and emailed—I moved to close the door, but the woman stuck out her hand to keep it open. The phone stopped ringing.

"If I don't get it off the street," she said, "someone'll run it over. There's no name or address on the tag." We both studied the dog as though we expected it to tell us something. Was it grimacing? A few minutes ago, it had been chasing squirrels across leaf-strewn November lawns, and now this martinet was cutting off its air. "I don't have time for this," she said. "I'm late for court. Can't *you* handle it?" She looked me over the way gainfully employed women sometimes looked at women dressed in exercise clothes in the middle of the day. In my case, purple shorts and a Rutgers sweatshirt. I had a hard time disagreeing with people who assumed their time was more valuable than mine.

"Fine, I'll take it to the borough hall," I said, out of sympathy for the dog.

"It *is* a cutie," she admitted now that it wasn't her problem. Her face softened as she picked up the dog under its front paws and passed it to me. It had surprising heft for such a small creature. I cradled it in my arms and rubbed its gray suede belly. One hind leg twitched with pleasure. "It likes you," she said, and I felt a nip of pride, though I knew she was assuaging her conscience. She was halfway down the sidewalk.

Alone with the dog, I tensed. It had been years since I owned one. My cell phone rang again. I ran to my office, the terrier jouncing in my arms. It was Frank. "Milly, did Jennifer text?" The faltering hope in his voice crushed something inside of me. Yesterday, our only child, twenty-three, had sent an email from her Christian mission post in San Salvador. She would not be coming home to New Jersey next month for the holidays as promised. We hadn't seen her in six months.

"Not yet," I said. "Maybe she's reconsidering."

I didn't believe that. I closed the door, put the dog down on the rug. He sniffed at the college catalogs stacked on the floor near the bookshelves. "Why don't *you* call?" I said. "Maybe she'll talk to you."

"Today's tough. Meetings." He was the director of student affairs at Bergen Community. He worried about Jennifer, but he tended to filter *his* unmanageable emotions through me. He'd read aloud the awful *Times* articles about San Salvador and cited gruesome statistics, while checking my reaction. He'd prod me to call Jennifer, and then counsel me through my fear, frustration, or anger, while—I suspected—working through his own. He missed the time they'd spent together, prowling yard sales and hole-in-the-wall shops for HO model train tracks and accessories. She'd lost interest in their shared hobby sometime during puberty, but he continued to add to the extensive tabletop railway in our basement. Winding rivers and pine trees, hollow mountain passes, pretty little houses. I didn't tell him I'd started to pack up her bedroom this morning in a fit of anger, boxing up her snow globe collection and the Laura Ingalls Wilder books, the painted ceramic crucifix that had hung over her bed since her eighth-grade year. The anger had passed. No need to parse it.

"We should go down," he said, not for the first time. "So we can get a good night's sleep."

"Depends on what we find." I imagined Jennifer putting on a brave face, denying her right to safety and family in the name of a higher purpose. That would be harder to take than tears or a confession of doubt. Each time Frank had suggested a visit, I'd shut him down. In the first three months, I said we should let her get settled; after that it was only a few months until Christmas. I hoped a visit home would break whatever spell she was under. "Let's talk later," I said. The dog clawed at the door, whining to be let out. "I have to go."

I don't know why I didn't mention the dog. I kept more and more to myself these days, innocuous things like running into an old friend or an amusing incident with a tutee. The effort of telling—or maybe it was the effort of extracting the aspect worth telling—was beyond me.

I needed a leash. I left my office and the dog followed on my heels. In the laundry room, I opened the cabinet over the juddering washing machine. The dog propped its front paws on the dryer, wet nose twitching. I rifled through the expired medicines and stale treats and found the leather leash wrapped around the gnawed wooden handle of a dog's brush. Tufts of ginger fur clotted the nylon bristles. Seven years ago, our golden retriever had choked to death after she'd snatched a bag of bagels from the countertop. When I'd entered the kitchen to make tea, I'd seen her pleading eyes and frothing mouth. Why was I holding on to this old stuff? Frank and I had promised: after Daisy, no more dogs. Maybe I didn't believe us. After I ditched the terrier, I would purge this cabinet. It was 2:10. If I walked the dog to the borough hall, a mile from my house, I could run home afterwards. One mile was better than nothing. Who the hell was I kidding? It *was* nothing. Sex without orgasm. Eggs without salt. I would take the car.

In the driveway, I opened my sedan's passenger-side door, and the dog leaped inside before I could bend to lift him. He rode shotgun like a pro. No jumping or barking or slobbering the window the way our golden retriever used to do. We all loved Daisy, but she was an ill-disciplined dog we were forever shoving behind doors and gates. Outside the middle school, children swarmed the sidewalk. Early dismissal? Without a kid in the system, I was out of sync with the neighborhood's rhythms. The sun, low in the sky, splashed the leafless trees and red brick school building with coppery light. The days were growing shorter; my opportunities for runs were shrinking into a narrower timeframe. I joined the long line of cars creeping over the two-lane bridge at the duck pond. A pale young cop directed traffic, his narrow hips swiveling like a salsa dancer's. The middle-school children waiting to cross were fat-cheeked babies. At their age, Jennifer had dominated our house like a storybook ogre, bellowing her demands, bawling her unhappiness. She'd felt things strongly: the quagmire in Iraq, the twelve dead coal miners in West Virginia, and Hurricane Katrina's devastation, all distressed her to the same degree as two-faced girlfriends and unjust teachers. An image surfaced from that time: talking to Jennifer's reflection in my bathroom mirror as I applied eye makeup for a night out with Frank, her body as rigid as an icepick, perched on the edge of my tub. What remained most vivid in my memory was my sharp impatience, the urge to escape the plaintive sound of her voice.

Our fault, Jennifer's religious conversion. After her friend's parents took her to the Methodist church, she rhapsodized about the teen group; these kids were way more passionate than her superficial classmates, she claimed. Our child needed an outlet for her crippling empathy, so we shelved our reservations and joined the church. We unlocked the god portal and pushed her through the wormhole. At first, she'd thrived in the youth group, her unhappiness trickling away with every selfless deed. In her junior year of high school, however, after a traumatic breakup (though she denied a connection), she'd sought a stricter interpretation of scripture. Her world had come apart and religion would be her glue. Without consulting us, she'd defected to Glen Valley Evangelical Church. Her new friends—Jess, the recovering addict, Lindy, the former petty thief—had worried us more than any shift in dogma.

As it turned out, we'd worried about the wrong thing. Last May, after she'd graduated from Bethel, the Christian college in Indiana, Jennifer had joined a missionary team based in San Salvador, a city controlled by vicious gangs. All her emails ended with: *Your Servant in Christ.* "What? No *love?*" Frank had mused after one of her early emails. "She's trying out a new identity," I'd said, hoping to sound reasonable. We were lapsed Catholics, suspicious of any outward displays of piety. Our daughter, the Holy Roller: pro-life, fan of school prayer. It couldn't last. I kept expecting her zeal to break like a fever.

THE BOROUGH HALL, A 1970s red-brick building was next door to the fire station and across the road from the duck pond. The dog sniffed at the bushes, added his scent to the lower branches, and bounded up the steps. Inside, he sauntered down the long hallway, nails clicking on the linoleum like he knew the way. I followed, amused, eyeing his wiggling hips and his carrot-shaped tail. I'd forgotten what good company a dog could be. The windowless health department office gave off an ancient sour smell: strata of sweat and obedience. The dog propped his paws on the desk where the plump clerk talked on the phone. Mariana, from the Methodist church. We'd worked together in the food pantry. A bossy woman, I remembered, prone to gossip. She pointed to the dog and then at the door before turning her back to continue her conversation. Outside, tail wagging, the dog sniffed his own urine on the bushes. I double-knotted the leash around the flagpole. He whimpered as I walked away.

Mariana was off the phone when I returned. "Milly Calabrese, long time no see. Is it five years?" She raised her hand to the pink patch on her neck, but stopped herself. "Dermatitis. Trying not to scratch."

"How're things at United Methodist?"

"Not the same." Her features pinched with displeasure. "The congregation has dwindled since...you know." The merger with the Korean church had taken place a month before we left. She lowered her voice, though we were the only people in the office. "They're standoffish. Have their own way of doing things. I've given up."

"Maybe they should call it the *Divided* Methodist Church," I said, mocking her bigotry. Her face darkened. "So anyway," I said, "how's your son?"

She glanced at the photo on her tidy desk—a young, attractive man in ski clothes—while absently scratching her neck. Augusto, she told me, lived in Colorado; he was helping a friend launch a snowboard business. She asked about Jennifer. "I still use the tote bag she made for...what was she raising money for?"

"Darfur." I examined her son's fancy ski goggles, helmet, and jacket. Is *that* what I wanted for Jennifer? "She's in San

Salvador, working with a youth group." Did I sound smug? I didn't feel smug.

Mariana grimaced. "I've been reading about the murders, those missing girls. What in the world made her want to go there?"

I couldn't speak. The chronic anxiety percolating in my gut bubbled up through my throat. Three months ago, in August, not far from Jennifer's mission post, a fifteen-year-old girl had been shot point-blank while walking through a traffic-clogged intersection on her way to work. She'd inadvertently entered a rival gang's territory. Frank had read the *Times* article aloud at breakfast, his chubby face draining of color, his dark eyes haunted. For once I'd wished I'd had faith. How liberating to believe: Jennifer's fate is in Jesus's hands now.

"Never mind. I'm sure she'll be fine. How can I help you?" Mariana was all business now. I explained about the dog. "Jagger," she said. "Belongs to the McGraths. I hear they're divorcing. They *claim* he digs holes under the fence." She smirked, pulling back her head, doubling her chin. "I don't get why they insist on keeping him in the yard when they're gone all day. It's negligence, if you ask me."

I agreed, but I didn't want her to think we were in league against the McGraths. I backed away and at the doorway said, "Nice to see you again—"

Her fingers came away bloodied from her neck. She must have seen my repulsion. "Not contagious," she said, wiping her fingers on the tissue she pulled from her shirt cuff. "Take Jagger home with you. I'll leave your address for the McGraths."

I froze. My second appointment was at six o'clock: I could fit in a thirty or forty-minute run at four o'clock after my first tutee. The sun set at four-thirty, but some light remained until 4:50—

"Otherwise, he'll sit in the cold until seven. Up to you."

I left the building. Outside, two squad cars tore out of the lot, sirens wailing. Jagger barked at the fat Canada geese, grazing in the distance. I hurried past him, unseen, to my car and drove home. A black Honda SUV blocked my driveway, forcing me to park on the street in front of my house. As I came up the flagstone walkway, I took in the peeling paint on the window trim, the leggy rhododendrons, the gray mold staining the roof shingles—when had we stopped keeping up appearances?—before I noticed the skinny redheaded boy on the porch, peering into the sidelight window.

"Gordon?" I said, coming up the steps. He wheeled around and flinched as though I'd hurled a rock. Three years ago, I'd tutored his older brother, now a pre-med student at Yale. When their mother hired me to help this son write his college application essay, she'd confided: Gordon's *sensitive*. In my experience, that meant *overindulged*. Also, less ambitious. For this first session, I'd asked him to bring a list of his interests, but he'd arrived empty-handed.

"Nothing? No embarrassing hobbies left over from middle school?" I said as I led him inside and down the hallway to my office. I was taking a risk: teasing loosened up some kids but made others homicidal. "Model trains? Pokemon, maybe?" I directed him to the overstuffed armchair. He fell into it, long legs spread wide. Steam rattled the old radiator. A dog barked in the street. I thought about Jagger tied to the flagpole and felt the energy dribbling out of me. I could not imagine ever running again. Gordon stared past me to the bookshelf. He projected an aloof arrogance I didn't buy. I asked him, with little hope, if he liked to read.

"Not really." He tore his eyes away from the books.

I asked about sports, told him he looked athletic. He blushed, a hopeful sign. "I played soccer, but I tore my ACL sophomore year."

"That's tough. At Rutgers, I strained my Achilles tendon halfway through my first cross-country season—" He yawned without covering his mouth. I felt the sting, but shook it off. "What do you want to study in college?"

"No idea."

"Do you want to go to college?"

"Do I have a choice?"

I told him he always had a choice, and he made a scoffing sound. "Not according to *my* parents."

I smiled with mock sympathy, though my hands twitched with the urge to throttle him. "What gives you pleasure?" I said, and he blushed again, which made my own face heat up. "Let me put it another way," I said. "What, when you do it, makes you lose all track of time?" He shifted, looked down at his hands. "I promise not to judge. The colleges want to know what sets you apart. My daughter, for example, works with a youth group in Central America where kids your age live with the constant threat of violence." My tone had turned aggressive. I *was* judging him. Apathy, like his, forced the Jennifers in this world to take on more than their fair share of compassion.

"Can't you just write the freaking essay for me?" He seemed on the verge of tears, which alarmed me more than his mild expletive. "Don't you have some standard thing? Isn't that what my mother's paying you for?"

Fuming, I dug through my files for the worksheet I'd designed for hopeless cases. We switched places: he sat at my desk, filling in the blanks, while I moved to the armchair with my phone. Still no texts from Jennifer. I fired one off: *Hello?*

Christmas? I looked again at the photo she'd sent last week; it had been taken at a market stall. She wore a white Youth Ministry T-shirt and baggy blue cargo shorts, her brown hair plaited in two braids. At five feet ten, she towered over the Salvadoran teens. I scrutinized their weary eyes and strained smiles. Most of them would be dead before they turned thirty-five, according to the statistic Frank had read to me a few days ago. All the photos she'd sent before this had been taken indoors—inside the shadowy church or a sparsely furnished classroom, sometimes a rustic kitchen—so why did this photo seem so familiar? I tapped on the screen to enlarge it, saw the bushels of green melons, the cobblestones, and realized it reminded me of the newspaper photo Frank had shown me a month or two ago: a gang member sprawled on the ground, a ribbon of blood unspooling from his body, winding between bushel baskets bursting with bananas.

My phone dinged with a text from Jennifer: *Pls stop. Can't come home. I'm needed.*

Gordon groaned. I half expected to see him reading over my shoulder, but he was still staring at the worksheet. She was needed? *We* needed Jennifer, her mother and father. I imagined shoving Gordon off my desk chair, opening my laptop, and booking our flight south. What was I waiting for? A reenactment of the prodigal son? My body felt charged with anger, frustration, and fear. Anything I texted now would only make Jennifer unhappy, so I didn't reply. It was 3:20. If Gordon left now, I could get in six miles before the sun set. I stood up and read over his shoulder.

1. What historical figure do you most admire? *Pee Wee Herman*

2. If your house were on fire, what is the one thing you would save? [He'd drawn a phallus. Or maybe a rocket ship with two sandbags hanging off it.]

3. If you had one day to live, how would you spend it? *Not filling in stupid worksheets.*

4. What is your greatest strength? *Not giving a shit.*

5. What is your greatest weakness? *Not giving a shit.*

"Please leave," I said. "You're wasting my time." He twisted to look up at me, his face bright with defiance. A pimple on his chin looked ready to blow. I had zero interest in this fight. When he saw I wasn't going to engage, he stood and dug into his jeans pocket and pulled out some wrinkled bills. "Keep it," I told him. "You seem to think I haven't earned it. Don't make another appointment until you're ready to work."

He glanced around as though searching for a place to hide. "Why are you being such a bitch?" he said. I struggled to keep my mouth shut, my expression neutral. He tossed the money on the floor and fled. I trailed him to the front door and slammed it behind him with relief. I waited until I saw his car leave my driveway. Clouds shifted and sunlight flashed in the sidelight windows. The house was a submarine surfacing in the murky sea. I opened the door and broke into a run the minute I left my porch, aware of the sun slipping lower in the sky. The grass—still summer green—was spongy from the previous night's rain. The air had grown cooler in the last hour. I couldn't take enough of it into my lungs. My quads were two blocks of concrete, and it would be miles before my Achilles tendon warmed up and stopped hurting. The few passing cars gave me a wide berth. My annoyance with Gordon fell away. If I had one day to live, I would spend it running.

I thought about Daisy. When I'd found her choking on the bagel, I'd shouted for Frank before escaping upstairs. Minutes later, he called for my help. I couldn't move. Jennifer wailed in her bedroom down the hallway. I wanted to go to her, but terror immobilized me. Frank shouted *Daisy* over and over again in a horrible anguished voice. I covered my ears until red lights flashed on the tiled walls. Men's voices downstairs, then a dark shape in the bathroom doorway. I flinched when Frank turned on the lights. He'd called 911. He needed a blanket to wrap the dog in. A blanket? I didn't understand. His eyes were red and swollen, his hand bleeding. "She's gone," he said. The look in his eyes. I couldn't bear it. In an email last August, Jennifer made one brief mention of the murdered fifteen-year-old girl, but she'd spared us the description of the corpse, sprawled for hours in the busy intersection as the morning commuters cut a wide swath. Frank had read those details to me from the newspaper. Her emails that month had been filled with the young gang member who'd knocked on the mission door in the dead of night, begging to be saved.

At the end of the road, I changed course and headed for the bridge. The cars were stopped for a Canada goose waddling toward the pond. Why walk when you have wings? The setting sun left a path of reflected light across the rippling dark water. I imagined the bird walking across like a web-footed Jesus. And, then I was thinking about my daughter's text. I knew what I had to do. I had to give her my blessing.

The terrier barked and strained at his leash when he saw me coming. Someone, probably Mariana, had left water in a silver take-out container. Three more hours before the owners claimed him. Tomorrow he'd dig another hole and spend another day tied up, waiting for their return. A police cruiser sped silently from the parking lot, lights flashing. After it turned the corner, I knelt to untie the leash. Jagger shook himself from side to side and gazed up at me, tail wagging. "What are you waiting for?" I asked him. "Go! I've set you free." I clapped twice. "Run!"

He took off, heading for the geese pecking at the hem of patchy grass along the shoreline. With pleasure, I anticipated the commotion: the honking, the sound of wings flapping as the geese rushed into the darkening sky. At the last second, Jagger veered left. Horrified, I realized my mistake. On the bridge, horns blared and cars swerved. I broke into a run but took off too fast. A searing pain blazed in my heel, and I slowed to a limping jog. Time became gluey as in one of my childhood fever dreams. Silver fur flickered between the moving cars. I limped closer. Another glimpse of fur. And then, Jagger was on the far sidewalk, nosing around a forsythia bush. I waited for an opening in the whizzing traffic, keeping my eye on his twitching tail. *He's safe*, I told myself, and I repeated it like a mantra until the light changed to green.

FEARLESS

WE WALKED OUR BIKES UP the long path to Baldini's Pizza in Marina di Castagneto, three fit American women in our mid-forties, dressed in skintight cycling kits. Peggy was in the lead, red hair radiating from her silver helmet. I struggled to keep up, while Freya lagged behind, purring Italian with Carlo, our guide. We propped our bikes against a split rail fence and sat down at a picnic table shaded by a vine-covered pergola.

"Only dogs eat outside in this weather," Peggy said, fanning herself. She'd been in some kind of a snit ever since we'd left Bolgheri Castle. If I'd had a tail, I would have wagged it, I was so relieved to get off the bike and out of the sun. I checked to see how Freya was taking Peggy's mood. She and Carlo sat across from us. Freya smiled dreamily, listening perhaps to the calliope music wafting from the carnival across the road. The Ferris wheel, just visible above the tree line, seemed unreachable.

The plump, middle-aged proprietor appeared with menus. Her hair was dyed an unnatural shade of red. Carlo introduced her as Daniella, his friend. He seemed to know a lot of people in Tuscany. He owned a small bike shop and had a stake in the local bicycle touring company run by a retired British racer. We were his first solo gig.

Freya and Carlo ordered first. I went next, mangling the pronunciation.

"*Cosa?*" Daniella said. She mimed puzzlement: shrugging her round shoulders, eyes opened wide, mouth drawn downward. Grimacing, I repeated my order in English.

"I always speak the language of the country where I am traveling," Daniella said.

"Good for you," Peggy said, thrusting her menu over her shoulder. "I'll have the Margherita, please."

Daniella turned to go, but Carlo asked her to wait for him. As he struggled to get up from the picnic table, she stole a glance at Freya. Was she measuring her own sallow fleshiness against Freya's voluptuous curves as I'd seen other women do, as I'd done myself? In the Westwood, New Jersey bike shop I managed, I was often mistaken for a teenage boy with my narrow hips and cropped bleached hair.

Carlo and Daniella walked off toward the kitchen, and Peggy leaned in and spoke in a low tone. "Is it just me, or was today's ride bullshit?"

Freya raised her eyebrows. "Define *bullshit*."

"I didn't break down my bike and haul it across the Atlantic for a touristy ride to a castle," Peggy said. "Did you, Julie?"

I shook my head, but I couldn't say with any certainty why I'd gone to so much trouble. I'd disassembled and rebuilt *two* bikes, my own and Freya's. On my first night in Italy, I'd woken at two a.m., convinced that back home both Anders and my mother would die. I couldn't breathe and fled the hotel room. My nightshirt clung to my skin as I paced on the second-story walkway under the yellow bug lights. Two months earlier, I'd moved my mother, against her will, into a nursing home. "You had no choice," Anders reassured me. When I neglected to visit her, he didn't judge. Instead, he'd encouraged me to travel, even though only eight months had elapsed since his final cancer treatment, even though it meant he'd be alone. In June, our only child had left for her junior year in Prague. Why *had* he urged me to go? I became aware of the smell of cigarettes, and saw Furio, the hotel owner's son—a coarse-featured man in his early thirties—standing half in shadow on the sidewalk below, watching me. His louche gaze stilled my racing thoughts, pinned me in place.

"Obviously," Peggy was saying, "Carlo thinks we're novices."

"He *did* compliment me on my efficient pedal stroke," I said with an eye roll. Only Freya laughed, but we'd all suffered the condescension of male cyclists. Our tight-knit female cycling community was a refuge from that undeserved contempt.

"You wrote him. What did you tell him about us?" Peggy asked Freya.

"That we're experienced A-level riders."

"Should've handled it myself."

Freya's eyes fluttered closed. The trip had been her idea, and since she was fluent in Italian, she'd handled most of the arrangements. Originally, six women had signed on, but three had dropped out at the last minute, leaving our odd trio. Undoubtedly, Irene and Vanessa's banter or Megan's self-deprecating humor would have had a leavening effect on this lunch.

"Let's not point fingers," I said.

"Our lines got crossed somewhere," Peggy said. "Maybe on *his* end. Italians have old-fashioned ideas about women." Her face was set in an angry pout, but she sounded abashed now. Attack first, apologize later. Even when her comments weren't directed at me, I felt the ghosts of old humiliations, and I was growing tired of it.

"It's only the first day," I said. "We've got seven more rides."

"Hear that, Peggy?" Freya said. "Seven opportunities to ask for what you want instead of complaining about not getting it."

Peggy looked down, folding her napkin into smaller and smaller squares until it was the size of a credit card.

"We'll tell him when he gets back," I said. "We're paying him enough. We should get what we want."

"What do *we* want?" Freya said. Her foot bumped mine under the table.

"If we were men, this wouldn't be an issue," Peggy said, tossing the napkin aside.

"If we were men, we wouldn't bother with a guide," I said. "We'd map our own routes. Get lost for the fun of it."

Freya smiled at me like she used to do, like I was special. This was what *I* wanted. This was why I'd shamefully crawled over the fragile bodies of my mother and husband to get here. Freya motioned for us to lean in closer. "He might not be up for it," she said. "Did you notice his little pasta belly?"

FREYA TENDED TO CULTIVATE brief, intense friendships before dropping them. After me, she'd taken up with Peggy for several weeks. Perhaps their breakup was why, in the weeks leading up to our departure, Peggy seemed overly anxious. Maybe she was looking for a way out when she'd proposed that Carlo was a scam artist who'd lit out for the Riviera with our deposit. But he'd been waiting for us in the chaotic, cacophonous airport, a short man, in his late thirties with a round, boyish face roughed up with a few days' growth of beard.

"He's a teddy bear," Freya said, propping her bare feet on the dashboard as we followed his van in our rented Panda. "This should teach you to have a little faith in people, Peggy." Her voice was throaty with fatigue, but her eyes were laughing.

"You talked to him for three seconds!" Peggy said. She was passing a Fiat doing eighty to keep the van in sight. "He could be taking off with our bikes, or leading us into an ambush. Right, Julie?"

I didn't answer. Folded into the cramped back seat, I felt trapped. Whatever I'd gotten myself into, there was no escaping it.

AFTER OUR PIZZA LUNCH we rolled out at a conservative pace, heading south for Piombino. Through the first few miles of rolling climbs, I stayed in my granny gear and thought longingly of my hotel bed. We'd made the sensible decision to set up base camp at our hotel, rather than bike from destination to destination trailed by our luggage stashed in a sag wagon. After a day of hammering and hill climbing, it would be comforting to return to a familiar place.

Ahead, Carlo and Freya rode side by side, chatting and laughing. This would have incited road rage at home, but here the drivers were more respectful. They hung back when the roads were narrow, waiting until it was safe to pass. Then they cut a wide swath, tooting their horns in friendly warning. Soon, I dropped my vigilance and surrendered to daydreams. Somewhere in San Vincenzo, I was picturing Anders at work, his open intelligent face hovering over a microscope, his lab coat sleeves too short for his long arms, until it hit me that the workday in the States hadn't begun. When I tried to calculate the hour, I couldn't manage the simple math. I felt unmoored and on the verge of tears. We were passing between fields of sunflowers. Behind me, Peggy was muttering again. As she peeled off the back of the pace line and made her way to the lead position, she looked at each of us with eyebrows raised above her sunglasses.

It was exhilarating, mind-clearing to be hitting twenty-three mph on a rotating pace line—heart straining, quads aching—but I worried I was expending too much energy too soon. Carlo took his turn pulling, but never for longer than four minutes. This worried me, too—he knew what lay ahead—and I shortened my time at the front. Freya did the same. Only Peggy hung onto the lead for longer and longer stretches.

At the end of a grueling mile-long climb we stopped in the Archaeological Park of Baratti and Populonia and walked our bikes across the rutted ground for the view of the gulf twinkling at the bottom of a gradual drop. The July heat struck me with its full withering force. We removed our helmets and guzzled water, while Carlo snapped photos.

Populonia was the only Etruscan city on the sea, Carlo had told us earlier. Now Peggy explained that when the Lombards attacked and destroyed Populonia, the survivors fled to the island of Elba. She pointed to the dark landmass on the horizon.

How pitifully unprepared I was for this trip, ignorant of the country's history and unable to speak Italian. I moved off and checked my cell phone. No messages from Anders. Freya and Peggy spoke in lowered voices now. I rejoined them, but they turned slightly away from me. Overcome by lightheadedness, I reached into my pocket for my PowerBar, the one I'd already eaten.

"Excuse me," I said. "Does anyone know what time it is at home?"

"Why?" Peggy snapped. "Do you have an appointment?"

"I don't know what time it is *here!*" Freya said. I raised my wrist, but she grabbed it before I could see my watch. "We're in Italy!" she said. "Time doesn't matter." Her grip was tight, but her eyes flashed with a teasing mischief. When she released me, I walked away. "Come back," she said. "We're joking."

"Let her go," Peggy said.

I climbed a grassy rise where a few sun-dazed tourists roamed with guidebooks. I felt detached from the landscape— the cypress and olive trees, the dusty wild sage and lavender—as though I were home looking at photos. I worked it out: Anders would have just woken up. I pictured my tall husband, loping barefoot down the driveway for the *Times* with Horace, our cat, brushing against his ankles. Not that long ago, Freya would have known I was worried about him. As for Peggy, illness was taboo. A year earlier, her husband, her partner in their engineering firm, had been unable to help his sixth-grade son with his math homework. A few weeks later, he had surgery to remove a brain tumor. His prognosis was good, but he had lingering difficulties with memory and vision.

In the near distance, the medieval fortress was bleached by the searing sunlight. I thought I would read the plaque, if there was one, then head back, but the path—a mottled pattern of grass and gravel—was too difficult to navigate in cleats. Halfway up, I lurched forward, breaking my fall with my hands and one knee.

"Ah, fuck!" I said, spitting into the dirt. A teenage girl glanced at me before hurrying past. I collapsed onto one haunch and examined my scraped palms and knee. I was absurdly furious and troubled by the vague sense I was making my life harder than it had to be.

When I returned, Carlo was photographing Freya in the yoga warrior pose against the blue backdrop of the sky. I sat on the stone bench and cleaned the gravel from my scrapes with my water bottle. Not for the first time, I wondered if Freya had mistaken me for someone more fearless, after seeing me in the shop, my hands smeared with grease and wielding a cable cutter. A few yards away, Peggy paced with her phone.

"Boundaries," I heard her say, giving instructions to a surveyor perhaps, or maybe to her mother, who was watching her three teenaged sons.

When we set off again under a cloudless sky, the pace was subdued. The sun baked my head inside my helmet. I gave up trying to catch Freya and Carlo. Peggy trailed behind me, complaining of a headache. When we arrived at the hotel she veered off to her room. Freya suggested we meet at the pool. I'd wanted to catch Anders on his drive into work but agreed. With Peggy out of the way, maybe Freya and I had a better chance.

A YEAR AGO, WHEN Freya first invited me to spend time with her apart from our cycling group, I was flattered but also cautious. I'd given up on close female friendships a few years earlier after Anders had pointed out that I tended to attract or to seek out (it wasn't clear which) women who looked to me for unreasonable support or validation. When I "failed" them, these women had lashed out by either freezing me out or by itemizing my faults. I limited myself to superficial connections like the one I had with my cycling group. But Freya's seductive phone calls and texts, the dog-eared volumes of Neruda and Akhmatova she left in my mailbox proved irresistible. On the inside cover of *Twenty Love Poem Songs and a Song of Despair* she'd written: Strong women make strong friends.

I was in a fragile state then: Anders had just been diagnosed. *His* type of cancer was the best cancer to get, he cheerfully told me, as though he expected congratulations. At first, I attributed his glib detachment to his profession— he conducted molecular biological research for Novartis—but then I came to see it as a distancing tactic. I wanted—no, I *needed* to support him, but he wouldn't let me in. First came

the surgery to remove his thyroid and then the radioactive io-
dine treatment that confined him to our basement guest room
for a week. Instructed by his doctors to avoid exposure, I left
his meals on top of the stairs and ran.

"You know what we're doing here?" he said during one
accidental encounter. He was hunched over like an animal,
one knee resting on the top step. His long face drooped, but
he sounded improbably upbeat. "We're radiocarbon dating!"
he crowed.

Not long after Anders' diagnosis, my mother's usual prick-
liness and self-absorption intensified. She'd call seven or eight
times a day with complaints and impossible demands like her
request for a ride to the DMV thirty miles away so she could
curse out the "rat" who had revoked her license. The cops had
sent her for a vision and driving test after she'd driven across
her neighbor's lawn. "I can't remember the rat's name," she said
when I suggested she call him. "But I'll know that son of a
bitch when I see him."

I would not find peace, Freya told me, until I learned to
accept uncertainty. She always had time for me: she worked
sporadically as a life coach, and her only child, an adult son,
lived across the country in Lake Tahoe. In the evenings, we
attended lectures and art openings in Manhattan. On my days
off, we took long bike rides, our conversations as meandering
as our routes. Freya mostly talked about her peripatetic childhood. Born in Paris to a British mother, a jewelry designer, and
a French father who owned luxury hotels and residences all
over the world, she'd lived in London, Amsterdam, and Rome.
Like the heroines of my beloved childhood books, she'd moved
through the world without adult supervision, smoking dope
in Amsterdam coffee shops, riding her Vespa in the Piazza di
Spagna, and clubbing in London with men twice her age. Her

stories were windows thrown open in a stuffy room. I was living the wrong life.

I'd fallen in love with her then, and when she withdrew, I was wounded in a way that was too embarrassing to admit to anyone but Anders. He suggested Freya's husband was behind it. He had a problem with Trevor. "The guy's a bully," he'd said in the car after our first and last meal together as couples. "He ordered her dinner like she's some kind of mail-order bride. You'd kill me if I did that." I shrugged. "You would," he insisted. He was all jazzed up, changing his grip on the wheel, shifting in his seat, as though each observation were accompanied by an electrical shock.

The dinner had been his idea after we'd bumped into Trevor and Freya at the Nyack farmers market in October, a week after his surgery. Trevor, a corporate lawyer, with the build and disposition of a bulldog, strode off when Freya laughingly showed us the obscenely large zucchini in her paper bag.

I'd feared Anders had fallen under Freya's spell, but after the dinner he was fixated on Trevor. "He kept talking over her," he said. "What's she doing with a guy like that?" Anders' usual keen powers of observation had malfunctioned. Freya's withdrawal was my fault, not Trevor's. I'd bored her with my worries.

Now FREYA APPEARED POOLSIDE, in a white bikini that barely covered her full round breasts and ass. She was carrying two wine glasses by their stems and a bottle of Bolgheri Sassicaia. I raised my eyebrows. "I have an admirer in the kitchen," she said.

We stretched out on chaise lounges at the edge of the oval pool, sipping the good Tuscan cabernet. The sun, low in the sky, turned the grass golden and glinted off the rippling turquoise water. The mothers coaxed their children from the pool, rubbed them with thick white towels. Their voices faded as they descended the hill behind us. I sipped my wine, feeling my head and chest grow warm. A pair of barn swallows swooped over the pool and disappeared into the trees. Worried I might say the wrong thing, I waited for Freya to speak first.

"Peggy looked so miserable," she said.

A hard knot dissolved in my chest. "Serves her right," I said, grinning.

"She'd rather keel over than admit she's wrong."

"Maybe now she'll let us enjoy the scenery," I said. "Instead of watching it zoom past at fifty miles an hour."

Freya drew her knees up and rested her chin on top of them. "I'm so glad you came. I thought maybe you'd back out because of Anders."

"What do you mean?" I said carefully.

"Trevor would've given me a hard time if he were sick."

"The doctors say he'll be fine. I have to get on with my life. *He* has."

"You don't sound okay with that."

I considered telling her that Anders's illness had magnified his independent streak, his slavish dedication to his work, and I worried about the distance growing between us. But if I'd wearied her with my fears before, I'd have to keep them to myself. "We can't let ourselves be defined by illness," I said. I drained my glass.

"That's good." She sounded unconvinced. "You've changed your thinking then. You used to say cancer was Anders's mistress."

"Did I?" I said, stiffening. "I don't remember that." I draped my towel around my shoulders and pulled the ends tight. "I didn't tell you, my mother's in the Crestview Nursing Home."

"Oh? That's new, isn't it?"

"Not really. It happened in the spring." I waited a beat to let that sink in, Freya's absence from my life. "It was too dangerous for her to live alone. She wouldn't listen to reason, so finally I had to get adult protective services involved."

"Are you feeling guilty?"

"I did what needed to be done. Anyway, she doesn't even recognize me anymore, claims she doesn't have a daughter."

"Oh, Julie. I'm sorry. That's really awful. How are you coping with that?"

"It's a relief, actually," I said quickly. "I can finally stop trying to get her to like me." Freya had a sly way of drawing me out, while she stopped short of revealing herself.

"How's *your* mother?" I said.

"Georgina!" She stretched her arms over her head and yawned. "She's moving to South Africa with her latest beau."

South Africa. Another place I'd never go. Once, when I'd asked Freya how she could bear living in suburban New Jersey, she'd said: "Life's a dream. It's a mistake to get attached to any of it." I'd pretended to know what she'd meant, but now sitting with her in the fading Tuscan sunlight I felt closer to understanding. This golden moment was slipping away, as were my life with Anders and my mother's memories of me. Where was the comfort in that? I was teetering on the edge of a drunken melancholy when Freya leaned in close and whispered, "He's watching us."

"Who?"

"Furio. Behind the bush. No, don't look." She laid a cool hand on my shoulder.

Shrubbery surrounded the pool. I slid my eyes toward the hedge, but saw no movement. "Who's Furio?" I thought to ask.

"The owner's son. The sexy ugly guy," she said, using Peggy's name for him.

I started to tell her how I'd caught him watching me the first night but realized she wasn't listening. She'd stood and was reaching around her back to unclasp her top. Then she wriggled out of her bottoms. How could two narrow strips of Lycra conceal such lushness? She tossed her hair over her shoulder and winked at me before diving into the pool. I turned to the hedge, but nothing.

Freya surfaced, her face shining with sunlight and water. "Let's give him what he came for," she whispered. "Take off your suit."

I looked at her, heart pounding, and then stood and swayed. Was I really going to do this? I rolled down my black tank suit and stepped out of it, telling my tipsy self that this was what a fearless woman would do. And even though I was convinced Furio hadn't climbed the hill to the pool to see *my* boyish figure—if he'd come at all—I picked up the wine bottle and toasted the bushes. "Here's to naked American ladies!" I took a long pull, enjoying the sound of Freya's jingling laughter.

"Give it here," she said, reaching up. I handed her the bottle then eased into the water. The cold sobered me. I'd been tempted to ask why she'd deserted me last year, but now I understood how pathetic that would sound. She had her back to the pool wall, scissoring her long legs. I faced her, submerged to my shoulders, and dragged my hands back and forth under the water, rippling the surface.

"I'm thinking about buying the shop," I blurted. It was more fantasy than truth—I hadn't mentioned it to Anders—but anything seemed possible now.

"Jack's selling? Why?"

"He's retiring," I said. "He approached a few of us. When I get back, I'm going to see about a loan." The fantasy assumed a more definite shape now that I was giving voice to it. "That shop is such a boys' club. I want to make it more women-friendly, get a better selection of bikes and clothing, hold more workshops."

Freya looked past me as I spoke, a smile playing on her lips. Whatever mood had taken hold of her prevented her from responding or looking at me. I felt close to knowing something important about her, but the wine and exhaustion from the day's cycling kept the knowledge just beyond my reach.

"What do you think?" I prodded.

"It's your decision." She gathered her hair in a ponytail and wrung the water from the ends. "I could never see myself tied down by a business. But it might be right for you."

I felt deflated. The sun had slipped behind the cypress trees. Chilled, we climbed out and dried off. I caught Freya studying me, and without thinking, I covered myself with the towel. She took a deep breath as though to say something, but then she sighed.

"What?" I said.

"Nothing. I'm just happy."

"Yeah, me, too." It was a lie, and I was certain she was lying, too.

DINNER THAT EVENING WAS a disaster. Freya and I had red wine hangovers and Peggy still suffered with a migraine. The restaurant Carlo had recommended for its view of the sea was pretentious. Peggy was convinced the waitstaff was ignoring us because we were Americans. She tugged on the waiter's jacket as he passed for the third time without acknowledging us. "Hey," she said. "Our drinks?"

Freya flashed a smile. "Dove sono le nostre bevande, per favore?"

The waiter nodded and left. Peggy started to complain again, but Freya cut her off. "Would you mind switching seats with me?"

"What for? I like my seat," Peggy said.

"Pretty please?"

After a few tense seconds of resistance, Peggy obliged. As she settled into Freya's chair, smoothing her napkin across her lap, Peggy said, "What was all that about?"

"I wanted to see things from your perspective," Freya said.

Peggy's face turned scarlet. "Are you for real?" She thrust out her chin. "Okay, Freya. What do you see?"

"I have an incredible view of the sea," Freya said, holding Peggy's gaze. "The moon's reflection looks like faerie lights." She turned to me, and I held my breath. "I see Julie's sweet smile."

I *was* smiling, I realized, and tried to stop. Freya's method was clumsy, but I grasped her intent. She'd done the same for me during the worst part of Anders' illness.

"Oh, for fuck's sake," Peggy said. "You have no idea what it's like to be me. You try running a business and taking care of three boys while your husband recovers from brain surgery. You wouldn't last two minutes in *my* world."

She stood and gestured at me, her top lip curling. "I have no idea why *she's* smiling. Who ever knows what's going on in her head. Have you ever heard her express an honest opinion?" She dropped keys on the table. "Take the car. I'll get a cab." She whipped her jacket from the back of the chair, rattling it, and then she was gone.

"Can you drive a stick?" Freya said. "I'm a little rusty."

I was too stunned to speak.

THE NEXT MORNING AT breakfast, Peggy avoided our eyes as she made her apology. "That migraine," she said. "I wasn't myself."

Freya rested her head on Peggy's shoulder. "It's nice to have you back."

I was still hurt but followed Freya's example of forgiveness.

At seven, Carlo arrived with Don Monsport, the retired racer, and Don's girlfriend. Gerrie was around twenty-five, half Don's age, and dressed in white Lycra. Peggy and I exchanged a disapproving glance as we rolled out. We were headed north toward Bibbona on roads winding through farmland. The morning sun chased the chill from the air and drew out the spicy scents of damp cedar bark and pine needles. Peggy and Freya sprinted ahead, ignoring Gerrie's attempt to hang on to their wheels. Carlo and Don, looking for free promotion through my bike shop, held me back with a long-winded pitch for the touring business. As we approached the first serious climb, they finally grew silent. Ahead, Freya and Peggy danced away on their pedals, side by side, up the hill. We caught up to Gerrie and the four of us climbed together. At the summit, Freya and Peggy were waiting, straddling their bikes, and laughing at something we were too late to catch.

"What's so funny?" I said, hoping I didn't sound jealous.

They grinned at each other and shook their heads. Before we could catch our breaths, they sprinted off again.

In Monteverdi, we parted ways with the racer and his girlfriend. Carlo led us to Mangia, a food shop on a quiet road bordered by vineyards. The shop was a colorful, aromatic place with cured meats hanging from the ceiling, shelves stocked with wheels of cheese, olive oils, and pasta. A stuffed wild boar stood atop a display case filled with Tuscan delicacies. The word *bamboozle* occurred to me as Carlo's friend, a handsome man in an apron and paper cap, launched into a manic performance, pouring wine, and slicing off wedges of cheese and pieces of sausages with a carving knife. Freya was always offered the first sample, and each time she directed the proprietor to serve us, the ugly stepsisters, first. The way she pretended to dislike the attention irritated me. I tried to make eye contact with Peggy, but she wouldn't look my way.

We left with pockets bulging with vacuum-sealed packages of wild boar and promises to return later with the car for more. But when we arrived at the hotel, I went to my room to call Anders. Our last conversation had been too brief—I'd interrupted him in the lab—but now I caught him before he left for work.

"Hey, you," he said, sounding out of breath. "I almost called you."

"Why? What's wrong?"

"I'm fine. Stop worrying. I was looking all over for my tennis racket. I'm playing with Chuck after work—"

I didn't hear the rest with the blood pounding in my ears. I managed to say, "Try the back closet—"

"That's where I found it. I'm cleaning off the cobwebs." The sound of his warm, raspy voice was the sound of home. I closed my eyes and saw his long Nordic face, his closely cropped salt-and-pepper hair, and I started to cry. The distance between us felt like the unnavigable distance of death.

He left off mid-sentence. "What's wrong?"

"I don't know why I came," I said. "I'm so homesick."

"Oh, Julie. You're not missing anything here. Try to enjoy yourself for once."

"What does *that* mean? I miss you, that's all. Can't I *ever* feel sad?"

"Wouldn't you rather have a good time?"

"You make it sound like I want to feel this way."

He didn't answer right away, and when he did, he seemed to choose his words carefully. "It's hard to hear you talk about homesickness when you keep leaving," he said. "All last year you kept taking off with Freya. You were never home. I thought that was over."

"But you were spending so much time at work."

"Because you weren't around."

I didn't think he was being truthful. Work comforted him better than I ever could. "Don't you miss me?" I said, hating the neediness in my voice.

"Of course I do."

A knock on my door released me from his impatience. I promised to call back.

I opened the door to Freya, radiant in a white dress and sandals, her wet hair leaving droplets on her bare shoulders. I invited her inside, but she said Furio was waiting. "He's giving me a lift back to that food place," she said.

"Furio? Is that a good idea?"

She frowned, but then her face softened with comprehension. "He's harmless." She touched my arm. "You all right?"

"I was just talking to Anders. *You* know how I—" She glanced at her watch, and I left off, worried about boring her. "We can talk later," I said quickly.

"You sure?"

I considered asking if I could come along to Mangia, but I didn't want to compete with Furio for her attention. "I'm sure. Go ahead—" I started to say when she leaned in close and kissed me on the lips. The soft hot pressure of her mouth startled me. I didn't know what to think. I watched her skip down the stairs and felt as though the blood were draining from my body with every step she took away from me. I went inside to lie down. It was dark when a knock on the door awakened me.

Peggy was dressed for evening in a denim jacket and white jeans, her wild, crinkly hair subdued in a tight ponytail. "What's the dinner plan? Where's Freya? She doesn't answer her phone. I left three messages."

I told her, and she groaned. "She left hours ago," I said.

We knocked on Freya's door and got no answer. We climbed the hill to the pool. I trailed behind Peggy, watching her red ponytail twitch on her neck like the tail of a fox stalking the henhouse. "Notice how she didn't invite *us*," Peggy said. "She's gotten that Neanderthal to fall in love with her, I bet. It's dishonest, don't you think?"

"I don't know what you mean," I said. But I knew.

We walked through the opening in the hedge. No one was in the pool. All the chaises were vacant. Our wine bottle and glasses lay toppled on the grass. "That's from yesterday, me and Freya," I said, dimly aware of wanting to hurt her. Her face soured, but before she could speak, I suggested we find Furio. We walked in silence to the office. He was on the computer beyond the reception desk, wearing a sleeveless T-shirt, a cigarette dangling from his lips. He didn't hear us come in and when Peggy banged on the bell, he looked up with annoyance, before he forced a cold smile.

"Where's Freya?" Peggy said. He gave her a blank look. "Our friend," she prompted. "You took her to Monteverdi?"

He grinned, relieved, it seemed, to understand. "Your friend, she asked for the taxi."

"Taxi?" I said, swatting at the cigarette smoke. "*To* Monteverdi or *from* Monteverdi?"

He approached the counter, and stubbed out his cigarette in the plastic ashtray. If he'd seen me naked, it hadn't made an impression: he looked right through me. "The taxi, it comes here."

"So, you *didn't* take her to Monteverdi?" I said. Someone was lying. "Did you see her return?"

"Ritorno? No, no, too busy." He gestured at the desk, looking nervous now.

"Let us into her room," Peggy demanded. He shrugged, took the key from a cubbyhole behind the desk. We followed him down the sidewalk and up the stairs. He unlocked the door but remained outside. The room appeared empty except for Freya's red Pinarello leaning against the wall. We all kept our bikes in our rooms, not trusting them to the storage shed. Peggy yanked open drawers, while I searched the bathroom. No clothes, no toiletries, no luggage. Not even a note. Peggy tried Freya's phone again. It went directly to voicemail.

"You didn't see her leave?" I asked Furio. "She would've had luggage."

"No, too busy." He offered to call Mangia, the food shop. But Peggy insisted the English-speaking waiter do it. Neither of us trusted Furio to provide an honest translation, one that could possibly incriminate him.

In the steamy kitchen, we gathered around the waiter as he placed the call. Furio's face fell when the waiter told us Freya had never arrived. He grabbed the phone, dialed, and spoke in rapid Italian. Polizioto was the only word I recognized.

We returned to the office where Peggy called the taxi company. "*Cosa?*" she said, and handed the phone to Furio. He turned his back to us and faced the plate glass window. Night had fallen, and the traffic speeding past on the rural road had taken on a menacing quality. He hung up and said, "The driver he's out of range. He'll call back."

A police car arrived with flashing lights. The polizioto had a flabby pockmarked face that made him appear sensitive but also untrustworthy. As Furio spoke to him in Italian, the policeman studied Peggy and me with evident interest. In broken English, he asked to see Freya's room. We all marched upstairs again.

"No passport. No luggage. The lady, she change her mind," the policeman said. "It happens every day." He looked to Furio as though for male corroboration, but Furio looked away.

Peggy and I remained in the room after the men left. She pulled one drawer clear of the dresser. A Euro coin rolled out and stopped near the bathroom. "Why did *she* get the bigger room?" Peggy said. The room was in fact the mirror image of my own. "Furio gave it to her, that's why," she said. "The only thing he's guilty of is lust. Looks like she just took off. But where'd she go?"

"She knows people all over Europe. Her mother's in Rome."

"Who leaves without saying anything?" she said.

"If she'd told us she was leaving, how would that have played out?"

"I would've been pissed," Peggy snapped before she registered my point. She tore the sheets from the bed and then sat down on the bare mattress. She tucked a strand of frizzy hair behind her ear. "I don't know how to say this without sounding pathetic." She avoided my eyes. "Did Freya come on to you like gangbusters then stop calling for no reason?"

I shrugged, resisting the comparison.

"Did you ever think you were maybe getting too close? Close enough to learn something awkward about her marriage? I only met him a few times, but that Trevor's a prick. I'm thinking she used us as an alibi to run away."

"I don't know. Maybe." It was easier to blame Trevor, but I couldn't do it.

The door swung open. I gasped. Peggy jumped up. It was Furio. He told us the taxi driver reported picking up an American from our hotel and driving her to the airport in Pisa. Behind him, Carlo gave a sheepish wave. "I come for the bike," he said. "I'm sending it to Roma."

"That's it, I'm out of here," Peggy said. "I'll get the next flight back."

"But *we* can still ride, can't we?" I said before thinking it through.

She looked nonplussed. "I don't know why I let her talk me into coming. My mother's losing her shit with the boys. My surveyor screwed up another job. I can't count on anyone."

"Shouldn't we maybe call Trevor?"

She blinked at me. "What the hell's wrong with you? Why would you want to get mixed up in their drama? If you need to worry about someone's husband, worry about your own. Go home." Peggy swept out, and Carlo followed with Freya's bike. Furio glanced at me before bending to pick up the wayward coin. He left with it clutched in his fist.

"She's living in Assisi," Peggy said. "Mistress to a bishop." We were in the bike shop, admiring the latest shipment of Treks. Four months had passed since our trip. At least once a week, Peggy dropped by to chat and share the latest outrageous rumors about Freya. On this sleety Saturday after Thanksgiving, the shop was crowded with women escaping the swamp of the long weekend. They crowded the espresso machine and gobbled my homemade blueberry scones. Later, if I got lucky, they'd line up at the register with armloads of winter gear.

In the end, our accountant had convinced me that a seasonal business was a bad investment. Anders sympathized with my lost dream, the dream I'd only just conceived in Tuscany. When the shop's new owner, a former hedge fund manager, offered me a ten percent share to run the "lady part" of the business, Anders suggested I take the money from our savings.

After the last customer left, I locked the doors. Soon I'd be home, eating leftover turkey with Anders, our warm kitchen a refuge from the cold, wet wind rattling the windowpanes. We'd speak kindly to each other over the click and clack of silverware. How relieved we were, after Italy, to come together again like castaways who'd washed up on opposite sides of a forested island.

Before I could leave, I had to count the money in the register and rehang the jerseys and jackets discarded in the dressing rooms. At the back of the shop, I tidied the mechanic's bench and checked on the bikes waiting for tune-ups. Among the muddy mountain bikes, the Pinarello caught my eye like a bright red Lifesaver candy. Without thinking, I swung around to look for her. But, of course, she must have brought it in on my day off. On the tag, dangling from the handlebars, I read her name: *Freya*. I checked my watch, and then hoisted the bike up onto the stand and got to work degreasing the chain.

CREATURE COMFORTS

A WEEK BEFORE THE FALL SEMESTER, Norristown Community offered me a section of English Composition. My C.V. was padded with volunteer work. I hadn't taught in over ten years. The college must have been as desperate as I was. A few months earlier, Larry's license to practice medicine and surgery in New York had been suspended. He'd been helping himself to morphine and Vicodin at the Valley Hospital pharmacy. After two patients filed lawsuits, I changed the locks, contacted a divorce attorney, and looked for work.

On the first day, I arrived fifteen minutes early to my classroom, wearing my orange pleated Jil Sander skirt, which usually made me feel as bouncy as a cheerleader. My hands trembled as I placed the roster and syllabus on the wooden podium. A girl wearing a red satin jacket sat in the back row, staring at me with wide unblinking eyes. I'd forgotten how unnerving that could be. As the other students shuffled in, I recalled the transcendent hopefulness of this moment. They were all potential geniuses, and I was their enlightened instructor. It could only go downhill.

A stubby woman with a prominent brow, dark skin, and bushy graying hair took a front row seat. She was in her late thirties, my age, and wore paint-splattered jeans, a purple polo, and plastic shower slides. She seemed familiar. A client at the food pantry where I volunteered? I smiled down at her, but she showed no sign of recognition.

I stepped out from behind the podium, and my skirt flashed in my peripheral vision like a traffic cone. "I'm Bonnie Starke," I said. "This is English Composition." The girl in the hijab groaned and left. Someone giggled. As I read the roster, working my tongue and teeth around the unpronounceable diphthongs and epiglottal consonants, no one corrected me. The woman in the front row was named Deeba Jagan. Her voice was braying, unpleasant, with an accent I couldn't place.

My contact lens had dried up from the air conditioning. I winked to keep it in place—confusing everyone I'm sure—as I read the rules and requirements. They sounded overly strict and punitive now that I was saying them aloud. It was a mistake to think I could return to teaching. Maybe I could try waitressing again. My blouse clung to me with sweat. Dry-cleaning was another expense I would have to cut back on.

"Any questions?" Fifteen blank faces stared back at me. Did they understand English? "Write a short introduction," I said. "Tell me your goals for this class. Why are you in college? What do you do in your spare time?" I kept firing questions. No one moved. "Write!" I said, flicking the backs of my hands at them.

Notebooks opened. Pens were fished from backpacks. A tall young man with a small head spoke with a Russian accent to the jittery man beside him. A pencil was passed across the aisle. Everything will be okay, I told myself. I resisted checking my phone, determined to set a good example. Larry's texts and emails had dwindled in the last week. Maybe he'd changed his mind about not checking into the rehab center recommended by the State Board of Medical Examiners. Maybe he no longer believed they were only *out to get him.*

If he could beat his addiction and also satisfy the board's conditions for reinstating his license, would I reconsider divorce? I couldn't imagine trusting him again. But I also worried about money. All my life I'd been told that money was the root of all evil—usually by people who didn't have any—but life, I'd found, was easier when you had some.

I PUT MYSELF THROUGH City College with student loans and various minimum-wage jobs, including waitressing, cleaning offices, and ringing up groceries at Fairway Market. My roommate, freshman year, was an accounting major who worked at Macy's Clinique counter. She gave me weekly makeovers, painting my face with her pots and pallettes, and she introduced me to the high-end thrift shops on the Upper East Side where we pawed through rich women's cast-off belts and blouses and shoes. During final exams week, we treated ourselves to haircuts at Henri Bendel's on the day the assistants offered their services at a steep discount. When I went home for Christmas break, wearing a secondhand camel-hair coat and Courtesan Red lipstick, my mother walked right past me on the train platform. In her glance I saw a flicker of something—respect maybe, or intimidation. She cleaned BMWs in a dealer's showroom to supplement my father's GE repairman paycheck. Her irritating practice of labeling certain behaviors low-class in order to encourage good manners and elevated speech meant that my two sisters and I could pass for upper class in any WASPy country club—if only they'd deign to admit us.

I was twenty-six and working my way through graduate school as a waitress in O'Sullivan's on Second Avenue and 84th Street when I met Larry Starke. One night, a rowdy group of men sat down in my section. "Don't waste time on them," one of the other waitresses told me. "They're residents from Lenox Hill; they never tip." Her blouse was unbuttoned to her lace bra and I gave up all hope. I wore a turtleneck and a below-the-knee hem to get through my shifts with minimal groping and proposals. I told myself I could handle those clowns. But one of the residents, a cocky redhead with a square jaw, patted my ass, and a crazy rage knocked me off balance. He'd singled me out as easy prey, I figured. I was pretty enough to warrant his attention, but because I was outside his social circle, I wasn't worthy of serious consideration. The abuse went on all night, and even though I told myself it didn't bother me, tears stung my eyes. When ginger boy tried to pull me onto his lap, I wriggled out of his grasp and spilled a platter of fried calamari in the process.

"Just let me do my fucking job, asshole," I said, and raised the empty platter over his head, prepared to do harm. He lunged for me, but Larry Starke jumped between us. I hadn't noticed Larry before. He pushed ginger boy back into his chair with an open hand and guided me outside into the chilly autumn night.

On the street, he gave me a wry smile. His face was fleshy, boneless; he had a sad comb-over. He said something, but an ambulance wailing past drowned it out. I guessed he'd just told me off, and I flushed with shame.

"Well?" He smiled with eager, watery eyes. "Do I have any chance at all?"

We were married six months later, and a few years after that we bought a faux French château-style house in Eagle Brook Estates, in Alpine, New Jersey, built on the rolling hills of a former golf course. I zipped around in a BMW sports car, the wife of a neurosurgeon. Our sex life, while not passionate, was at least warm and friendly. After I got pregnant at thirty, I left my teaching assistantship at City College, abandoned my dissertation on radical women's writing in 1930s America, and never looked back.

Life was good for a while, but then Larry was hit with a malpractice suit three years ago. He began to spend more and more time at the Upper East Side apartment he shared with two other doctors.

At the end of the first class, a knot of students blocked my escape. One after another told me about the double shifts and second jobs, sick children and elderly parents that would interfere with their studies. Deeba was the last in line. We were alone.

"Get them to talk more." Her voice was like metal hitting a power saw blade. "They need practice. Especially the Mexican ladies."

It came to me where I'd seen her: waiting in the local bus shelter with the other house cleaners. "You know them?" I said.

"The three Mexican ladies work for me. So does the African girl. I have a cleaning business. New construction mostly. You know the Santo brothers?" I shook my head. "We work a lot for them." She dug into her jeans and handed me a wrinkled hot pink business card, which I dropped into my briefcase without reading. She continued, "Most of them will end up going back where they came from."

"What makes you say that?"

"They don't have what it takes. You have to stop making excuses, work hard, and speak English." She gave me a defiant look. "I'm saving for a house."

"Good for you," I said.

"This book you want us to buy—"

"You won't need it this week. Read the handout for homework." I held up my cell. "If you'll excuse me."

After she left, I took my time packing up, so I wouldn't risk running into any of my students. I felt hopeful, and I didn't want anyone to spoil that.

Later, when I was driving my nine-year-old home from her after-school care, the hope began seeping out of me. I couldn't believe I had to go back in two days. Campbell asked about my students, but I was at a loss. I remembered the essays and told her to read one.

"Really? I can?" She sat up straighter.

I hesitated, remembering the intimacy of reading another's thoughts. Her father's last text: *If I go 2 rehab they'll take everything. I do this 4 us. Delete this.*

I'd told Campbell her father had gotten sick from bad medicine, and he was getting help. She'd seen through the lie, I was sure. Like her father, she had an intuitive brilliance. As young as seven, she'd asked me why her daddy was so sad. On his rare visits home, I would be shocked at the change in him: he'd put on weight and was disheveled; he gave off the sweetish odor of shit. I monitored their time together, deflecting his obsessive questions. Were her teachers or friends' parents talking about him? What did they say? Did she love him? How much?

"Maybe read just one." I stopped for the light and watched her lift my briefcase onto her lap.

She held up a ragged-edged sheet. "This one. It's got purple writing." She sniffed it. "Grape!"

"Are you going to read it or eat it?"

She rolled her eyes. "Dechontee Sirleaf," she read. "Is that a girl or a boy?"

I shrugged. Campbell read:

I was 12 when I came to US after first Liberian Civil War in 2000. My uncle got hands cut off by Charles Taylor's soldiers

then my mother and fater get killed, my aunt lets me live with
her in Newark. In my spare time I worked at Newark lickor on
Bloomfield avenue but a man come with a gun. I too afraid to goes
back so now I clean. I come to college for a degree in business to start
my own business like Deeba.

We drove in silence. When we pulled through the stone
gates of Eagle Brook Estates, Campbell said, "I wish I hadn't
read that. I feel sad."

I touched her knee. "Sorry."

I STRODE INTO MY classroom, three days a week, like an ac-
tor reprising a beloved role. So much of teaching was acting.
Stanislavski—or maybe Darwin—said the external expression
of an emotion deepens it. I worked hard to project a confident
image, so why wasn't it taking root inside me? At least it didn't
take long to match up the names in my roll book with the faces
in front of me. Dechontee Sirleaf was a tall, elegant twenty-
eight-year-old woman who spoke in a whisper. The three young
Mexican women who worked for Deeba were named Marisol
Guzman, Lupe Castillo, and Esperanza Diaz. They took turns
sitting in the desk hidden behind the tall cart that held the overhead projector I never used. Every class, I'd coax one of them out
of hiding. The male students stuck together: Glen Lopez, Jerrick
Brown, Leo Domashev, and Abdul Nasir. I'd lost three students
after the first class and a fourth after her mother fell ill.

The eleven remaining students were all struggling. Our text-
book was partly to blame. The essays were dense, complicated,
and presumed a base knowledge few students had. Maybe that
was why they kept forgetting to bring it to class. More likely,
they'd never forked over the ninety dollars to buy it.

On a gray Monday in October, I gave up trying to explain
Walker Percy's "The Loss of the Creature" and sent Deeba to

the copy room with the *Times*. As we waited, I listed on the board the Middle Eastern and Northern African countries affected by civil wars and protests in the Arab Spring.

Deeba returned and distributed the Thomas Friedman article. "It's about how education is important," she told her classmates. "I read it while I made copies." Dechontee, Marisol, and Esperanza nodded. They wore identical lime green T-shirts from a colon cancer charity run. Lupe's red sneaker poked out from behind the cart. As usual, the men looked bored.

"Yes, in part," I said. "It addresses the leadership vacuum after the Arab awakening. But you're right, Deeba; it also discusses how Arab dictators neglected education. Young Arabs can't compete for jobs in the private sector."

Abdul's sleepy dark eyes shifted from me to Deeba with agitated interest.

"That's what I said," Deeba told me. She turned back to her classmates. "Read the last paragraph. It says three years in a row of a bad teacher can screw up a kid for years, but one year of a good teacher can make them successful enough to the point where they can buy their own house."

The article said nothing about real estate. And Friedman used the example of teachers to make a point about effective leadership. But the students were all reading, so I let it alone.

A FEW DAYS LATER, I was driving home in a flash flood. My wipers could not keep up, and I peered at the road through a waterfall. That morning, my director had encouraged me to apply for an open full-time position, which she privately assured me I'd get. I needed the money. Larry had drained our joint savings. There were other accounts, but I didn't know how to access them. I had to get my act together. Larry was never going to rehab. The day before, one of his roommates, the orthopedist, had called to say he'd changed the apartment locks while Larry was out. Valuables had gone missing—a watch, an iPad, the TV. I pictured Larry ripping a flat-screen TV off the wall. What did it say about me that I was still married to a man like that? The orthopedist went on to say he wasn't pressing charges, but I should also change my locks. His superior tone called up the images of private schools and beach houses, deals brokered by handshakes in exclusive clubs. I told him I was way ahead of him and hung up.

I drove slowly. The wind and rain ripped leaves from the trees, turning the road slick. A mile from home, I spotted a hunched hooded figure walking in the distance. Cars were swerving, honking. I slowed and pulled over to the curb after I recognized Deeba in the rearview mirror.

"Lucky I came along," I said as she climbed in. "I don't even like *driving* on this street."

"Bus never came. I couldn't wait." Her voice was even more grating in the confined space. Wet, she gave off an earwaxy smell. She removed her hood and looked around. "Nice car."

I pulled into traffic. "Where're you going?"

"Leather, isn't it?" She stroked the seat. "I like the Range Rover. That's what Nancy drives."

I didn't know who Nancy was. "Where're you headed?"

"I watch the Gerbers' kids until Nancy gets home."

Why didn't I know this? After reading her rambling essays, I knew she'd emigrated from Guyana in her twenties, cared for her mother who had colon cancer, and ran that business she was always talking about. And, as everyone knew, she was saving for a house.

"Where do they live?" I said, losing patience. "Am I going the right way?"

"Don't you know the Gerbers? They live at the end of your street."

I snapped my head around. "How do you know where I live?"

"I see you outside. I've been watching Becky and Adam since they were babies. I run into Dr. Larry sometimes in Dunkin' Donuts. I tell him: better stop eating all those jelly donuts. You'll pop your buttons."

I stiffened, waiting.

"He pretends they're for your little girl," she said. "Big fat liar, I call him." She grew quiet. "I haven't seen him in a long time. He okay?"

I hesitated: the house-cleaner grapevine was notorious. "He's very busy," I said.

I made the turn through the stone gates of Eagle Brook Estates. We ascended the first hill, and the mansions with their stone turrets, slate roofs, and four-car garages came into view. Seeing the neighborhood through Deeba's eyes made me uneasy. I thought ahead to when I'd be alone again. If I left Campbell in the after-school program for another hour, I could get a jump start on grading essays.

As though reading my mind, Deeba said, "Who watches your girl when you have to go out?"

"What?" I felt my face heat up. "I don't see how that's your business—"

"I only meant I can watch her," she said with no trace of offense. "I'm good with kids. Ask Nancy. It's got to be hard if Dr. Larry—" She leaned forward. "There he is. I was going to say he's never home."

I whipped my head around, but she blocked my view. I pressed hard on the gas, flinging her back in the seat. By now Larry would have realized I'd changed the locks.

"Here, turn left here." She stuck her arm in my face, pointing. I drove up the long, curving driveway of the shingle-style house. Now I remembered Nancy. She'd wave whenever our paths crossed at school or the country club, but lately she pretended not to see me.

My phone was ringing in the briefcase at Deeba's feet. It had to be Larry. "See you in class," I said, my hands gripping the wheel.

"Aren't you going to get that?"

I ignored her.

"Could be your little girl," she said.

"I'll get it after you leave." I smiled, until she got the hint and opened the door.

"My rates are reasonable," she said before getting out.

By the time I could check my phone, I'd missed two calls from Larry but no messages, texts, or emails. All the way home, Campbell complained about some classroom injustice. I wasn't listening. I was on the lookout for Larry's black Jaguar. It wasn't like him not to leave a single message. Sober or high, he was a chatterbox. I used to love that about him back when he made sense.

I scrutinized the interior of the garage before pulling the car in. I'd changed the codes for the garage doors and alarm as well as the locks, but I wasn't taking any chances. Larry would need a place to sleep now that his roommates had locked him out. Inside, I went from room to room, checking doors and windows. Campbell followed on my heels, whining that she was hungry. I hadn't been to the grocery store in a week. In my bedroom, I pulled the shades. The wind rushed down the chimney and blew open the glass doors on the fireplace, making me jump. White ash swirled and settled on the soft leather vamps of my Chanel boots. I bent down to take them off.

"What's blow?"

I spun around. Campbell was stretched out on my bed, chin propped in her hand, eating a piece of the good dark chocolate I stashed in my night table. She must have sensed my alarm, because she popped up to a sitting position, watching me. I ignored the chocolate; though it disturbed me that she had her father's lack of impulse control.

"Why do you ask?"

"Brandon's father said Daddy can't be a doctor because he does blow."

Brandon's father, an anesthesiologist, was on the school board. If he knew about Larry, everyone knew, and not just the fourth grade. I sat on the bed and stroked her frizz of curls. I stared at the photos on the mantelpiece: birthday parties, Christmases, a rare family trip to Grand Canyon National Park—all were at least five years old.

"You studied substance abuse at school, right?" I began with no idea of how to continue. The ringing phone cut me off. I stretched to reach it.

"Where you been?" Larry said. "I couldn't get inna house. My keys won't work."

I hadn't spoken to him in a month. His voice plunged me into misery. I let the silence build.

"Bon, you there?"

"Yes,"

"Listen, I'm in a li'l bit of trouble. I'm at the police station."

"What did you do?" I stood; Campbell watched me, alert.

"Nothing. I swear," he said. "Self-defense."

I started down the hallway. "Oh, shit, what did you do?"

"One of 'em shoved me. Every man for himself."

"Did you hit a cop?" I glanced back. Campbell peeked around the doorframe. I ducked into the guest room.

"You gotta come. They're gonna kill me." He lowered his voice. "There's cash. In the garage. Tennis ball cans."

"Jesus, Larry, you have to get help. Do it for Campbell. Kids at school are saying things. Is that what you want?"

The silence stretched out. I'd walked to the farthest corner of the guest room. The pillow was still indented from his head. He let out a sob. "I love Campbell," he said. "She knows, right?" There was a shuffling sound. "They're making me get off. Are you coming, Bon?"

"I don't know, Larry." I was crying, too. "I don't think I can do this."

Campbell followed me down the stairs into the kitchen, asking "Who was that?"

"A friend," I told her.

"What did your friend want? You look scared."

"My friend needs help," I said. "I'm not scared. Just worried."

I sliced a banana on the granite countertop for her cereal. From now on, I would do better. Campbell deserved at least one good parent. It nagged me that maybe I'd given up on her father too soon.

While she ate, I went into the garage. His car had been missing so long the space had filled with bicycles and recycling. I climbed the stepladder to reach the shelf and popped the lid on one of the Wilson cans; it was stuffed with cash. I counted ten hundred-dollar bills. I shoved them into the pockets of my Stella McCartney jacket and opened a second can. Same deal. I opened a third and froze. I pulled out three plastic bags filled with white powder. A wave of nausea hit me. Was he using *and* selling?

The door swung open; Campbell gaped at me. I shoved the bags into my pockets with the money and climbed down.

"What're you doing, Mommy?"

"Never mind." I steered her back inside. "Get started on your homework."

I went into the bathroom, locked the door, and flushed the powder. Clouds of it settled on the toilet seat, the floor, my jacket; I cleaned it up with dampened tissues. How could he do this to us? Campbell knocked, asking for help with her math.

"One minute!" I rinsed the empty bags, and caught my reflection in the mirror. My dark roots were growing out. My face looked as gaunt and drawn as the migrant mother's in the Dorothea Lange photo. Wet clumps of tissue dotted my jacket where I'd wiped it.

In the kitchen, I coached Campbell through a long division problem while making my own calculations. The teenage babysitter wasn't available on school nights. My sisters lived an hour away. I could take Campbell with me, leave her in the car, but that alternative seemed worse than the choice I kept bumping into and rejecting. I gave in and reached for the phone and the school directory.

Nancy said Deeba was on her way out. She didn't bother to cover the mouthpiece when she shouted, "Can you watch Bonnie's daughter right now?"

I heard Deeba's strident voice. "Yeah okay." A pause. "Who's Bonnie?"

"Mrs. Starke from down the street."

"Professor Starke? I'll walk over. I know where she lives."

Nancy laughed. "She's on her way. For some reason, she's calling you professor. How do you know her?"

"I'm her professor." I let that sink in. "I have to ask. Can I trust her with Campbell?" I grasped the irony: the cokehead's wife worried about trustworthiness.

"Deeba? Oh, my god, yes. Just watch out. She'll rearrange your furniture and then your life."

The doorbell rang five minutes later. Campbell pushed back her chair and skipped ahead of me to the door. I'm sure she imagined some cute college girl, because she took one look at the stubby woman in the soaked black hoodie and ran up the stairs.

"Go on," Deeba told me. "I'm good with kids. You'll see."

I DROVE AROUND EAGLE Brook Estates in the rain, working up my courage. The people who lived in these artfully landscaped mansions probably believed they were insulated from this kind of nightmare. Larry had grown up in a Westchester neighborhood similar to this one. Both his parents were doctors. Life was supposed to be easy, but his nerdy intelligence and his ungainliness had made him a target. He didn't come into his own until college when his cleverness was sought out by friends and rewarded by professors. I suspected the malpractice suit had dug up the sense memories of being bullied. All those years of achievement teetered. I sympathized, but I also knew I couldn't let him drag Campbell and me down with him. That was what I'd tell him after I paid his bail. But Larry's lawyer had gotten there first. He was gone. A part of me regretted that Larry hadn't trusted me to show up.

I was home less than an hour after I'd left. The house was fragrant with baking brownies. Deeba and Campbell were huddled inside a blanket fort in the family room. I stood outside it a few minutes, listening to Deeba read about Justin Bieber's romantic Bahamas trip, before announcing myself.

Campbell begged me to let Deeba stay. "We didn't eat the brownies," she said.

"Another time," I said, taking the *People Magazine* from her hands and returning it to Deeba. I sent her off to bed. Deeba's eyes bulged when I pulled the wad of cash from my pocket to pay her. I offered to call a taxi, but she said she would stay at Nancy's.

"You have a nice house," she said at the door. "Nancy's is bigger. She's got a two-story family room. I can still see all the action, even if I'm stuck upstairs with the kids."

"It's late, Deeba."

She peered around my shoulder and lowered her voice. "Dr. Larry called. He's a drinker, isn't he?" I shook my head. "He said to tell you he'll make Campbell proud, even if it kills him. I think that's what he said. It was hard to understand."

I looked away, lips pressed together to stop myself from crying.

"Oh, Professor." She hugged me hard. When she released me, I felt unsteady. "When I used to see you in town, I'd think, there's a sad lady. But when I came to your class, I thought, this is not a sad person. She's always smiling. She's really happy when we understand."

After that night, I distanced myself from Deeba, assuming an aloof manner, but if she sensed a change, she never let on. We limped through the semester, dissecting the complicated essays in our text. In mid-November, I revisited Percy's "The Loss of the Creature." It was tricky explaining how Percy's ideas about independent thinking might be applied to the American dream when American products and experiences continued to dazzle them.

"I drive boss's Lexus SUV," Leo Domashev said with his usual passion. "And I see for myself is superior car."

"I'm not buying anyone else's ideas either," Deeba said. "I went to the Grand Canyon with the Gerbers last year, and I was as amazed as that Spanish explorer."

I sagged behind the podium. I'd come to think of the wooden structure alternately as a life raft and a shield. "The

Grand Canyon is a metaphor," I said. "It shows how we see things based on whether they measure up to what we've heard."

"Heard from who?" Dechontee said.

"From the so-called experts," I said. "Me, for example."

"I understand," Deeba said. "You could switch the Grand Canyon for Leo's Lexus or Eagle Brook Estates," she said. "Same thing."

A strange, guttural laughter took us all by surprise. The students turned. My view was blocked by the overhead projector. I stepped out from behind the podium. Larry was leaning in the doorway. I hadn't heard from him in two weeks, not since the night of his arrest.

"Nicely put, Jelly Donuts!" he said, clapping. "Brava!" His pupils were dilated and his greasy blond hair hung past his collar. His shirt was torn and dirty as though he'd slept outside.

Deeba must have seen my panic, because she gave me a nod and strode toward him. "Dr. Larry!" she said. "Let me take you where you need to be."

"It's all a crock of shit, Jelly Donuts. The American nightmare. Eagle Shit Estates. I worked so hard, and where did it get me?" He looked at me. "Why are you doing this to me, Bon?" His shoulders shook, and he began to weep.

What am *I* doing? I wanted to ask, but I'd lost my voice.

"I made a good life for us, didn't I?"

I looked down at my scuffed boots. Leo climbed to his feet, hands balled in fists.

"Come with me, Dr. Larry. You need to rest." Deeba took his arm, and to my great relief, he allowed her to steer him into the hallway. "They all just fuck me up the ass," he wailed.

When his voice had faded, my students turned back to me. They deserved an explanation. I wished I had one. I couldn't say why life fucks some people, why innocent girls like Dechontee lose their parents to mad dictators, why Lupe would eventually return to Mexico in defeat, why my brilliant, privileged husband resorted to drugs when life got too hard. I didn't know for sure why I'd taken the lazy way out by marrying Larry.

I dismissed the class early and took my time packing up. I thought of the night, so many years ago, when Larry had rescued me from that jerk at O'Sullivan's. I closed my eyes and saw Larry's anxious, hopeful smile. It came to me that he'd wanted me to rescue *him*. I'd let him down.

I left the classroom. Leo, Abdul, Marisol, Esperanza, and Dechontee were waiting for me in the hallway. "I'm okay," I said. "Go on home." Without a word, they followed me through the front doors and into the parking lot. A new layer of silvery snow waited for our footprints. The cold seeped into my collar. I'd left my Hermès scarf behind. A police cruiser flew by, heading for the school building. I imagined Deeba in the Dean's office, holding Larry's hand. This was new territory for all of us. We were all explorers. As my students watched, I drove away, grateful there were more days left in the semester to make up for this one.

TABOR LAKE, 1993

Ｆ ROM THE LIFEGUARD'S CHAIR Katherine notices the
white pickup truck entering the lake property. It rattles
down the gravel road and stops about a hundred feet away.
The driver, a short, body-builder type in an orange T-shirt,
jumps down from the cab, stirring up some dust. It's un-
usual to see an outsider in the private lake community on a
weekday afternoon, but it's especially weird if that stranger
is male. Most of the able-bodied men leave their cottages
on Sunday night and don't return until late Friday, if they
come back at all. This muscular guy in the orange T-shirt
saunters over to the old oak at the edge of the water like he's
thinking about bench-pressing it. The tree reaches at least
thirty feet into the sky, and its branches sprawl out over the
water. The trunk is so enormous a skinny decrepit man can
hide behind it, apparently, because here comes Mr. Hurley
seemingly out of nowhere to shake the stranger's hand. She
loses interest then—the lake president is older than the tree
and one hundred percent duller—and returns her attention
to the swimmers and to nursing her perfect misery.

After weeks of faulting Teddy, she blames herself now,
which makes their breakup a little easier to bear. If she hadn't
gone to work at that stupid upstate New York camp, they
might still be together. She accepted the job months before

they met in February. It was supposed to be her big adventure since, unlike most of her friends, she isn't going away to school in the fall; instead, she'll be commuting to the state college with her older brother who owns a car.

How could she know then that losing her virginity to Teddy would so thoroughly uproot her? The first few times she phoned him from the camp office, he sounded disengaged like he was working out a calculus problem or building a model airplane while he talked to her. Worried she was losing him, she told him about all the fun she was having with the two local boys who worked in the camp kitchen. Any moron could have predicted how that would turn out. Every time she called his house after that, his mother said he was out. After the last futile call, Katherine sank to the floor and sobbed in front of the moose-faced secretary who, smiling to herself, continued typing. It makes Katherine cringe now to remember it. With two weeks remaining in the session, she quit the camp and took the train home, only to discover Teddy was still "out" every time she called.

When the shouting starts on the lake road, Katherine turns toward the commotion grudgingly. The voices are muffled by the shrieks and screams of the swimmers, but it's clear someone is mad about something. It's the heat. The late August humidity presses down on northern New Jersey like a steaming iron, flattening everyone's spirits. There are three men by the tree now: Mr. Dinardo, the beach manager, wearing his usual Hawaiian swim trunks and red bandana, has joined old Mr. Hurley and the muscle man. She considers Mr. Dinardo her friend even though he's old—at least sixty-five. Tall, lanky, and quick with a joke, he shows up every day at one o'clock to relieve her while she eats lunch and uses the bathroom. He appears at other times of the day too, and he always brings her a cold Coke. She thinks he might be lonely. He lives alone; his wife is dead.

For some reason, it appears Mr. Dinardo is preventing the muscle man from reaching his truck. When the younger man steps closer, Mr. Dinardo takes a swipe at him and misses. Katherine stands in her seat, the whistle touching her lips. If they fight, she thinks, Mr. Dinardo will definitely lose to that bruiser. She looks around for help and meets the eyes of Mrs. Sheehan who's nursing her baby on a beach chair.

"I was afraid it would come to this," Mrs. Sheehan says. "They've been fighting over the tree since June." She's stocky, and her flame-colored hair is held back from her round, sensible face by a white headband. She's the type of woman Katherine's mother calls *frowzy*. As she struggles to her feet, her breast swings free into the open air. It's crisscrossed with blue veins, and the nipple is large and dark and rubbery-looking. Katherine looks down with fascinated revulsion as Mrs. Sheehan shoves it inside her swimsuit. I'll never let that happen to me, she thinks.

"Looks like Tom's trying to pull a fast one," Mrs. Sheehan says, shading her eyes. Tom is Mr. Hurley. It disorients Katherine to hear people call him that. It makes him sound young, which she can't imagine him ever being. "What do you mean?" she says.

"He can't do anything until the stockholders' meeting," Mrs. Sheehan says. "Some of us want to save that tree; some of us remember jumping off it when we were kids."

"You?"

Mrs. Sheehan looks amused. "Yes, me! I wasn't born this old, you know."

She blushes. "I'm sorry. I just thought it was against the rules. What's wrong with the tree?"

"Gypsy moths, and now some kind of fungus—" Mrs. Sheehan breaks off. "Oh, boy, here we go," she says.

Katherine swings her head around. The driver is making an end run around Mr. Dinardo to the back of his truck. He lowers the tailgate and reaches into the bed to lift out a chain saw. Mr. Dinardo takes a step toward him but stops when the man jerks a cord and an angry snarl fills the air. In the next instant, Mr. Dinardo is running for the tree.

"Jesus, Mary, and Joseph," Mrs. Sheehan shouts over the roar. "He's climbing it!"

Katherine presses her fingers to her mouth to stop herself from smiling. It makes sense: he's from the Sixties, when people made grand gestures to protect the environment. But it's a lost cause. They'll just cut it down after Labor Day when he returns to his Florida condo.

Mrs. Sheehan hoists her fat baby onto her shoulder like a sack of sugar. "Time for a little female diplomacy," she says. "Don't you think?" Before Katherine can answer, Mrs. Sheehan is making her way down the stretch of sand, barefoot and bottom-heavy, her progress slow.

In mid-June, after the graduation parties, Teddy talked Katherine into trespassing at Tabor Lake to jump from the tree. They parked on the other side of Route 53 and walked under the stars down the gravel road to the lake. The night was humid, and the air was rank with stinkweed and algae blooms. Woods surrounded the small lake on all sides, but there were about forty cottages on the hill behind the beach; their lights shone faintly through the trees. Her swim team friends often bragged about sneaking into the lake after hours, but she'd never had the nerve to join them. That night with Teddy she hung back on the lake road, fearful of getting caught.

In mock military tones, he said, "Shape up, soldier. Life's not a risk-free operation." He was taller than she was and more beautiful, she thought, with a halo of blond curls, sleepy brown eyes, and a carnivorous grin. He carried an Army blanket from his house and a flashlight, which he shone in her face, until she made him shut it off.

"My parents will *kill* me if we get caught. You have no idea."

"Come on," he said, dragging out the words seductively. "They're never going to know." He pulled her by the hand, but she resisted.

"We're trespassing. It's against the law."

"If it makes you feel better, we'll have an exit strategy," he said. "I'll make a break for the woods. And you? Let's see." He tapped his chin with his index finger. "You can jump in the water and hold your breath until the coast is clear."

A lightning bug flashed past her face and flew out over the lake. The moon illuminated clouds of gnats hovering over the placid surface. In a small voice, she said, "Why can't I come with you?"

"You don't know anything about military maneuvers, do you?" He draped an arm across her shoulder and steered her toward the tree. "It'll be harder to catch us if we separate."

She kept silent, thinking she'd follow him into the woods if they were chased. She would follow him anywhere. Whenever they were separated for any length of time, she felt crazy with lust or love or a busted heart. She had no words to describe the terrible feeling of missing him. If she could get out of the camp contract, she would, but the director was her father's old college roommate, and she couldn't back out without disappointing people.

At the tree, Teddy pulled off his gray T-shirt and running shoes. He grabbed hold of a gnarl and planted his foot on the trunk to pull himself up. He moved as fluidly on land as she did in water. She envied his grace, athletic and otherwise. If she couldn't *be* him, she could love him. As he stepped onto the branch, the wood creaked under his weight, and he flexed his knees to bounce the branch.

"Timber!" he said.

She laughed to hide her dread. In the next instant, his pale skin flashed in the darkness, and his splash shattered the silence; she held her breath until he surfaced.

"Come on in," he said, treading water. "Don't be such a chicken."

She looked down the shadowy road. No one rushed from the cottages with shotguns and bloodhounds like she'd imagined. While Teddy floated on his back, spouting water from between his teeth, she peeled off her black Nike tank behind the tree trunk. He was always telling her how much he loved her swimmer's body, her broad shoulders and narrow waist. She climbed the tree wearing only the opal necklace he'd given her for their graduation, thinking, *I'll show him who's chicken.*

With trembling knees, she inched out along the branch, grasping the slender branches above for balance, grimacing at the creaks and groans of the old tree. She glanced down into the inky water, into Teddy's admiring gaze. If it weren't for him, she wouldn't know what it was like to be suspended, naked, between the water and the night sky. She took a deep breath, trapped it in her lungs, and leaped. When she surfaced from the roily darkness, nose stinging, gasping for air, the first thing she saw was Teddy's grin.

"That's how I like my women," he said, swimming toward her. "Naked and wet."

She thinks of all this now as she watches the bodies, a swarm of children and a few women, moving in the shimmering heat toward the tree. Mr. Dinardo, perched on the outstretched branch, swings his legs, and grins like a dunk tank carnival clown at the gathering crowd. The chain saw is quiet now, but the air still vibrates. Mr. Hurley and Mrs. Sheehan are trying to push the kids away from the tree, but they keep pressing closer, and more keep arriving. They jump and jostle each other, made giddy by the sight of an adult's misbehavior.

An approaching siren drowns out all the voices. The squad car stirs up dust, scattering the crowd. It doesn't take long for the big-bellied cop to clear the area. Katherine knows it's not a crime to climb a tree, but still she's worried for Mr. Dinardo. When the kids return to the beach, she tucks her whistle inside her bathing suit and follows them into the water. "What did the cop say?" she asks Jeremy, the freckled twelve-year-old. He blinks and shrugs. When he wades into the water, she follows, and swims out to the raft behind him. "What did the cop say?" she asks the boys on the raft, but they move away, shaking their heads. She sits down on the sandpapery boards, her feet dangling in the cool water, and wrings the water from her heavy brown ponytail.

Back at the tree, Mr. Dinardo is gone. The cop is talking to Mr. Hurley, Mrs. Sheehan, and the man from the truck. The sun glints off the squad car windows, making it impossible to see if there's anyone inside.

The boys are leaping from the raft, performing backflips and cannonballs, splashing her over and over again. Watching their tanned bodies fly through the air reminds her of Ed and Louie, the boys from the camp kitchen. *Townies*, they called themselves with a smirk, giving her the impression they resented the designation. They were, like her, recent high-school graduates, but only Louie was going to college. Ed was going to trade school to be an electrician. On her breaks from lifeguarding, she visited them in the kitchen where they washed dishes and prepped for meals. They let her forage through the pantry, teasing her about her man-sized appetite. A few times, she went with them to the woods behind the art pavilion to smoke a joint and to listen to their epic tales of disaster and calamity; their stories were close enough to the ones Teddy and her friends told to make her long for home. It felt like a mental breakdown, that longing. Most nights she cried herself to sleep.

On her next-to-last day at the camp, she went with the boys to the reservoir, hitching a ride on the back of Ed's blue Suzuki. He seemed to have a crush on her, but she pretended not to know. At the same time, she encouraged him. That day she wrapped her arms around his waist and rested her cheek against his worn Grateful Dead T-shirt, inhaling his sweet, grassy sweat. And, even though her insides were twisted with missing Teddy, she felt something close to joy as Ed banked for the hairpin turns.

The reservoir was cold and tasted like iron. Dragonflies swooped. The boys horsed around, ducking and splashing each other, while she swam elegant circles around them.

"Don't go, Kat. Stay 'til August," Ed said after Louie swam out of earshot. Did they arrange that, so Ed could be alone with her? She felt trapped by his sadness as well as her own. They were two heads bobbing on gray water. She moved closer, kissed his blue lips. He reached for her, but she ducked under the surface and swam away.

Later, when they were lying on the flat rock at the edge of the reservoir, passing a joint, she touched her throat and discovered she'd lost Teddy's necklace. She tried not to cry as the boys dove over and over again beneath the algae-clotted surface to look for it.

Louie gave up first and stretched out on the flat warm rock beside her. "It's a sign," he said. "I wouldn't go home if I were you."

She ignored him.

Ed was poised to dive again. "One more time?" he said. Strands of algae clung to his cutoff shorts. He was a sweet boy with sharp cheekbones, ears that stuck out, and a goofy laugh. If she were not so crazy in love with Teddy, she might have kissed him sooner.

"Don't encourage him," Louie said, propping himself up on his elbows. "I know this guy. He'll never give up. We'll be here all night."

"He exaggerates," Ed said. "As per usual."

She hesitated before answering. She was due back at the camp to help out with swim lessons. "Forget it," she said, fighting back tears. "It's only a necklace."

She touches her throat now where the necklace used to be. It should make her feel better that another boy likes her, but all she can think about is Teddy. To be loved and desired by Teddy is like getting an invitation to the best party in the world. She can't accept that they'll never make love again under the orange fishing net suspended from his bedroom ceiling or in the wee hours in the woods behind the junior high school. The time the cops chased them after they'd both climbed from their bedroom windows to meet.

The raft tilts into the water, and then rocks back the other way. Behind her, two boys are locked together, wrestling. She blows her whistle, makes them sit down next to her. "What's happening at the tree?" she says. "Where's Mr. Dinardo?"

"Dunno," Mason says, shivering so hard the raft vibrates. He raises his chin. "Look." The police car crosses the tracks on its way out of the lake property. The truck follows close behind.

"Dinardo's going to jaaa-il," Jeremy sings out. "Dinardo's going to jaaa-il."

The other two pick up the chant, jumping up and down on the raft behind her.

"No, he's not," she shouts, climbing unsteadily to her feet. "You don't know what you're talking about. Stop it. Shut up."

She dives into the water before the boys can see her tears. Behind her, Mason calls out, "Can we go in? Can we go in?" She swims until she can touch the silty bottom with her feet.

Mrs. Sheehan and the other mothers are gone; the snack shack is shuttered. She checks her watch: it's five o'clock. She hates not knowing what happened to Mr. Dinardo, but there's no one to ask. She dries herself off, then pulls on her brown shorts. The savory scent of barbecued meat drifts down from the cottages, worsening her hunger pains as well as her loneliness. She lowers the flag from the mast and folds it into a tight triangle the way Mr. Dinardo showed her. He seemed surprised no one had taught her how to do it. "How did they ever let you into college, an ignoramus like you?" he said, making her laugh.

She returns the flag, the buoys, and the rescue board to their shelves in the lodge. Dusty sunlight pours through the screens and through the chinks in the old boards. Two girls are playing Ping-Pong at the far end of the lodge. Their volley goes on forever. She uses the payphone to call Teddy's house and hangs up after six rings. She wants to say goodbye before he leaves for the University of Vermont, she tells herself. Even when they were together, she didn't believe he'd ever leave. That's what love did to her. It deranged her mind.

Something stings her calf, and she spins around to see the Ping-Pong ball bounce under the table, and the girls running from the lodge, giggling. Katherine picks up the phone again and calls information. She makes a collect call to the camp kitchen. It's a risky move, but luckily Louie answers and accepts the charges.

"Hey, traitor, I thought we'd never hear from you again." He sounds hurt.

"Sorry," she says, trying to hide her irritation. Can't he think of anyone beside himself? "I got another lifeguarding job. It's only me, eight hours a day, seven days a week. I'm pretty worn-out."

"Sure it's not your boyfriend wearing you out?"

She stays silent.

"Ed's not here," Louie says. "He made a run into town for potatoes."

"I called to talk to you," she lies. He snorts, and she realizes Ed must have told him about the kiss. They have a few minutes to talk before his boss comes back from a cigarette break. As he fills her in on the parties and the most recent counselor couplings, she feels detached, far away.

Before they hang up, Louie says, "Ed'll be pissed he missed you. Give me your home and work numbers."

Outside, the sunlight blinds her. She gives a last blast on her whistle. No one pays her any mind. She unlocks her bike from the flagpole. But then, remembering her towel, she returns to the lifeguard's chair. She smiles with relief when she sees the can of Coke, dripping with moisture, still cold. She spins around to look for Mr. Dinardo, but he's already gone.

THE NEXT MORNING, SHE gets a late start. Her house is chaotic with everyone trying to leave for work at once: Daniel in his UPS uniform, Lisa in her camp counselor T-shirt, her father in his rumpled suit, and her mother wearing what she calls her "teacher outfit," black slacks and a silk tee. Only Natalie doesn't

work. She's eleven, but she has a list of chores to perform, before she walks to her summer rec program. When Katherine
complains at breakfast that she's the only person who doesn't
get a day off, her parents exchange weary, amused smiles.

"Try to enjoy your last days," her father offers. "Next
week, when you're cooped up at school, you'll wish you were
back at the lake."

She should know better than to look for sympathy from
either of them. Her mother teaches three summer classes
and tutors a kid for his SATs. Her father is balancing the
Bark Avenue dog groomer's account books as he finishes up
his bacon and eggs. The small, hot kitchen boiling over with
children gives further testament to their industry and their
sacrifice. "Life's hard," they repeat often. "Get used to it."

When she steers her bike onto the lake road, she's out of
breath, but relieved to see the tree still standing. Blue jays explode
from the highest branches with loud squawks as she pedals past.
She looks back at the road in time to see a squirrel dart in front
of her wheel. She swerves to avoid it and skids sideways in the
dirt. In the next instant, she's on her back with the bike resting
on top of her. Tears come, not because she's hurt, but because
her life seems so pitiful. She climbs to her feet, brushes the dust
from her clothes, and walks her bike the rest of the way.

The lodge phone is ringing. She throws her bike down
and runs up the path, hoping against all reason that it's Teddy.
"Tabor Lake, Katherine speaking." Her voice is a whisper.

"Kath-er-*ine*! Kath-er-*ine*!" Her heart dips. It's Ed and
Louie. They must be on the speakerphone in the kitchen.

"Ed cried when I told him he missed your call," Louie
said. "The crazy bastard is still looking for your necklace. He
rented scuba gear and everything."

All her pent-up tension releases in a loud, honking laugh.

"Don't listen to him, Kat. He's full of shit. As per usual." Ed's tone is mild.

"You don't have to tell *me*," she says.

"How's that boyfriend of yours?" Lou says.

She hesitates. "He's okay."

"You missed the best party last night," Ed says. "You remember Benny, the psycho cook? He scored some excellent weed. Louie was so wasted he thought he was Neil Fucking Armstrong. You should have seen him, Kat. He wanted to climb up on the roof."

"Look who's talking," Lou said. They both laugh until they're out of breath, making her wonder if they're stoned now. Lou says, "Don Juan Eduardo, here, won't shut up about you."

"He exaggerates," Ed says. "As per usual."

"He *loves* you," Louie says. "Poor bastard. You *have* to come back, Kat."

She hears a banging sound, pots crashing, and grunting. Lou cries out, "Hey, cut it out, man. Get off me. *Shit.*"

She listens to them scuffle and realizes she's smiling. She inspects her skinned elbow, waiting, but the line goes dead.

All morning, she fantasizes about returning to the camp. She could hide in their cabin during the day and hang out with them at night when the director goes home to his family. By the time one o'clock rolls around, however, she admits to herself it's Teddy she misses, not Ed.

When Mr. Dinardo arrives, she jumps down from the lifeguard chair to greet him. He's got heavy bags under his eyes, and patches of gray stubble dot his chin where he missed with the razor.

"Well, if you don't look like the cat who swallowed the canary," he says, handing her a cold Coke. "Come on, fess up. What'd you do?"

She pulls the tab, releasing a hiss of air. She feels shy all of a sudden. "The tree," she says. "It's still here."

He lets out a long sigh. "The tree," he says. "It's a hundred years old. Did you know that?" She shakes her head. He says, "Did you ever jump off it?"

Her face grows warm, and she fiddles with the end of her ponytail.

"Off the record," he says, cutting the air with his hand.

"Okay. Yes. In June, with my boyfriend."

His eyebrows lift in surprise. "Good for you!" he says. "Everyone should know what that feels like." He steers her toward the low concrete wall where they sit in the shade of the beech trees. "Did I ever tell you about the time my daughter carved her initials in the trunk. With a boy's?"

She looks at his heavy, creased face. "I don't think so," she says.

"Tom—Mr. Hurley, caught her red-handed. I scolded her, and she cried her little heart out. Oh, my god, she bawled for hours. I felt like such a heel," he said. "She was in love for the first time, and I'm all hung up about a damned tree."

"How old was she?" Katherine says, relieved she wasn't dumb enough to leave her own permanent record.

"Younger than you, thirteen or fourteen," he says. "My wife finally pulled it out of her. She wasn't crying because I scolded her. She was crying because the boy loved another girl."

Katherine thinks it now: Teddy loves another girl.

"You can still make out the initials. North side, knee-high, where the bark is split." He climbs to his feet with a grunt. Then he squints down at her, deciding something. "Okay, look," he says. "I'll deny I said this, but you and your boyfriend should take one last jump. Don't put it off. Do it soon. Tonight, if possible."

His words devastate her on too many levels. "Why?"

"They've moved up the stockholders' meeting to tonight." He grits his teeth. "I've got a bad feeling."

"But everyone loves the tree," she says. "You're going to win. I know it!"

"Katherine," he says, resting a heavy hand on her shoulder. "I like your spirit."

AT THE END OF the workday, she pedals away from the lake with a crazy idea. She'll bike to Teddy's house. "Hey, guess what," she'll say as casually as she can manage. "They're cutting down that tree. I'm going over there tonight. Wanna come?" She rehearses these words, with subtle variations, as she follows the back roads to Teddy's neighborhood. It's a five-mile trip to Boonton, and as she nears his street, she stops to untie her ponytail and dig in her pocket for her lip gloss. She wishes she didn't smell like lake.

When she gets back on her bike, her heart is pounding like it wants out of her chest. Turning into his road, she sees his silver Capri in the driveway, and she forgets everything she planned to say. She feathers her brakes to slow herself down.

The dozen or so times she's driven her mother's car past his house since she returned from camp, it was under the cover of night. Once, she saw someone taking out the trash, but she drove on, too scared to see if it was Teddy.

She drops her bike on his lawn and walks up the sidewalk to the front door, smoothing back her hair with both hands. "Hey," she rehearses silently. "I thought you'd like to know." She presses the bell with the horrible feeling she's being watched from an upstairs window. The door opens after a few seconds, and her stomach drops. But it's only Mrs. Powers, a pale, fragile-looking woman.

"Hello, Katherine," she says, looking pained. "Teddy's not home."

"But his car's here," Katherine says, feebly.

Mrs. Powers releases a small sigh that sounds like a bike tire going flat. "Yes, but Teddy's not here. *He's out.*"

"Are you sure? Because I feel like maybe you've been covering for him," she hears herself saying. Her face is hot with shame.

"I'll tell him you stopped by." Her smile is strained. It's not clear whether she's offended.

Katherine picks up her bike from the lawn and sees him coming up the road, maybe fifty feet away. His arm circles the waist of a petite blond Katherine doesn't recognize. They are deep in conversation and don't see her. Her head tells her to pedal away fast, but her body will not move. He sees her. Their eyes meet, and in the brief instant before he looks away, she sees fear. In one smooth motion, he turns the girl around, and they walk the other way.

When Katherine arrives home, her head aches from holding back her tears. "A boy called you," Natalie announces. She stops in the kitchen doorway. "Was it Teddy?"

"Dunno. But he sounded kind of funny." Natalie continues to distribute silverware around the table, whispering to herself. She has white-blonde hair and a dimpled chin and talks to imaginary friends; her life is a mystery to Katherine who'd preferred real friends to pretend at age eleven.

"Did he leave a number?"

Natalie looks up, interested no doubt by the strain in her older sister's voice. She shakes her head. "You can check the call log thingy. He called a few minutes ago."

She runs to the hallway. Daniel, still dressed in his brown UPS uniform, is talking on the only functioning phone. She points at herself and then the phone. He turns his back, continues talking. Lisa plays scales on the piano in the living room; the notes are like flicking fingers on her skin.

"Please!" She yanks his sleeve. "I need the phone. It's important."

He looks at her for a long, measuring moment. "Can I call you back?" he says. "My sister's going crazy." He listens and laughs. "Yeah, probably a guy."

"Daniel!" she screams.

The bathroom door swings open. Their mother starts toward them, looking tired and irritable. She's wearing shorts and an old Rowan University T-shirt, her face still made up from her summer school job. Katherine snatches the phone from her brother before their mother can intervene. Daniel opens his mouth to speak, but clomps off instead.

"Put the phone down and go hang your wet towel outside," her mother says. "You are not going to ruin my furniture."

"I have to make a call," she says, pressing buttons for the call log.

"No. Do it now. And pick some tomatoes for a salad." She heads down the hallway as she talks. When she passes the living room, she shouts, "For god's sake, Lisa, practice later. You're giving me a migraine."

She carries the handset outside, hidden under her wet towel. From the garden, with her back turned to the house, she calls the unfamiliar number. A woman answers. It doesn't sound like Teddy's mother, but Katherine isn't ready to give up hope.

"This is Katherine Reilly," she says, brightly. "I got a call from this number? My sister said a boy asked for me?"

The silence drags out for so long, Katherine thinks the woman hung up, but then she says, "You're the girl from the camp, aren't you?"

"Yes," she says, her eyes filling with disappointed tears. It's the camp secretary, she guesses, though the voice is still unfamiliar.

"This is Louie's mother. He can't come to the phone. But—oh, honey, he was calling about Ed. I don't know how to tell you this. Ed died this morning. A motorcycle accident in Freedom Plains. Outside the park there. He skidded out—"

Katherine doesn't hear the rest. A roaring fills her ears. She drops to her knees in the dirt and hears herself say, "Thank you for calling. Thank you."

She stares at the tomato stalks, but sees Ed's sweet grin, remembers how she gripped his waist and laughed into his shoulder as they took the turns on his bike. She tries to remember his goofy laugh, but it's gone. She closes her eyes and concentrates on his mouth, the plump lower lip, the crooked front teeth. But it's no use. She hears instead his nerdy "as per usual." And, then she's remembering the kiss. It's my fault, she thinks. If I'd stayed at the camp maybe he wouldn't have been riding so recklessly. Her chest and shoulders heave.

The back door opens and through her tears she sees a tall brown figure silhouetted against the sun. Her brother crosses the lawn, but stops when he sees her. He comes closer, head cocked at a worried angle.

"Is it Teddy?" he says, bending down for her. "Did you break up?"

She shakes her head no, even though she knows the right answer is yes.

ON LABOR DAY, WHEN she steers her bike onto the lake road, she senses something missing before she realizes the tree has lost its branches. The stump looks tragic, like an amputee. Two men in orange T-shirts are tossing branches into the back of their truck. They pause to watch her pass. A third man starts up the chain saw and a bitter green scent reaches her nose as she pedals past. It's the sap; the tree had more life in it. It could have been saved.

Out beyond the raft, old Mr. Hurley swims his morning laps. Mason, Jeremy, and Mike kick a soccer ball around on the sand, waiting for her. It doesn't seem possible that Ed's gone. Her mind won't let her believe it. She will imagine him diving for her necklace over and over again.

She chains her bike to the flagpole and crosses the road to the lodge. Out of habit, she pauses at the payphone, her fingers digging in her shorts pocket for the quarter. Then catching herself, she continues on to the shelves for the rescue board, the buoys, and the flag.

All morning, she keeps looking over her shoulder for Mr. Dinardo. She sits on her folded towel atop the concrete wall, twirling her whistle on its long red cord, to the left and then to the right, wrapping it around two fingers. The day is hot and still. The sound of hammers rings out as a few of the fathers secure battens over the screened windows of the lodge and the snack shack. Two men struggle to remove the diving board from the concrete platform. When they cart it away, the empty space looks like the gap in a child's smile. Despite all the preparations, Katherine has difficulty believing in the coming winter.

When Mr. Dinardo arrives at one o'clock with two Cokes, she feels a hard knob dissolve in her chest. He smiles at her with tired eyes. The red bandana circling his neck seems less jaunty now and more like a bow on a wilting bouquet. He joins her on the wall, and they watch the water, sipping their cokes. Four boys leap from the raft over and over again as if the summer has no end.

"Can you believe this heat?" he says. "Hottest Labor Day on record."

She presses the cold can against her sweating forehead. "Are you leaving today?"

"Nah. I'll stay through September. Maybe October. The lake's beautiful in the fall. I've got the space heaters. I could maybe hold out until December." He bends to scratch his ankle. "I hear the ice fishing's pretty good."

She can't tell if he's joking. "Won't you be lonely?"

He pulls back to look at her. "Maybe a little bit."

He grows quiet, and she worries she's said too much. They never discuss his dead wife or his daughter who lives someplace far away.

He sighs. "Every year, it gets harder and harder to leave."

She wants to talk about the tree, but she will not be the one to bring it up. And though the men are making a racket at the truck, Mr. Dinardo doesn't mention it either.

"Of course they'll have to cut it down," her father said when she asked him about the gypsy moths. "It's a death trap. A lawsuit could wipe them out." He would never climb a tree to save it. Maybe her life would be different if she had a father who would. When she quit the camp, he told her he didn't raise her to run from her responsibilities, not even for love.

The doors on the pickup slam shut. The engine starts up. "I guess Mr. Hurley's happy now," she says before she can stop herself.

He gives her a tight smile. "It's okay."

"Oh, I know," she says, hurriedly, to cover up her awkward sympathy.

"No, Katherine. I mean it. It's a tree."

"But you climbed it—"

"I can be a little melodramatic sometimes," he says, grimacing.

"But I thought you *loved* the tree." She's embarrassed by the strong emotion in her voice.

"I do. I mean I *did*." He looks at her. "Ah, Katherine. Don't be sad for me. In the great scheme of things, it's nothing." He snaps his fingers. "A blip."

Her throat constricts; she doesn't trust herself to speak. He puts an arm around her shoulder and pulls her close. "Hurley's right," he says. "It wasn't healthy. It had to go."

She doesn't know what to say. She sits as still as possible, so he won't take his arm away. Its warm, heavy weight on her shoulder steadies her.

He says, "Will you look at that. The little squirts are pitching in. Who would have thunk it?"

The boys are pushing the raft to shore, their feet churning the water behind it like a motor. When they get closer, Mr. Dinardo jumps up and wades out to help. They struggle in knee-deep water to haul the raft onto the sand with Mr. Dinardo pushing from behind and the four boys pulling from the other side.

"Come on, you're not even trying!" Mr. Dinardo says. "Put some muscle into it."

Their legs scissor. Sand flies.

"Need help?" she calls out.

"This is *men's* work," Mr. Dinardo says with a wink. "Right, boys?"

They answer with growls and grunts.

"That's all you've got?" Mr. Dinardo shouts. "What are you? Men or mice?"

When the raft bumps over the sand, the boys collapse around it, groaning. Out of the water, the raft looks strange.

The anchor is a large galvanized bucket filled with concrete attached to a long, rusted chain. The gray pontoon tubes are stained with mold and algae. She never bothered to wonder what kept the raft afloat. Now that she knows, it's disappointing somehow, like seeing the strings on a marionette.

Mason runs up to the lodge and returns with the putty-colored tarp. The boys help Mr. Dinardo cover the raft with it. He shows them how to secure the ends with the bright yellow rope. Mrs. Sheehan arrives with her baby. She nods at Katherine and sets up her chair a few yards away.

A cloud passes over the sun. The long shadows from the birch trees darken on the sand, giving Katherine a moment's relief. Only three hours remain in the season. In a few days, she'll be sitting in a classroom with people she doesn't know, starting her new life.

The boys are chattering, and Mr. Dinardo crouches on the other side of the raft out of view. She steals a peek at the place where the tree used to be. In years to come, people will forget it ever existed. They'll forget her, too. But she'll never, ever forget this summer.

When Mr. Dinardo reappears on the far side of the raft, he's wiping his glistening face with his red bandana. He looks pale, dazed by the heat.

"Everything okay?" Her voice sounds wobbly.

He flashes the thumbs-up sign.

She returns the gesture even as her eyes fill with stupid, ridiculous tears. She'll leave without saying goodbye, she decides. It's the only way she can do it.

WILDERNESS
OF GHOSTS

I'VE LEFT THE UNIVERSITY of Maryland three-quarters through my freshman year. My mother drives me home and does most of the talking. We cruise north on 395 and she catches me up on people I've never met. I nod off in Delaware and snap awake on the New Jersey Turnpike when the stink of burning rubber hits my nose. It's two hundred and forty miles from College Park to Closter, New Jersey, but it feels like I've traveled to another galaxy. The refinery plants with their globe-shaped storage tanks and convoluted pipelines are space stations. My mother's hair, tinted green from chlorine, comes from beyond the Horsehead nebula. My troubles are light-years behind me.

We land at 27 Magnolia Lane, the only house on the street with Christmas lights. The only house with newspapers in the driveway. Snow on the walkway. A burned-out bulb in the lamppost. Nothing's the way I remembered it.

My bedroom, after the shared dorm room, feels spacious. The walls are mossy green and the furniture is from IKEA: *Ektorp*, which means cheap crap in Swedish, I'm sure. My mother waits behind me in the doorway, holding a crate of my notebooks. "We'll redecorate," she says.

"I like it the way it is." I fall back on the bed. There they are: the North Star, the Big Dipper, and Cassiopeia—the glow-in-the-dark stars my father stuck to the ceiling when I was fourteen. "Anyway, I'm not staying," I say, hoping I sound convincing. "I'm just taking a break."

MY ROOMMATE HANGED HERSELF from the shower rod in our double suite. Sometime during the night, she looped my rhinestone belt around her neck, the belt we'd argued about the day before. In the morning, before my contact lenses were in, I saw her in the mirror over the sink. She hanged herself in another dimension, a reverse world where antimatter ranges free.

At school I majored in history. I had two good friends, Miranda and Jackie, and there was a guy named Blade in my Contemporary U.S. History class that I flirted with despite his ridiculous name and dopey soul patch. I made the honor roll my first semester, and I was an editor on *Stylus*.

When my mother calls me to dinner, I pretend to sleep. A few minutes later footsteps sound on the stairs, and then the smell of Bengay wafts in my room. Once the door clicks shut, I open my eyes. The stars glow pus-yellow in the dark. I hated Hillary Nesbit. When I told her I wished she were dead, it wasn't so I could start liking her after she was gone. But I'm sorry I said it now. I'm even sorrier I wrote it on a Post-it note and left it on her bed before I went to sleep.

I feel like I'm drowning, like I'm gulping water without taking a breath. I have to open the window. A police car whizzes past, red light flashing through the pines; the siren exists in my head. I lie back down. If I focus on the North Star, I can be fourteen, safe in my bed, my parents downstairs. Nothing bad has happened yet.

Two DAYS LATER, A Thursday, my mother drags me out of bed at seven a.m. A triathlete, she's all about action. We're back in the Volvo, heading for the Englewood medical arts building where she's an internist's nurse. She's arranged a job for me with the foot doctor on the third floor.

"The job's yours. He just wants to meet you. He's sort of desperate, actually," she says as though I might be worried, as though this crazy detour is a part of my life plan.

"And I apparently need this reassurance for a lame job I don't even want?"

Her smile fades. I wait for her to call me ungrateful, but she switches on the radio and starts to hum, which makes me feel worse.

Dr. Gutch has curly black hair and a large head. We face each other across a desk messy with files and plaster casts of feet.

"My last assistant left for a teaching job in Philly," he says. "You're probably wondering why I don't hire a nurse."

I shrug; not my business.

"The two that worked for me—we're talking years ago— were disasters, messing up my systems, sticking their noses in. I prefer smart young women I can mold."

He looks at me, waiting for something. Proof I'm not a nurse? Easy to mold? I'm sweating inside my mother's tweed blazer. I say, "I'm taking a semester off to figure things out. I thought I wanted to teach, but now I'm thinking maybe medicine."

The lie seems to satisfy him.

"Does this bother you?" He's holding a glossy black-and-white photo of a foot with a bunion the size of a doorknob. The toenails are cracked. Most of the toes are crossed as though for luck.

I relax. No one has told him about the things I've seen. "Not really," I say, giving a short laugh. "Probably not as much as it bothers the poor guy it belongs to."

His smile is a brief meeting of his top and lower teeth. He passes a pen and a sheet of paper across the desk. "Please write *bilateral debridement of plantars*."

I do my best to sound out the words, then pass the paper back to him. He looks at it without expression. "You can tell a lot from handwriting," he says.

I'm skeptical but also interested in what my neat, Catholic-school hand says about me, because I need all the clues I can get.

"You can start on Monday," he says.

I HAVE MY MOTHER's car for the day, but nowhere to go. By default, I end up at the edge of the Hudson River. It's March so all the slips in the Alpine Boat Basin are vacant; the pilings rise up from the water like tombstones. In high school, we came here to smoke weed and to plan the rest of our lives. If you want to make god laugh, tell her your plans, my history professor once said, but she was talking about the U.S.'s goals in Vietnam.

The George Washington Bridge is just south, but you can't see it from here. To the north, the Palisades cliffs where in the 1920s they filmed *The Perils of Pauline* and the term *cliffhanger* was born. In good weather, my mother cycles here with her team. The car smells like her chlorine-soaked Speedo. In the rearview mirror, I see her blue gym bag on the back seat. She'll need it for her lunch hour swim. I start the engine and head back to Englewood, happy to have a destination.

HERE'S MY DILEMMA: I can't bear my parents' scrutiny, but I don't want to be alone. For years, they've made a sport of disagreeing, but they seem to agree now that the best way to behave around their traumatized daughter is like happy robots. It leads me to believe they've consulted the mental health counselor at my father's school, which makes me sad for them. Their time would have been better spent at a marriage counselor's.

"Here's an interesting tidbit," my father says at dinner. "Constellations appear fixed, but they're actually changing very slowly. In hundreds of thousands of years, the Big Dipper is going to look different than it does today."

"They'll have to call it the Big Bucket," I say when the silence goes on too long. I don't have the heart to tell him I haven't been interested in astronomy since the ninth grade.

He laughs like I'm the next Tina Fey. He looks older than I remember. His brown hair is thinning on top and his blue eyes look tired behind his nerdy wire-framed glasses. He's a high school math teacher and the astronomy club advisor, which he founded *hundreds of thousands of years* ago in 1998.

"Roger, you are a *fount*." My mother starts to clear the table. I get up to help. My father leaves the kitchen, returning after a few minutes with the broom and sweeps around our feet.

So, NOW I AM a podiatrist's assistant. Monday morning my mother and I drive to Englewood, wearing mint-green scrubs under our coats. The traffic is heavy, but orderly. The morning sky brightens as we near the medical arts building. Despite everything, I have that good, nervous feeling I got at the start of every new school year.

Inside my mother walks right past me at the elevators, heading for the door marked *stairs*. "It's good for the glutes," she calls over her shoulder. Fine. I follow and stop on the third floor, but she keeps climbing and rounds the corner. A feathery panic flutters in my chest.

"Good luck," she calls down the stairwell.

Dr. Gutch is late. I wait outside the door like a stray. The young women who pass by, wearing bright-colored scrubs or tailored suits, look settled and self-possessed. A psychotherapist's office sits across the hall and I wonder whether this job is a ruse to get me into therapy.

When Dr. Gutch arrives, sweat drips from his hairline down his temples and he's out of breath. He fumbles in his pockets for his key, cursing under his breath. I look away. Down. His feet: they're too small for his body. Penguin feet. He waddles inside, switches on the lights, and gestures toward the reception desk.

"Elizabeth Whatley, my old girl, left instructions." He readjusts one of the pink Post-its on the filing cabinet. The workstation is littered with Post-its. A few are curled at the edges; some reinforced with yellowed tape. I must look lost, because he says, "It'll all make sense in time. The *most* important thing to remember is you must collect payment before the patient leaves. Once they're out of here, it's twice as hard to collect. Simply smile and say, 'Will that be cash or check?'" He pauses with a finger raised and I wonder if he expects me to repeat his words, but he motions with the finger for me to follow him. "If there's one thing I cannot tolerate," he says, leading me into his office, "it's loose ends, loose ends." He opens the desk drawer, and with a flourish, hands me a key.

A buzzer sounds. "Our ingrown toenail is here," he says.

BEFORE HE LEAVES FOR lunch, Dr. Gutch gives me a stack of bills to mail. I walk the quarter-mile to the center of town, wishing I'd worn a coat with more coverage. I avoid my mint green reflection in the windows. The breeze carries a whiff of spring, the scent of dirt and tubers. When I left Maryland, kids were wearing flip-flops and shorts to class, even though snow still fringed the quad. The classrooms smelled like chalk and rain. New couples were cropping up at the student union and at the frat parties. I was hoping Blade and I would be one of them.

I wait in the long line at the P.O. A poster catches my eye, an artist's rendering of a young woman's face. She looks familiar, not best-friend familiar, but maybe salesclerk familiar. When the line moves, I get a closer look and discover she's a Jane Doe, an apparent murder victim who washed up on the Jersey side of the Hudson a week or so before I moved home. I try to picture her face at Target's cash register, and then I try to imagine her on the other side of the glass at the movie theater ticket booth.

Not until after I finish paying at the counter do I realize the clerk is Jerry Farina, our old mailman. He's pretending not to recognize me in my baggy uniform to spare me the embarrassment, I think.

On the drive home from work, I start to tell my mother about Jane Doe.

"Jane?" she says, distracted by the rush-hour traffic and god knows what else. "Is this a girl from high school?"

"Yep," I say and drop it.

IN RELIGION CLASS BACK when I was in junior high, the teacher talked about a place called Limbo. That's where I live now. It only looks like my hometown, but it's the edge of hell. At the dinner table, my parents don't stop me from talking about fungus toenails and the yellow calluses Dr. Gutch shaves from the soles of feet like Parmesan cheese. "It falls on the paper with such a satisfying plop," I say.

"Well, I sure hope you washed your hands," my father says.

My mother gives a little laugh and picks up her fork. "Let's change the subject," she says. Flushed after her run, she looks pretty. On Mondays and Wednesdays, my father cooks so she can work out with her team.

"You'll never guess who I saw the other day," I say.

"You're right," my mother says. "So tell us."

"Jerry. He's at the Englewood post office now."

"Jerry who?" She starts to clear the table, even though my father is still eating his Dover sole.

"Farina. Our old mailman." I send my father a wry smile, before I tell her, "Better known as your old boyfriend."

"Oh, *him*," she says, making a racket at the sink. She runs the water and hums what sounds like "Hotel California."

"Excuse me." My father gets up from the table.

She watches him go with the dish towel clenched in her fist. "Oh, for god's sake," she says. "What's his problem with Jerry?"

She's looking at me, but I have no answers.

"Do me a favor," she says on her way out of the kitchen. "Take care of the dishes."

I clear the table and load the dishwasher. I start to leave and make it as far as the staircase when I hear shouting upstairs. Back to the kitchen, where I wipe down the table and sweep the floor. The old boyfriends are a family joke, the way they pop up all over town, still smitten with my mother. When did it stop being funny?

It feels like I've wandered into the second act of a play, and all the important action is taking place offstage. The hidden things are scarier than the ones in plain sight: the raised voices in the next room, for instance, or the afterlife. A door slams. The walls and windows vibrate with the aftershock. I look around for more to clean, but the kitchen gleams.

I crawl into bed without turning on the lights. Jerry. He was a troublemaker, like the Bad Hat from my *Madeline* books, my mother told me. He drove his dirt bike into the cafeteria once and streaked through the auditorium during the Christmas play. In the summer, he serenaded her outside her bedroom window, playing Christopher Cross songs on his guitar until my grandfather called the police.

Jerry sounds like a loser. Maybe my mother started to think so too. After high school, they drifted apart, she says. Like two rudderless boats on the Hudson. In the end, she married the debate-team captain that she'd followed to Rutgers University, and they settled down for a lifetime of spirited arguments.

There's a knock on my door. "May I come in?" my father says.

I sit up. "Sure," I say, but I'm afraid. Of what, I don't know. He leaves the door ajar. In the light from the hallway, he crosses the room and settles into the canvas butterfly chair by the window. Crashing and banging noises come from down the hall. It sounds like my mother's moving the furniture around in their bedroom. He tilts back his head and looks at the stars on my ceiling. He's grown a small paunch since I last saw him at Christmas.

He says, "All the planets orbit the sun counterclockwise, if you're looking from above. All but Venus, Uranus, and Pluto, that is."

"But who's looking from above? That's stupid." What I want to say is: you think Jerry is orbiting your wife and all you want to talk about is Pluto?

"Good point," he says in the way that used to make me feel precocious.

After a short silence, he says, "If you ever want to talk, Ellie, I'm here."

His gentle tone pierces something hard inside me. Tears come and my throat closes up. "Thanks, Dad," I finally manage to say.

He opens his mouth to speak, but closes it when a loud crash shivers the window panes.

"What's she doing in there anyway," I say.

"Looking for her wetsuit."

"In March?"

"She's talking about a swim camp in Sarasota."

"Sounds expensive," I say, giving him an opening. Money, in particular the amount of money she spends on sports equipment, is a recurring debate.

He grunts.

"Well, speaking of swimming," I say, "did you read anything about the dead girl they found in the water at Ross Dock?"

"Uh, no. Not that I recall. Why?"

"I saw her picture in the post office. She's a Jane Doe, but I have a weird feeling I've seen her somewhere."

"I'm always seeing people I think I know. I saw my brother Jim in a blue Chevy the other day, picking his teeth with a matchbook like he used to do. There's only a finite number of face types, I think. And those get passed down from generation to generation."

"Maybe."

I don't tell him I also saw my dead Uncle Jim. In Target. He was slipping something, maybe dental floss, into his shirt pocket when he thought no one was looking.

"But I've been thinking about it," I say, "and I figure she's either someone I saw every day like the cafeteria ladies or the janitors who become sort of invisible after a while. Or she's someone you can't quite look in the eye, like the judge at traffic court."

"When were you at traffic court?" he says with mock sternness.

"Oops."

"*Anywho,*" he says, dragging out the word, "if she did hold one of those jobs, she probably has people to keep track of her. No, it's more likely she's a prostitute or someone mixed up with—"

I wait for him to continue, but he seems to be listening to my mother who's in the hallway, talking at a loud volume.

"I'll come by tomorrow after work," she's saying.

In the mirror across from my bed, I see her pause outside my door, the phone held to her ear. She bursts out laughing. "Me, too. I looked all over before I remembered you borrowed it."

I feel myself relax and sense my father's relief, too. He says, "I wouldn't worry too much about her."

"It's not *her* I'm worried about," I say before it dawns on me he's talking about Jane Doe. I quickly add, "It's just a loose end. I hate loose ends."

"Get used to it," he says, chuckling. "The older you get, the more life unravels in ways you never expect."

IN APRIL, MIRANDA CALLS from school. I've been texting with her and Jackie nearly every day for the past three weeks about dumb stuff like *The Bachelorette* and *The Great British Baking Show*, but this is the first time she's phoned. There's heavy bass and laughter in the background when she puts me on speakerphone. Jackie shouts, "Hey Ellie girl, what's up?" like it's any other Saturday afternoon in Easton Hall. I picture her at her desk, following a YouTube makeup tutorial on her iPad. Miranda is stretched out on her twin bed, munching sunflower seeds and flicking the gray hulls. When

Miranda asks me about life in New Jersey, it doesn't feel half as real as Maryland does in this moment. I don't mention my new job. Instead, I tell them about Jane Doe, about how I think I might recognize her.

"It's hard to tell from the drawing, but she looks around our age," I say. "My dad thinks she's probably a drug addict or a sex worker. But he thinks that's what happens to everyone who doesn't go to college."

Miranda laughs, then grows quiet. She says, "Look, I wasn't going to say anything, but Jackie thinks I should."

I take a deep breath and grip the edge of the chair.

"People are talking shit about you and Hillary Nesbit. They're making her out to be some kind of saint."

"I don't care," I finally manage.

"Don't worry," Miranda says. "Jackie and I are telling everyone how she was always taking your stuff without asking. Like your MacBook—"

"And all your clothes," Jackie says.

"It doesn't matter," I say. "I'm over it."

After a short silence, Miranda says, "I miss you, dude."

"It's so boring here without you," Jackie adds.

"I can't wait until next fall," Miranda says. "You, me, and Jackie in our own apartment. We'll have the best parties."

"It's going to be awesome," Jackie says.

"Awesome," I say.

After we hang up, I borrow my mother's car and drive past my high school, the Closter movie theater where I used to work, and my old boyfriend Nick's stucco house. I was so hot to leave this town behind, but after I got away, I'd cry into my pillow, missing it. For a while my two lives ran on parallel tracks. In the end, I had to let one go. Every day I stay in Closter, I fall farther behind in my life in Maryland.

Jackie and Miranda will have college degrees and careers while I'm still billing patients and massaging feet. Thinking about my friends makes me feel like someone's holding my head underwater.

I don't want to go home, and I can't go back to school. So, where does that leave me? I'm halfway down Henry Hudson Drive before it occurs to me that Jane Doe's murderer may be lurking in the woods. Along with her ghost. The woods are full of ghosts—from the nineteenth-century moguls who built their cliff-top estates here, to the ordinary New Yorkers, including my grandfather, who traveled by the Yonkers ferry to swim at the Undercliff Beach. You can't travel two feet in the park without bumping into the past. You're never alone here. History can be a comfort but also pretty damn spooky.

I pass the turnoff for the Alpine Boat Basin and head up the road past the stone parapets and the WPA bridle paths to Ross Dock. A swarm of cyclists approaches from the other direction, and I slow down to let them pass in the traffic circle. I follow the long winding road down to the river and park facing the George Washington Bridge. The bridge is slung across the belly of the sky like a silver belt. I imagine a body tumbling from the upper level. A murder can be solved, but a suicide is a story without an end.

MY FATHER INTRODUCED ME to astronomy the year I was fighting a lot with my mother. She's addicted to action, but she made it her mission to stymie mine, giving me a ridiculous ten o'clock curfew and checking in with my friends' parents every time I made plans to go out. He took me outside on the deck after I'd made her cry at dinner one night. I jumped up and down to keep warm, waiting for him to tell me off, so I could get back to my big, important life.

He said, "Look up."

I raised my eyes to his, waiting, but he said, "No, Ellie. Up, up." I tilted my head back. *Stars.* How predictable. I didn't bother to hide my yawn.

"Kind of puts things into perspective, doesn't it?"

Nice try, Galileo, I wanted to say, but I didn't dare.

He pointed out the constellations, told me the life story of the universe. It turns out he was right. Thinking about a galaxy measured in hundreds of thousands of light-years did make my problems seem puny and stupid.

I GET OUT OF the car and stand at the seawall. The brackish water laps at the lichen-covered rocks piled below. Something white flashes below in the water. Though I lean over the wall, the ebb and flow of the river won't let me get a long enough look. I take off my boots and socks, and roll my jeans over my ankles. The wall is easy enough to scale, but the icy water makes me gasp. The foot has thirty-three muscles, but I can't feel any of them. I get down on one knee and snatch at the white thing. It's a cotton glove, the kind worn by waiters at fancy restaurants—or by murderers who don't want to leave prints. I wring out the water and try to pull it on.

"I don't think that's such a great idea." From behind the seawall, a Parkway cop glares down at me—buzz cut, reflector sunglasses, the full regalia. I recognize him as a patient, Bob Meliora. Fungus toenails. Fallen arches.

"Come here," he says. I obey, grabbing his offered hand as I swing a leg over the wall. He asks, "What were you doing, ma'am?" He doesn't recognize me, or is pretending not to.

I give him the glove. "I saw this in the water. I thought maybe it had something to do with the dead girl they found here." I'm shivering from feet to teeth.

"Get your shoes on before you catch pneumonia."

I sit on the wall to pull on my socks and boots with shaking hands. He watches me like I'm someone who needs watching, a suspect or a suicide risk. I slide down from the wall and say, "Do they have any leads?"

"What's your interest in the case?"

Is there irony in his tone? I can't tell. Reflected in his lenses, I look small, windswept. "I think I recognize her," I say.

He removes his sunglasses and squints hard at me, and I want to take it back. "You know something?" he says.

My face heats up. "No. I don't know anything."

He puts his sunglasses on. "Well, keep us in the loop. Let us know if you uncover any more leads."

"But she *does* look familiar. It's driving me crazy, trying to figure out where I saw her."

"Okay, ma'am you work on that and get back to us. In the meantime, stay away from the water. We don't want to be fishing *you* outta there."

By the end of April, I no longer cringe when I massage feet, not even the cracked and crooked ones. The old ladies don't call me "new Elizabeth" anymore. A couple of days ago, Ivy Barnes trapped me in the examining room, squeezed my arm with her knobby fingers, and said, "You're the best nurse he's ever had. Don't go leaving him like Elizabeth did."

"Don't worry," I told her, patting her arm. "I'm not going anywhere."

It's true. Is this how it happens? Is this how people get stuck?

Every other week, I assist Dr. Gutch at the Crestview Nursing Home. The place reeks of Mr. Clean and urine, and the inmates slumped over in their wheelchairs under musty afghans make me sad. Looking into their vacant, shrunken-apple faces is like skipping ahead to the disappointing end of a good book. Is that it? Is this all we get?

I try to take my cues from Dr. Gutch who is a different Dr. Gutch in the nursing home. He cracks jokes with all the men like he's at a Rotary Club meeting. Most stare blankly back at him, but he doesn't seem to mind. He compliments the women on their hairdos and clothes, while massaging their insteps. They close their eyes and smile faraway smiles. He's more relaxed when there's no money to collect.

On the ride back to the office, he'll refer to the patients by name. Today, he says, "It doesn't look good for Evelyn. She's going to lose those toes. Remind me to check in with her doctor."

"Evelyn? Which one is she? The one who was in the Air Force?" I have trouble telling them apart. They're all so pale and blurry like half-erased drawings.

"No, that's Maggie," he says. "Evelyn buried four husbands."

"No wonder her toes are all messed up."

He sends me a quizzical look.

"Isn't that what marriage is about? Stepping on each other's toes?"

He doesn't answer. I slide down in my seat, certain I've breached some podiatry code of civility. When we return to the office, he says, "I hesitate to say this, Ellie, because you're doing such a bang-up job, but not everything's a joke. Imagine for one minute what it would be like to be Evelyn or Maggie. Imagine you've been waiting all week to see us."

He's wrong about me. I can imagine it all too well.

I HAVE A LUNCHTIME routine. Most weekdays, I hit the post office with a stack of bills and insurance forms and give Jerry the stink eye before heading down East Palisades Avenue for lunch at Starbucks or Omar's, depending on my mood.

I blend in with the Englewood Hospital staff now that I've replaced my mother's mint-green scrubs with a navy blue pair. At Omar's, the hot young Lebanese waiter calls me Doc.

"*Ahlan*, welcome, Doc," Gabir says when I arrive, and, "Tank you, Doc," when I leave. If he ever works up the nerve to ask me out, I'll have to set him straight. Or maybe I won't.

Every day I pass the same sandwich board sign: *Tarot Card * Palms Read * Psychic * one flight up*. Every day I try to work up the nerve to go in. One night I dream Hillary speaks to me in the high frequency squeaks of a bat and decide it might be time to see what the future holds.

At the top of the stairs a door stands open; it's painted midnight blue like the sky over Paris in *Madeline's Christmas*. I enter a tiny room with mismatched chairs, and a second later, an overweight redheaded woman appears, biting into a drumstick. She's wearing a long black skirt and a purple T-shirt with *Cancun* printed in glitter across her sizable breasts. She startles when she sees me.

"Are you the psychic?" I say, thinking I've barged into someone's house.

"You scared me."

A real psychic would have known I was coming.

"Tarot is twenty, palm ten," she says.

"Palm, I guess."

She motions with the drumstick for me to follow her into a room that's just large enough for a desk and two chairs. Over the desk hangs a picture of Jesus holding a heart encircled in thorns.

"Pay first," she says, dropping the chicken on a plate and wiping her hands on her skirt.

I dig inside my quilted bag for the ten intended for my lunch and hand it over. She stashes it in a drawer, and we both sit.

She looks me over. "You a doctor or nurse?"

"*You* tell me," I say, laughing. It's a mistake. A sour look alters her face.

She takes my hand and runs her thumb along my lifeline. She raises her eyes and looks at me too long before speaking. "You are carrying a great weight. A heavy sadness. Is that right, young lady?"

"Yeah, I guess."

She encloses my hand in her two, and her eyes bore into me. "In your life, you are feeling trapped. Stuck."

I nod.

"I'm picking up an older man. A guide. A teacher, maybe."

"My father's a teacher."

"It could be your father. This man will help you out of your trouble." She slumps in the chair with a sigh of exhaustion. "I can't help you any further without the cards."

"Okay."

"That's twenty dollars more."

"No thank you." I pick up my bag and get out of there in a hurry. I have enough change for a cup of coffee. With a few tablespoons of sugar and a half cup of cream, it should tide me over until the end of the day. From about fifty yards off, I spot my mother sitting outside Starbucks. The pool must be closed. I quicken my pace, surprised at how happy I am to see her. I won't tell her about the psychic. She'll only worry; she'll say I wasted my money. As I get closer, I notice there are two grande cups on her table and hang a U-turn.

ONE MORNING IN EARLY June on our way into work, my mother's face is pinched with worry; I don't want to hear whatever it is she has to say. When she asks what I'm doing for lunch, I lie. "I'm assisting Dr. Gutch at the nursing home."

"Maybe you could get out of it?" she says.

"Don't you swim anymore?"

She narrows her eyes. "My shoulder's bothering me," she says tightly. We drive in silence, passing by the hospital and its massive parking garage. I want to ask her what she does with her lunch hour now that she doesn't swim.

"Listen," she says, "your father tells me you've been talking about the woman they found in the river. What's that about?"

I'm surprised they're still talking, even if it is only about me. "I mentioned it once, over a month ago. I thought I might've seen her somewhere."

"Where?"

"Just around. It doesn't matter."

"Tell me the truth: does this have anything to do with your roommate?"

I look at her. "How could it? Hillary was already dead when they found the other girl."

"Ellie, really, come on. You know I'm not talking about a connection between the girls. I'm talking about you."

"Well, I don't want to talk about me. Okay?"

Later, at the end of the workday driving home, my mother is completely quiet. Most evenings, she'd be yakking away about one of her pet topics: gruesome medical cases or her triathlon training. If she's angry about lunch, I don't care. Where was she all those days I ate alone? This summer, I'll walk the four miles home, I decide, planning a future I don't want. I slump in my seat and watch the houses speed past. It's not until we're making a left on Knickerbocker Road instead of our usual right that I catch on: she's up to something.

"Where are we going?" I sit up straight.

"Promise you won't freak?" She keeps her eyes on the road. "I've made an appointment with a hypnotist in Teaneck."

"Why?"

"To help you remember where you saw that girl."

"Really?"

"Sure, if it's bothering you—"

I don't let her finish. "Forget it. I'm over it."

She gives me a sad smile. "I'll go first to show you there's nothing to be afraid of."

"I'm not afraid. I'm just not interested. Why would *you* need a hypnotist?"

"Well, to tell you the truth, I'm having trouble with transitions."

"Transitions?" I brace myself for the divorce announcement, but she says, "I get nervous in the transition zones, dealing with the change of equipment. Sometimes I freeze up."

Triathlons. "What about Dad? Isn't it your night to cook?"

We're approaching a busy intersection. The light changes from green to amber. She floors the gas and runs the light.

"He's perfectly capable of getting his own dinner."

"By the way," I say, watching her. "I'm supposed to tell you the Wilma Rudolph stamps are in."

"Thanks," she says brightly, betraying nothing.

"You know, Mom, Jerry's not the answer."

She pulls her head back and laughs in apparent surprise. "Well," she says, seeming to mull over my words, "that would depend on the question, wouldn't it?"

The shingle outside the rundown ranch-style house reads: *Pierre O'Connor, Hypnotist.* We park behind a rusted green station wagon propped up on cinder blocks. My mother presses the bell, and an ancient man wearing a yellowed undershirt and pressed slacks opens the door.

"Mr. O'Connor? I'm Mary Ann Delaney and this is my daughter, Ellie. We have appointments to be hypnotized."

A bubble of nervous laughter rises in my throat.

"That would be my son," he says, stepping aside to let us in. The house is too warm; it smells of cooked meat. A television, tuned to a game show, provides the only light in the living room. A Budweiser waits for the man on the TV tray shoved between two armchairs. He disappears down a hallway, calling out, "Pete, Pete. You've got customers, Pete."

Pete? I look at my mother. "What happened to Pierre?"

"It's a nickname. So what."

"I'd like my mind control done by someone with a more formal name," I say.

"Oh, stop it."

"Look at this place," I say.

"Don't be such a coward." Her tone is sharp.

I sniff, hurt. She thinks I'm a coward. I expected her to be as appalled as I am by the seediness of the house and the old man. It's not like her to shell out hard-earned money for something so flaky.

The old man is back. "Pete's ready. Who's first?"

"I guess I am." I gape at my mother who nods encouragement.

Pete's father leads me down the dark hallway. "In there," he says before turning back. I knock on the door, and a middle-aged man with thick silver hair and a beaky nose opens it.

"Come on in," he says in a deep, friendly voice. His blue-eyed gaze is intense, and I wonder if he's reading my mind. But after a short pause, he says, "Mary Ann?"

"I'm Ellie, her daughter." I look around the bedroom and move to the straight-backed chair he holds out for me. "This is all my mother's idea, by the way."

He nods and smiles. I feel at ease with him. Maybe it's because we're both living with our parents. Though his tattoos, the faded blue snakes and anchors adorning his arms, hint at a past more complicated than mine.

"She told me about the dead girl, that you think you recognize her." He leans back against the dresser, crossing his blue arms over his concave chest.

"Yeah, she thinks I should figure out where I saw her. But I'm actually over it."

"You're *over* it?" he says as though he's hearing the expression for the first time. I nod. Behind him on the dresser, there's a matching tortoiseshell hairbrush and comb, a wooden box with inlaid mother of pearl, and a carton of Marlboros all lined up the way they might be in a barracks or a prison cell.

"How long have you been doing this?" I ask.

"Maybe fifteen years?"

"Who's your typical client?"

"I've helped all kinds. Fatties, two-pack-a-days, blackjack junkies, you name it."

"So, you help people with addictions?"

"Among other things."

"Why do *you* still smoke?"

He jerks his head back. "Because I *like* it. I don't want to quit. Besides, I'm no good at hypnotizing myself. Some are, but I never got the hang of it."

"Where did you learn to do this, anyway? Is there like a hypnotist school where you start small with chickens and rats and stuff?"

"Look, if you're not going to take this seriously, you should probably leave. You're wasting my time."

"I told you this was my mother's idea. I don't really care about the dead girl."

"I heard you. Why are you still here then?"

"So what if our paths crossed. Life's so random. I pass by hundreds of people every day, but I'm not responsible for what happens to any of them. Right?"

"Depends. You want to help the cops out? Or the girl's family?"

"I don't want to sound cold, but no, not really. I sort of have my own problems."

He looks at me, waiting.

"Something bad happened at school. I want to, but I can't go back."

He crouches down until he's eye level with me. He has heavy bags under his eyes. In a low voice that I feel like a vibration in my breastbone, he says, "What's keeping you here?"

Tears swell, but I do nothing to stop them. A truck changes gears on the road outside. Canned laughter drifts in from the television.

"Tell me what happened," he says.

"My roommate hanged herself in our room. I'm the one who found her."

He lowers his eyes and nods sympathetically.

"I probably should've been nicer to her. She didn't have a lot of friends. She was weird. She kept taking my things, even after I asked her not to. It felt like she was taunting me, seeing how far she could push me. I tried ignoring her. Even after I caught her wearing my favorite sweater, I didn't say anything. But that made it worse."

I breathe deeply from my gut. He nods encouragement.

"Then she took my MacBook. When I confronted her, I saw she was wearing my belt. It was a birthday present from my best friend. I went a little berserk. A stupid belt. If I could build a time machine and dial back to February

27th, I'd just give her the fucking thing and the MacBook. We could go our separate ways and nobody would be dead."

"Ellie." He touches my hand, startling me. My last words vibrate in the silence. I was shouting.

"Why don't you follow the second hand on my pocket watch?"

I look down. He's holding a gold watch like the one Alice's rabbit has in Wonderland. The second hand clicks in slow motion from one faded Roman numeral to the next.

A second later, it seems, Pete is shaking my shoulder, calling my name. I raise my heavy head and wipe the drool from my chin. "I'm so sorry," I say, mortified. "I must have dozed off."

"That's sort of the idea."

"Oh, I see." I'm disoriented, stupid with sleep. "What happened? What did you do?"

"The thing you said you wanted? I helped you focus your attention on getting it."

I stand up, dazed. The streetlight casts a long shadow across the twin bed. I feel a profound exhaustion as though we've switched bodies and now I'm the middle-aged man living in my father's house. I stumble toward the door, anxious to leave.

"Good luck, sweetie," Pete says as I start down the long, dark hallway toward the flickering blue TV light. As though sensing my approach, my mother stands, her eyes searching the darkness.

I wave both hands over my head—like someone drowning, I realize. Like someone who wants to be saved.

COYOTE

FRANKIE WAS HAPPIEST WHEN she was being useful. In June, as a favor to her older sister, she flew to California to stay with her nephew for a few days. A cold fog darkened Teresita Boulevard when she climbed out of the taxi at her sister's house. On the stoop, a blond man in a loose-fitting camouflage jacket stood hunched over the lock. She panicked, glanced back at the taxi, but the driver gunned the engine and sped away. The man turned at the sound. *Not a burglar. Not even a man.* Her nephew had shot up four inches since Christmas.

"Carey! When did you grow up?" She spoke in a loud, emphatic tone, her default mode whenever she was fatigued or uncertain.

He blinked behind his tortoiseshell eyeglasses, too small for his long face, then hopped down the steps, a key swinging from his neck on a leather cord. Over one shoulder, he carried a muslin knapsack, an accessory that would've gotten him beaten up in any New Jersey middle school. "You're early," he said. "Is Uncle Bruce—"

"You're so tall for twelve, taller than me. What are you, five ten?" She held out her arms for a hug, but he grabbed the suitcase handle instead.

"Actually, five nine and three quarters, and I'm thirteen. My birthday was two weeks ago."

She yanked him into a hug and smelled the pencil-shavings boyness of him. "I know your birthday, you nut." It had slipped past her. Last year, she'd given him a set of Tolkien novels; god only knew what he was into now. She released him, and he went up the steps with her suitcase. She marveled at his height: he'd been conceived with the help of an anonymous sperm donor, so every non-Mulroney trait raised the specter of that stranger.

Inside, the house had a cedar and eucalyptus smell she liked and associated with San Francisco. A quick glance at the modern furniture, bare hardwood floors, and chilly abstract art reassured her nothing had changed since her visit the year before.

"We'll celebrate your birthday tonight," she said. "What's your favorite restaurant?" He didn't like eating in restaurants, he told her. "Takeout, then. Pizza? No, wait, you like tacos, right?"

"Actually, I'm not hungry." His faint smile gave her the impression she'd confirmed an unflattering opinion he had about her, her overeagerness to please, probably. "I'd like to work on my project," he said.

After his bedroom door clicked shut, she rolled her suitcase down the hallway to her sister's room. A patchwork quilt covered the bed, an incongruous homey touch. It was ten degrees chillier in the bedroom. Three tall windows, opened slightly, looked out over Glen Canyon, Oakland, and a sliver of bay, but now a dense marine layer of clouds obscured her view. It was a relief she wouldn't have to go out or feign interest in middle-earth hobbits or whatever floated her nephew's boat these days. Though the flight had exhausted her, she'd been drained before she'd boarded the plane. Naïve to think moving her seventy-two-year-old husband to the nursing home would ease her burden.

She stripped off her black turtleneck and jeans and changed into a pair of soft gray sweats. Her phone dinged with a text from Nora. A selfie taken on Waikiki Beach: her sister's wind-blown coppery curls—just like her own—obscuring half her face. Nora was attending a conference in Hawaii on women's economic empowerment. When her usual babysitter had backed out, she'd contacted Frankie, thinking she could use the break from her "nursing home drama." Probably, her sister hadn't been thinking about her at all. If she'd learned anything during her sixteen-year marriage to Bruce, a renowned Mark Twain scholar, it was that successful people put themselves first and seemed happier for it.

Frankie texted: *All's well in SF*, then crossed the hallway and knocked on Carey's door. His muffled answer sounded like *come in*. He sat at his desk under the window, shoving papers into the drawer. After raising two spymaster stepdaughters, she was inured to teenage subterfuge. "I heard from your mom."

He swiveled to face her. "Why won't you let Uncle Bruce live in your house?" He sounded angry. He and Bruce had formed the He-Man Chess Club, an excuse, really, to escape the women's pleas for help on holidays.

"*Let?* Don't tell me you didn't notice a change in him at Christmas. He hardly spoke to you." It came out more harshly than she intended. She tried again, "It's for his own safety. You heard about the fire he set in our kitchen? Did your mom tell you he left the house in February without his coat and shoes? If the police hadn't found him, he could've died."

Carey scowled. "You could keep a better eye on him."

"You sound like Jean." Her younger stepdaughter had accused her of giving up on Bruce. So easy to judge from across the country, from Seattle. "That's because you don't see what's going on. Ask Clara. She's there all the time.

She'll tell you; we'd have to lock Uncle Bruce in his room to keep him safe."

"Just lock the front door," he said, sounding less certain. "That's what my mom did when I was little."

"He's not a toddler—he's a big man. I can't control him when he gets agitated. He took a swing at the orderly the other day." Her nephew's shocked expression gave her guilty satisfaction. "He needs constant supervision; if I didn't put him in the nursing home, I'd have to give up my life."

He swiveled back and forth on his desk chair, looking unhappy. She returned to her sister's room, sadness eclipsing her anger. She didn't have much of a life to give up: a book group that met sporadically; Jenny and Hal, friends and fellow editors at the university press where she was employed part-time. Bruce would continue to suffer these bouts of belligerence until he'd permanently lost his mind, the doctor had told her as though it were something to look forward to.

God knew she needed something, but not that. She craved companionship, intimacy. Ten years ago, she'd had a brief affair. She'd kept track of Kip Jones over the years since, the way she'd keep track of the exit signs on a turbulent jet: after Princeton University, he'd landed a tenure-track position at the University of Texas at Austin. From there, he'd accepted a year-to-year contract at Berkeley. If he'd figured into her decision to come to San Francisco, she didn't want to examine it too closely. She lay on her sister's bed, watching the fog lift from Glen Canyon. Once she could sell the Princeton house, she'd rent an affordable apartment near the nursing home so she could visit Bruce for the remainder of his life, which could conceivably be ten more years. She was forty-three.

When she'd set her sights on Bruce Shay sixteen years ago, she would never have guessed it would end this way. She was the twenty-seven-year-old office coordinator serving the entire Princeton English department, but after Dr. Shay's wife died from breast cancer, she'd made his frantic, often last-minute requests her top priority. To show his gratitude, he treated her to lunch off campus in Palmer Square. Before long the handsome, fifty-seven-year-old professor was lending her novels and volumes of poetry. At Stockton State, she'd been a mediocre English major, more focused on boys than on her classes. If she'd had a professor as brilliant and encouraging as Dr. Shay, she would've paid closer attention.

One afternoon in October, he asked her to stay with his girls while he attended a reception that had slipped his mind. She canceled her plans with Larry—the thirty-five-year-old assistant in alumni relations who lived with his parents and wore his glasses during sex—and drove out to the Shay farmhouse on the canal. Two rosy-cheeked, sturdy girls, aged twelve and ten, opened the door wearing aprons. "We're baking apple pies," Jean, the younger girl said. "You can help." The overheated house was a charming mess of books, craft projects, and potted green plants. Bruce's familiar tweed blazer hung from a doorknob, and she stroked the woolen collar in passing. In the steamy kitchen, bowls crowded the countertop; a cookbook was propped open with a warty gourd. Clara, the older girl, opened a closet, and from the jumble of rubber boots and jackets, exhumed a navy-blue apron imprinted with constellations. "It's Mommy's," Jean said in a reverential whisper. How could Frankie refuse?

THE NEXT MORNING, SATURDAY, Carey slept past noon. Awake for hours, she'd taken a run in Mount Davidson Park, ignoring the sign at the trailhead: WARNING! COYOTES

ARE CLEVER, QUICK, AND OPPORTUNISTIC. Now, she lay in wait for Carey in the kitchen.

"Tell me about your project," she said when he appeared, rumpled from sleep. "Has your mom seen it?"

"It's just a graphic story for the school assembly." He took a bowl from the cabinet and filled it with cereal. "I didn't show Mom. She'd just give me one of her Buddhist lectures."

"Why?"

"I used real kids as characters."

His secrecy made sense now. "You're not worried about hurting someone?"

"No. They're mostly morons who think sneaking beer from their house is a lifetime achievement." He went to the refrigerator and took out a carton of almond milk. "Anyway, I won't see them after Monday. No one's going to my private high school."

"I don't think that lets you off the hook. Why don't you let *me* see it?"

He stomped out of the room. Did she blow it? A few seconds later, he returned with crumpled legal-sized papers. They sat at the table, and he passed the pages to her, while eating his cereal. The story, drawn in pen and ink, began with a scene in a school cafeteria. The students were anthropomorphized rats (boys) and cats (girls). She admired his artwork, the impressive detail, but said nothing about the trite plot: geeky boy wins girl from popular boy. Also disappointing: his depiction of the girls as trophies or mirrors for the boys' egos. She imagined her sister objecting to this more than anything else.

"It's hard for me to judge. I don't know any of these animals," she said. "Are you willing to accept the consequences?"

"Okay, sure," he said, as though he didn't believe there would be any.

LATER, IN THE AFTERNOON, they drove to West Portal in her sister's Audi to buy his art teacher a gift. The art store was in a lively shopping district. He chose an inexpensive box of pastels. Outside, they joined the families and young people enjoying the warm day. A disheveled, bearded man walked alongside them for half a block. Cleaned up, he could have passed for Ken Carbone, the American Studies guy who'd grabbed her ass years ago near the faculty mailboxes. Only this man muttered "bitch" and wore filthy rags; the sun's heat intensified his rank odor. She felt lightheaded, needed to sit down.

"Too bad you don't like restaurants," she teased. "I saw this great ice cream place—"

"Ice Cream Castle?" He fought back a smile. "Doesn't count."

They entered the shop and joined the long line waiting for tables. Three attractive girls, slightly older than Carey, waited ahead of them. They stole glances at Carey, and whispered and tittered amongst themselves. Blushing and frowning, Carey suggested they buy cones and eat them outside. The hostess beckoned; Frankie shot Carey a consoling smile, and they followed the broad-shouldered young woman. The tables were crowded with boisterous teens. Why wasn't her nephew among them, she wondered? They sat down and opened their sticky laminated menus.

After they ordered, Carey pulled his phone from his camouflage jacket. She asked him about his high school, but he didn't want to talk about it. When they were served, he dug greedily into his sundae, trailing his sleeve in the fudge. She ate her banana split without tasting it. Eating in silence with Bruce off in a daydream had become routine for her. No wonder she'd failed to notice his decline for so long. In the first years of their marriage, she'd discovered the extent of his absentmindedness, his self-absorption. She could get him talking if she asked about his past—his working-class childhood in Chicago, his scholarship to Harvard where he'd met Annaliese, the Munich exchange student, the girls' mother; his travels abroad for conferences, his National Book Award. Most days, he holed up for hours in his study or wandered through the house, book in hand, muttering to himself. She'd made a game of it, directing the girls to be silent and stand still as their father drifted through the room. As time passed, though, it became less of a game and more of a test he failed over and over again.

"Brain freeze." Carey grimaced.

She instructed him to press his tongue to the roof of his mouth to warm it. When that didn't work, she told him to tip his head back.

"*Why* am I doing this?" he said.

A crumpled napkin struck his ear. His head snapped forward; color drained from his cheeks. "Don't look back," he said. "Two rats are behind you."

"Two what?"

"Andrew and Sahil from school." He sounded more disgusted than worried. How different Clara and Jean had been at his age. Self-confident, impervious to insult, her stepdaughters had taught her to fight fire with fire bombs. They were all still close, which Frankie counted as one of her greatest accomplishments. She considered texting Jean for advice about Carey, but he was watching her. "Headache better?" she said.

"What do you call a group of snakes?" he said.

"I don't know, teenage boys?"

"No, but that's good. It's a *bed* of snakes. What about a group of guinea fowls?"

She shook her head, stumped.

"A *confusion*," he said. "Surprised you didn't know that."

Off-putting, his smug tone. How did it play with his peers? Another balled-up napkin struck his head. Behind her, the boys tittered. One came over to their table. This boy's brand of adorable—small nose, plush lips, and a shock of dark hair falling over his wide-set blue eyes—would appeal to girls who'd recently surrendered their teddy bears. "I'm having a graduation party next Saturday," he told Carey. "Everyone's invited." He turned to her. "I'm Andrew."

"She's my aunt," Carey said. "I'm busy on Saturday. Thanks anyway."

After Andrew left, she said, "Is *he* the rat that got the girl? He's nothing special. No Carey Mulroney, that's for sure." Carey looked at his phone. "You should go to the party. It might be the last time you see these kids." She watched him type. "Or are you hoping for a clean break after you insult everybody? That only works in the movies, you know. In real life, you *always* run into the people you never want to see again."

When he didn't respond, she took out her phone to mirror his rude behavior. She texted her sister about the party. Magical things happened at parties, even at those Princeton gatherings where she'd felt conspicuously young and un-credentialed. Her conversion from office coordinator to Bruce's wife had offended most of the female faculty. Four years later, when Kip Jones was hired, she'd gained an ally. *Who are these stuffed shirts?* his conspiratorial smiles implied. What little she'd managed to say to the attractive, fifty-year-old newcomer was designed to shock or amuse. After five months of watching each other, they'd kissed at the dean's New Year's Eve celebration. It was midnight and everyone was kissing everyone, but the pressure of his hand on the small of her back made his intentions clear. Two weeks later, they became lovers.

ON SUNDAY AFTERNOON, FOG rolled in, and the house floated inside a cloud. When Carey woke at noon, she scrambled eggs for their lunch. He volunteered to clean up, and while he washed and she dried, he told her about the street art he'd seen in the Mission District. All of yesterday's tension had dissipated; that was how it went with teenagers, she remembered. Afterward, he returned to his room, and she went into the living room to read the *Times Book Review*. She was pleased when Carey appeared with his project. He laid out the pages on the coffee table, dropped to his knees, and got to work. Occasionally, he'd read aloud a clunky caption, and they'd figure out a pithier one together. When the ringing phone broke into the thick, comfortable silence, they both looked for his cell under the pages of his project. "Mom," he said, looking at the screen. He headed for his room with the phone; he closed the door.

She regretted texting her sister about the graduation party. What if Nora was nagging him now, undoing all her progress? She left the couch and stood at the window. The attached houses across the street were veiled in mist. A white-haired man appeared in one window, then disappeared. Frankie pulled her phone out of her pocket and called the nursing home. In the few minutes it took for the orderly to locate Bruce in the arts and crafts room, she pictured her husband, the National Book Award-winning biographer bent over popsicle sticks with Elmer's glue. She was tempted to hang up, but then his deep, soothing voice was on the line. "Sweetheart," he said, "where are you?"

She imagined his handsome face. In his later years, his dimples had deepened into long creases, giving him an expression of perpetual amusement. His top lip had thinned, but the bottom was plump and sensual; it was still a pleasure to kiss him. She reminded him she was in San Francisco, watching Carey. "Our nephew," she added, helpfully.

"Carey. Good kid." After a short pause, he said, "Where did you say you were?"

Five o'clock in New Jersey, too late in the day for lucidity, but she only wanted to hear his voice. "California, Bruce. Remember Kip Jones, the Irish lit guy?"

"Sure, I remember Kip. Good kid."

Kid. He'd be close to sixty now, slightly older than Bruce when they'd married. "Turns out he's at Berkeley. Thought I might see him while I'm here."

Silence. Was he having a memory lapse or a memory jog? The affair had lasted only four months, not long enough, she hoped, for her distracted husband to catch on. At the end of the spring semester, Kip had left Princeton without a goodbye. Rumors had circulated about the dean's wife, but Frankie had refused to believe them.

"I probably won't have time," she said. "Doubt he'd remember me anyway."

"I wish you'd come, darling," Bruce said. "Clara's here every day, getting in my hair; manuscript's a mess. I could use your help. Can't make sense of—. Sweetheart, will you please come?"

"On my way, honey," she said. It did not escape her notice that Bruce had addressed her younger self, his amanuensis. "Be there soon. Get some rest."

She took her phone to her sister's room and emailed Kip at his UC Berkeley address, filling him in on Bruce's health crisis. Then she stretched out on the bed and ran her hand over the patchwork quilt, the stitched calico squares, old dresses or blouses from another lifetime. That January afternoon when Kip had surprised her at the house, she had been copyediting Bruce's biography in the drafty study; she'd answered the door in her pink thermal long underwear. With a sly grin, he'd slipped the pencil from behind her ear and circled her nipple with the eraser. She was thirty-two, married to a man who would soon collect social security, stepmother to defiant teenagers, and until that snowy afternoon, she'd believed the best years of her life were behind her.

Within minutes of sending her email, the phone chimed. Her news about Bruce had devastated him, Kip wrote, such a tragic loss. After a decade of no contact, they were emailing back and forth. He asked about her stepdaughters, and she inquired about his teaching. What she really wanted to know was whether he was in a relationship. Finally, she held her breath and typed: *I'm in SF at my sister's, leaving Tues.* Within seconds, he suggested they meet the next day, Monday, for lunch at noon. That left plenty of time to get back for Carey's four o'clock assembly. They exchanged cell phone numbers, and he sent an address for a restaurant in Berkeley.

On Monday morning after Carey had left for school, she went for a run through Mount Davidson Park. In the near distance, the tall grass rustled violently. She was a strong runner, but not strong enough to outpace a coyote. She came to a dead stop, backed up a few steps, and headed back the way she'd come. At the house, she showered and changed into jeans and a black turtleneck. She found a pair of chandelier earrings in a ceramic bowl on the vanity; her hands shook as she slipped the wires through her earlobes. Her reflection stared grimly back at her; the turtleneck was the problem. In Nora's closet, she found a white silk blouse with pearl buttons, only a little tight in the bust. Satisfied with her softer, sexier reflection, she left the house. The Audi was parked on the street; she tossed her pocketbook on the seat and started the engine. Before she could enter the restaurant's address into the navigation system, her phone rang. Kip.

"Sorry, love, can't make lunch," he whispered. "Something's come up." She imagined him hiding in a closet from his girlfriend or wife, and she felt angry and absurdly ashamed. She stared out at Teresita Boulevard, unable to speak. The road climbed steeply to the horizon before it ended in what looked like the edge of a cliff. On the phone, Kip was suggesting a six o'clock dinner, same restaurant, and she heard herself saying *yes*.

THE SCHOOL ASSEMBLY WAS a three-ring circus. In the library, tables displayed artwork and science projects. In the solarium, a poetry reading. She found a seat in the dark auditorium where a slender girl played one of Chopin's nocturnes on the baby grand, pouring more passion into the notes than seemed possible for a girl her age. Kip's whispered phone call had unsettled Frankie, and as the piano music washed over her, she relived the gutted, lost feeling that had followed his sudden, mysterious departure. The long aimless drives she took to escape Bruce and the girls, Coldplay on the CD player, tears blurring her view of the road. Without her secret life, marriage and motherhood had become, for a time, unbearable.

The pianist left the stage, and a boy entered. Andrew, from the ice cream place. He carelessly dangled his violin as though it were a baseball bat and he was approaching home plate. When he raised the instrument to his shoulder and played "Amazing Grace," he looked and sounded angelic. Why would her nephew have a problem with *this* kid? An only child, Carey spent more time with adults than with children his own age. At family events, he lurked around the women until someone, never his mother, shooed him away. God knew the things he'd heard. They were all grateful to Bruce for taking the boy under his wing. If she couldn't find a friend for Carey to go home with, she'd have to bring him to her dinner with Kip; the conversation would have to be confined to the safer, less satisfying territory of the present. What she wanted from Kip, she realized now, was the intimacy of shared memory, the very thing she was slowly losing with Bruce. The music ended; Andrew left the stage.

A screen descended from the ceiling as the lights dimmed. She lowered her eyes, afraid to look, and saw Carey center stage bent over a laptop on a folding table. The first story panel appeared, and he read the caption, his voice barely audible despite the microphone. The audience grew restless. She shushed the whiny boy beside her. In the next panel, a rat farted on the lunch line, and the children in the audience went ape shit. Her little seatmate fell off his chair; his mother had to scoop him up from the floor. Carey's narration grew more confident as he neared the final scene, and he was rewarded with wild applause.

She followed the crowd shuffling into the gym where a few tables had been set up with juice and cupcakes. Andrew made a beeline for Frankie, trailed by a stunning, silver-haired woman who introduced herself as Sally, the boy's mother. "I wanted to meet the East Coast aunt," Sally said. "I lived in New York City a *thousand* years ago, before my husband—" She broke off when Carey approached. "Our talented artist!"

"You were a hit!" Frankie gave his shoulder a squeeze. He mumbled thanks and frowned at her blouse as though trying to work out where he'd seen it before.

"Awesome performance, Andrew!" The pianist was passing with another girl. Andrew blushed and turned away. Carey looked stricken.

"Andrew?" his mother said, "Why didn't you thank Lyra?"

"*Whatever.* I messed up a part."

"Boys!" Sally rolled her eyes; Frankie smiled knowingly, though she didn't have a clue. Then a stroke of luck: Sally invited Frankie and Carey to her house. Sahil and his mother were coming, too, she said.

"Sounds like fun," Frankie said. "Unfortunately, I've got plans, but Carey's free."

"What plans?" Carey broke away from the boys.

"It's personal," she said, without thinking.

"Actually, I'm busy too."

"No, you're not, silly! Go, celebrate with your friends. I'll come for you later." She noted his worried expression before turning to Sally. "Is nine okay?"

CAREY WOULD BE FINE, Frankie told herself, as she drove over the Bay Bridge, heading for Berkeley. It wouldn't be the last time he'd have his heart broken, and if the boys couldn't get along, Sally had Frankie's cell number. By the time she entered Claudine's on Durant Avenue, she'd almost convinced herself she'd made the right decision. The maître d' led her to Kip's table beside the tiled fireplace. His back was turned: his neck under the stiff blue collar had thickened and his dark hair, flecked with gray, had been cut close to his scalp, exposing a small bald patch. These diminishments made her feel tender. Discreetly, she undid the top button on her blouse. He turned, and she saw more changes. His skin was ruddier, looser around his jawline. Deep creases cratered along his cheekbones when he smiled. He rose and pulled her into an embrace. "You haven't changed at all," he said. "Still so beautiful with that lovely chestnut hair." His compliment put her at ease.

Ordering dinner and deciding on wine occupied the first ten minutes. Then he caught her up on his last ten years. Occasionally, she'd feel something brushing her neck and swat at it only to remember her sister's earrings. She drank too much wine and lost the thread of his monologue—a fellowship, summer course at Trinity. His impersonal patter strained her patience; they had so little time. "Why did you leave without saying good-bye?" She wanted to take it back the instant she saw his stunned expression.

"You didn't know about Ginny? I thought everyone knew." The dean's wife, the plump opera singer. "She'd turned the story into a damned aria. All her idea, the skinny-dipping. Robert came home early. Ugly scene, one I'd rather forget, if you don't mind."

He must have noticed her distress; he touched her hand on the table. It occurred to her that an irate husband had probably chased him out of Texas too, and that was why he'd settled for the adjunct position at Berkeley.

"Ginny meant nothing to me." He glanced quickly at her cleavage and back at her eyes. "You were always the one. I can't tell you how happy I was to hear from you. But curious too. Why now? This can't be the first time you've visited your sister."

She flinched, felt exposed. "I thought you should know about Bruce."

He sat back, teeth gritted, and ran his hand over his head. "I'm crap at keeping in touch. Doesn't mean I didn't think about you. Bruce, too. Love that guy. Who didn't, I mean, *doesn't*? He mentored half the junior faculty." He paused, a helpless, lost look on his face. "Too late now, isn't it?" He fidgeted with his phone, flipping it over and over on the table, avoiding her eyes. She remained silent, left him to twist with his guilt.

"Funny how things turn out," he said. "I mean, we all envied Bruce with his prizes and his sexy, young wife and now..." He trailed off when the waiter arrived with their dinners. Steak au poivre for Kip and confit de canard for her.

As the waiter stood between them to refill their wine glasses, she rebuttoned her blouse. Kip made her sound like one of Carey's trophy felines. She picked at her duck, remembering how queasy she'd felt when Ken Carbone had cupped her behind with his sweaty hand in the faculty mail room, but she hadn't made a peep of protest. Out of her depth on the Princeton campus, she'd sensed her youth and sexuality were her most potent superpowers. No wonder the women had been so cold. When the waiter left, she said, "So, tell me, are you in a relationship now, or are you still sleeping with other men's wives?"

He left off cutting into his bloody meat. "Don't think I like the sound of that, darling." She raised her chin and held his gaze. "Right. I'm sort of engaged," he said. "Her name's Madison." She rolled her eyes without thinking. He smirked, got her point. "She's twenty-seven."

She waited for more; it didn't come. "Please tell me there's more to her than that."

He wiped his mouth with his napkin, and she noticed dark stubble under his nostril his razor had missed. Eyesight's going, she thought with some satisfaction. "She's a physical therapist," he said. "Took care of my arthritic knee."

"She sounds perfect for your golden years."

He snorted. "I used to call Bruce an old goat. Guess *I'm* the old goat now." He didn't seem too bothered.

"If the hoof fits..."

His smile was affectionate. "Madison reminds me of you. She's goofy."

"I was never goofy. I was *young*."

"Don't you remember all the fun we had moving things around at those parties? Scotch bottle in Robert's pajama drawer. Ginny's birth control tablets in the freezer."

She shook her head, though the memories were coming back. An odd and disappointing thing to remember when all she'd ever wanted was to be taken seriously in her black turtlenecks.

"I also remember us fucking at the arboretum," he said. "You were always up for adventure." He pointed his knife at her with one eye closed as though taking aim. "I so loved that about you."

She'd flinched at the word "fuck." He had pushed her into taking risks. Eager to please and blinded by her own wild appetite, she'd often given in to him. Easy to mistake that heart-stopping fear for something more meaningful. When she'd balked at sex in his campus office, he'd called her a prude. She doubted the skinny-dipping had been Ginny's idea.

"And look at us now." She meant they were like the other boring, middle-aged couples in the restaurant, but his self-satisfied smile told her he saw things differently. "You're happy," she said. "I'm happy you're happy." A lie. Why should he get a second chance? In Carey's graphic story, Kip would be a coyote, taking everything he could get his greedy paws on.

"Why wouldn't I be happy? I'm having dinner with a gorgeous woman." He brushed a curl from her eye. Without thinking, she grabbed his hand and held it against her cheek. He'd always known the right thing to say. They locked eyes for a titillating second. "I'm not sure I can handle this," she said, her voice catching.

"Ah, Frankie, you'll be fine. You'll do what needs to be done. But you must've known this day was coming. You're an intelligent woman."

She pulled back, stung. That was *not* what she'd meant. "Oh, sure, just like *Madison* knows she'll be changing *your* diapers in a few years."

He laughed, but she hadn't meant to be funny. His phone chimed. He read the text with a smirk, and typed a long response. She took out her own phone and saw two missed calls from Sally. She shoved back from the table and stood, knocking over the empty wine bottle. Without a word, she left the table and pinballed through the maze of tables to reach the door. On the sidewalk, she plugged a finger in her ear against the traffic noise and listened to the message. Carey was at the hospital. The boys were *messing around* at a construction site, the framed-out house next door—he tried to jump across beams and fell. The call was cut short, and she moaned.

Kip strode out of the restaurant toward her, clutching his napkin like a flag of surrender. "Is it Bruce?"

She held him off with a raised hand and listened to the second voicemail. "A broken arm, a fracture. No concussion," Sally reported. "The doctor spoke to your sister. You can pick him up at my house." She gave the address again. "I should warn you, he's loopy on painkillers. Keeps telling us he loves us!"

LATER THAT NIGHT, SHE lay beside her sleeping nephew in Nora's bed. His cast rested on his stomach—his right arm, his drawing hand. In the lamplight, she read his classmates' names scrawled in green marker on the plaster. Andrew had answered the door, apologizing. Sally handed over Carey's broken glasses zipped inside a baggie.

Kip had offered to drive her to Sally's, but she'd sent him home to his fiancée. No doubt he'd make more two-timing phone calls from his closet, but none to her. She preferred her curated memories of him to the trickier reality. She imagined telling Bruce about her dinner and turning Kip into a joke, but in her secret heart, she would continue to think of Kip as a necessary interlude in her otherwise faithful marriage.

She touched Carey's shoulder to wake him. With eyes half closed, he sat up and took the offered pain pill. She raised the water glass to his lips. "Tell the truth," she said. "Did someone push you?"

"Nobody's fault. They thought I wouldn't jump across to the beam, but I showed them." He lay back with a smile. "For a second, I was actually flying."

"In your next story, you could be the hawk, swooping through the cafeteria, snatching French fries." He snorted. An instant later he was asleep, blissfully unaware of the trials and compromises that lay ahead of him.

She switched off the lamp. Lights glimmered in Glen Valley like distant constellations. Three thousand miles away, Bruce was asleep in his single bed. If he dreamed about her at all, which version of her did he dream about? The sexy office assistant who'd flattered him with attention? The eager, infatuated student seated across from him in the café? Or the clever Mary Poppins who'd rescued his family? It came to her that *she* had been the coyote. Clever and quick, she had taken everything.

That first year, married to Bruce, she'd nearly lost her mind, keeping Clara and Jean occupied while their father worked on his second book. In the farmhouse on the canal, where he'd taken over the screened-in porch for his study, his dark, fuzzy figure would occasionally appear behind the screen, watching them, wading in the algae-clotted canal for crayfish, chasing butterflies with nets through golden yarrow and Queen Anne's lace. "Wave to Daddy," she'd say, but the girls would be too caught up in their adventures to mind her. Oh, but what an idyllic picture they must have made, like a scene out of *Tom Sawyer*. Or so she had liked to imagine. It was the sort of thing that had made her happy then.

OPEN HOUSE

THE REALTOR HAD LET HERSELF into the house on Sunday morning while Frankie slept—overslept, rather—and baked something sweet-smelling. Now she was darting around the kitchen, opening cabinets and banging them closed, while monologuing into her Bluetooth earpiece about escrow or maybe escarole. Frankie only half listened; she lurked in the doorway in her black turtleneck and jeans, damp hair pulled into a low ponytail, saying a silent goodbye to her kitchen, the only room in the one-hundred-year-old farmhouse that reflected her taste. Last year, she'd been forced to renovate after her husband, seventy-four and thirty years her senior, started a fire in the toaster oven. The fruit and rooster wallpaper swapped for a blue-and-white floral, the cherry cabinets for white, the brown Formica countertops for pearly granite. Pleased with the brightened results, she'd replaced all the gold appliances with stainless steel, though it had busted her budget to do so.

"Smells good in here," Frankie said when the realtor ended her call.

"Toll House cookies!" Suzy said. "Trick of the trade." In her mid-fifties, blonde and conventionally pretty, Suzy wore a navy pinstriped suit, the jacket cut close to her narrow waist. "Out of all the senses, smell is the most evocative."

"That's true. I remember the first time I met my step-daughters. They were making pies right here. They wore these adorable little—"

"You wouldn't happen to have a cutting board, would you? I'd hate to scratch this gorgeous countertop."

Aprons. What was Suzy's deal? The realtor stood to earn a healthy commission: the least she could do was listen to one measly memory. Frankie crossed to the lower cabinet, slid out the wooden board, and slapped it onto the counter.

"I looked all over for that little rascal," Suzy said. "Usually, it's right next to the knife block." She picked up the knife. "So, what was I saying? Oh, right, sense of smell. I challenge you to find even one person who associates baking smells with something bad."

She could think of one: someone who was raped in a bakery, but she kept this to herself. She'd repressed quite a few noxious comebacks these past weeks, while submitting to the realtor's endless instructions for cleaning, painting, staging, and landscaping. At times, she'd felt cornered, even bullied, into going ahead with the sale, despite her growing ambivalence. The timer dinged. Suzy slipped on the blue oven mitt, and smiling tensely, waited for Frankie to step aside.

"We'll just let these cool a minute." Suzy slid the baking sheet out from the oven and rested it on the countertop. "Would you like to take this batch to the nursing home?"

"Sure, thanks," she said, thinking: Here's your hat, what's your hurry. "Don't you want to put them out for the people?"

"Actually, no. I just need the baking smells. The cookies make a mess. Crumbs everywhere—" The doorbell rang, and Suzy looked at the oven clock, her face creased with annoyance. "For goodness' sake! Early birds?" She looked older and sadder. Like a different person.

FRANKIE OPENED THE DOOR to her twenty-nine-year-old stepdaughter, Clara, who was dressed like an acrobat in a black V-neck sweater and leggings. She had inherited her German mother's tall, sturdy frame, fair complexion, and fawn-colored hair, which she wore in a single braid, thick as a fist, down the center of her back.

"Stupid truck's blocking the driveway," Clara said, thrusting a take-out coffee at Frankie. Behind her in the October mist, two landscapers planted yellow chrysanthemums along the walkway. "They couldn't do this last week?" Clara said. "Talk about last minute—" She broke off to sniff the air. "You're baking?"

"Hello, to you, too."

"Sorry." Clara reached around to pat Frankie's back. "How're you doing? Is this hard?"

"A little." She peeled back the plastic coffee lid. "I may be having second thoughts—"

"It's brighter in here." Clara moved past Frankie and took in the spacious living room. "I like it. What'd you do?"

"What? Oh—well, this rug's new, and the linen drapes. What else?" She sipped the scalding coffee and examined the room, her gaze falling on the scratched wood floor, the buckling walls, the chipped newel post. All the flaws that had stopped registering long ago were obvious and intolerable now that strangers would be eyeing them.

"Basically, I de-cluttered," she said.

"It's called staging," Suzy called out from the kitchen.

Clara's eyes bugged out; she mouthed, "What?"

"Thanks, Suzy!" Frankie shouted. "Forgot the word." She pressed a finger to her lips and beckoned Clara to follow her to the far corner. "The realtor. I'll introduce you in a minute. I'm curious to know what you make of her."

Clara's judgments were often hasty and harsh. Without evidence, she'd accused the nursing home staff of abuse last week after Frankie mentioned seeing a bruise on Bruce's arm. Apart from Clara, however, she had no one to ask. After her layoff from the university press the summer before, she worked from home on freelance editing projects and only occasionally met up with her former co-workers. Her book group, formed during Bruce's Princeton tenure, was slowly unraveling as the older members moved away or lost interest.

At a louder volume, in case Suzy guessed they were talking about her, Frankie said, "I put away those needlepoint pillows, your oma's. You can have them if you want."

"Oma Lilly was a straight-up bitch. You should just burn them."

"Really?" she said, taken aback. "You think Jean would want them?"

"No fucking way."

"Well, if you're sure. What about this painting?" She gestured toward the dark oil painting, a forest scene inside an ornate gold frame, hanging over the fireplace. Clara's mother had brought it from Germany. "Do you want it?"

"No." Clara hitched her tote strap higher on her shoulder. "Burn that too."

"You sure?" Clara's answer surprised Frankie: though her stepdaughter was unsentimental, she had adored her mother. "It's old, might be worth something," she tried.

"Then sell it. I don't want it. Don't look at me that way, Frankie. That painting gave me nightmares when mom was sick. Ask Jean. I dreamed I was lost in that forest. I mean, I dreamed I was trapped *inside* the painting."

"Wish you'd told me. I would've taken it down. I hate it, too." She had made no changes to the décor when she moved in with Bruce and his two daughters sixteen years ago, though the late Annaliese's somber art and heavy antique furniture had oppressed her. "I don't want to erase the girls' mother," she'd told her new husband. But at twenty-eight, she'd had no decorating preferences; she tried on other people's opinions and tastes. If she had it to do all over again, she would redecorate every room. Outside, rain lashed the windows. A pale maple leaf pressed against one pane like a small hand. She felt drained, thinking about the long day ahead.

She opened the breakfront drawer, took out a lime-green Game Boy, and handed it to Clara. "The cleaning crew found this behind your dresser." Frankie remembered how Bruce had nagged thirteen-year-old Clara at the dinner table, in the car, and at bedtime to "put that thing down." In private, Frankie tried to make him understand: to ease his own grief, he'd had his adoring Princeton students and his bottomless Twain research. And Frankie, the English department administrator, a much younger woman, to satisfy needs that fell well outside her job description.

"What am I supposed to do with this?" Clara handed the Game Boy back to Frankie.

IN THE HEAVY DOWNPOUR, Clara cruised through Sunny Vista's small parking lot, the car's wipers on top speed, searching for an open space. Frankie held the Tupperware container on her lap, a Target bag filled with new undershirts and briefs wedged between her feet.

"Are you going to tell Dad about selling the house today?" Clara believed her father should know, but she'd promised not to interfere.

"I'm not sure," she said, though she was leaning toward never telling him. He'd soon forget everything, including the house. And what if Suzy couldn't find a buyer, or Frankie changed her mind about selling? She would have upset Bruce for nothing.

Clara began a second loop around the parking lot. Sundays were the busiest at the nursing home, and rain increased the visitors' numbers. Last Sunday, another washout, a woman in her late fifties with pinched features and over-plucked eyebrows had asked Frankie if it bothered her dad that there were so few men at the home. Frankie had been standing over Bruce as he studied the receipt from the grocery bag she'd used to carry his books—Augustine's *Confessions, A Connecticut Yankee in King Arthur's Court, Paradise Lost*—books he'd requested from his personal library in a moment of increasingly rare lucidity. The titles, she'd hoped, were an ironic acknowledgement of his monthslong confinement, but it was the receipt that claimed his attention while the books sat neglected on the side table.

"He's not my *dad*; he's my husband," she'd snapped, forcing the woman to stutter an apology and hurry off.

A reasonable assumption, she thought now. So why had she taken offense? Maybe it wasn't offense she'd felt. *Paradise Lost* had been one of the first books Bruce had lent her. They'd discussed the poem for hours and hours. She pried open the Tupperware lid and took out a chocolate chip cookie. Clara thrust out her hand and Frankie placed a cookie on it.

"You wanted my opinion?" Clara said, chewing. "About that realtor, that Suzy Q?"

"Suzy Whitacre. Yes, tell me," she said, with no expectation of deep insight or revelation; Clara had spoken briefly to Suzy, grilling her about the Princeton real estate market. Clara slammed on the brakes. Taillights had lit up on a white Cadillac parked in the row closest to the building, only fifty yards away. Waiting, Clara brushed crumbs from her lap. "So, this Suzy Q—"

"Suzy Whitacre."

"*Whatever*. She looks like a fake person."

"Fake? As in shallow? Or fake like a replicant?" She half hoped for the latter. Suzy's studied courtesy, her self-conscious cheerfulness had a Stepford Wife quality.

"Replicant?" Clara made a face of disbelief. "Jesus, I'm not insane." She pulled into the vacated spot so fast, Frankie feared they'd hit the parked cars. Clara shut off the engine and twisted in her seat, leaning her back against the door and tucking one leg beneath her. "I mean fake like a casting agent's idea of a cheerful, selfless mom. Was she on one of those Nickelodeon sitcoms Jean and I used to watch? I swear I've seen her somewhere."

"You're probably thinking about her advertising signs. They're everywhere." Frankie had stared at one on her grocery cart last week for five minutes before she'd connected the pretty face with Suzy. She yawned. If only they could pass the afternoon inside the warm Honda, chatting and eating cookies. She preferred visiting Bruce alone. Easier that way to numb out, to practice denial.

"Nope. Not the signs." Clara reached for her umbrella on the back seat. "I'll Google it. You'll see, she's one of those perfect moms."

"Perfect mom." She scoffed. "What an oxymoron."

"What are you talking about?"

"A contradiction in terms. If you and Jean judged me against those sitcom mothers, well…" she trailed off, feeling unexpectedly emotional.

"I know what the word means." Clara met Frankie's eyes. "Listen, we were practically feral when you showed up. I mean, who leaves an eleven-year-old in charge of a house and her nine-year-old sister? Dad was AWOL for like two years. Believe me, we were thrilled to have you take care of us. No one ever judged you. Okay?" She gave Frankie's shoulder an awkward pat.

She nodded, grateful. Clara had told her this before. So, why did she need to hear it over and over again?

IN THE MEMORY WING, Clara went on ahead to the solarium where the inmates—her name for the residents—received visitors, while Frankie popped into the staff's break room. Once or twice a week, she brought the staff bagels, pastries, or donuts. Clara called this her don't-hurt-my-husband bribes. They'd both seen the viral videos, the orderlies abusing or manhandling the slow or uncooperative residents. In one black-and-white video that Jean, her younger stepdaughter, had sent, an aide slapped an elderly man's face hard every time he slumped over in his wheelchair. Idiotic to think a raisin bagel would deter a sadist. If Frankie found a second bruise, she would hide a camera in her husband's room—Jean's suggestion. Jean, twenty-six, lived in Washington State and played clarinet with the Seattle Symphony. Her husband, Wendell, a software developer, had offered to hook them up with some "sweet" surveillance equipment.

For now, Frankie would rely on trust and kindness, though she couldn't help thinking that Annaliese, Bruce's first wife, a mathematician, would have opted for something more rigorous, like an official investigation. She arranged the cookies on a scratched yellow plastic plate. Without attribution, the cookies would be pointless. She took a Bic pen from her pocketbook and scrawled across a brown paper towel: *Enjoy! From Frankie Mulroney!* She laid the note on top of the cookies, but then picked it up again and scribbled *Shay*, a name she'd never taken as her own.

RAIN DRUMMED THE SOLARIUM's glass roof and muffled the visitors' conversations. She guessed there must be thirty or so people in the room. The air, clammy and close, smelled faintly of ammonia. She spotted Clara hovering behind her father who was seated at the card table across from another man, a stranger to Frankie. Male residents came and went at such a dizzying pace that by the time she learned their names, they were gone from the nursing home and maybe gone from the world. As she drew nearer, Frankie discovered that the two were actually playing cards and betting with cellophane-wrapped hard candies. Her husband's opponent had a pile of Jolly Ranchers and Starlight peppermints twice the size of Bruce's. He also had an astounding protuberance, like a small doorknob, on his forehead over his left eye.

"He's got two pairs," Clara whispered to Frankie. "Tell him; he won't listen to me."

She smiled at her husband's card partner before bending down to eye level with Bruce. His face brightened when he saw her. The bruise on his forearm had faded, and she saw no new marks. A quick assessment of his silver hair, ruddy skin, and navy wool pullover—all clean, all neat—reassured her. She moved closer for a kiss, and he opened his dry lips. Still enjoyable to kiss him. They hadn't had sex in two and a half years, but she remembered their physical life with pleasure. Bruce's unhurried, attentive lovemaking, after all her younger, greedy boyfriends, had been a revelation. She pointed out his pairs. He wriggled his eyebrows playfully and tossed two peppermints into the pot. His partner folded, and Bruce used two hands to sweep the small pile of candy toward himself. The other man stood, filled his pockets, and took off—probably to fleece another, more debilitated resident.

"Does he ever talk, that guy?" Clara dropped into the vacated seat.

"Excuse me, young lady," Bruce said. "Maybe *she'd* like to sit." He had forgotten their names again. He met Frankie's eyes, a wry smile deepening his long dimples. It was their old way of communicating in the girls' presence, mutely expressing their affection or frustration with the children.

Clara, looking sheepish, rose from the chair, but Frankie gestured for her to sit. She set down her shopping bag, pocketbook, and empty Tupperware on the card table, and circled behind Bruce to massage his tight neck and shoulders. His lifelong sedentary habits had not changed: tall and lanky, he'd grown a little belly, and his legs were thinner, frailer. He avoided all the chair exercise classes—just as he'd ignored his doctor's orders to exercise when his health had started to decline at sixty-four. Instead, he'd holed up in his study preparing lectures and burning through weekends writing his second book; he'd flown to conferences during the winter and spring breaks.

Now she wondered if he had been racing the clock—his father had succumbed to Alzheimer's at seventy—but at the time, she'd fixated on her own resentment and loneliness. That made her an easy mark for Kip Jones, the new faculty hire, a seasoned flirt. When the intense four-month affair ended with Kip's abrupt departure for another teaching post in Texas, she'd felt limp and empty, a purse turned inside out.

"So, old man," Clara said, stretching out her long legs. "What's new?"

"New?" He chuckled. "What do you think? I'm stuck in this...this cuckoo's nest." He sounded amused and resigned. In recent weeks, he'd stopped pleading to be taken home, which should have been a relief but felt like a betrayal. The old meticulous Bruce with his subtle, logical mind would've been—*had been*—horrified to find himself trapped here.

"What's new with you?" he asked. "You married yet?"

Frankie's hands froze on Bruce's shoulders as she watched her stepdaughter's grimace soften into a patient smile. "Not until I find a man as wonderful as my father," Clara said.

He laughed. "Smart girl." He gave her a thumbs-up. "So, how's…how's work?" Bruce had always connected with his daughters through their academic careers and later through their professions. Clara was a data analyst in the Rockefeller Foundation's grant office. Now she told her father about a global commission to end energy poverty.

"Energy poverty," he repeated, nodding thoughtfully. As Clara elaborated on the project, he continued to repeat the odd word or phrase, an old teaching technique, Frankie suspected, meant to reassure the speaker that he was listening, that her ideas had merit. When Clara reeled off some figures, he twisted in his chair to view the room behind him. Clara raised her voice, as though his hearing was the issue. He pushed back his chair, and Frankie staggered out of the way. She reached out for him, heart racing, when he struggled to a standing position. It was muscle memory from the winter evenings when she'd had to stop him from leaving the house in his pajamas. Once she'd found him teetering at the top of the staircase, his arms loaded with books.

"Do you need the bathroom?" she asked, taking his elbow.

"I need…I need…" He looked around with a panicked expression. "Where'd that fella go? The one with the…um…" He touched his forehead.

"He's with his daughter." Frankie gestured toward the couch where the card shark sat with the woman she'd rebuffed last weekend. She brought her iPhone out from her pocket-book. "I have Jean's latest recording. The symphony? Come sit, Bruce. Take a listen."

Clara got up to help lower her father into the chair. Frankie handed him her AirPods; he looked with a bewildered expression at the two white plastic devices resting in his palm. She shot Clara a worried glance before calling out Bruce's name. He looked up, and she pointed to her ears. He inserted the earbuds one at a time. She found the recording on her playlist. He closed his eyes and settled back in the chair with a contented smile on his still handsome face.

"He seems out of it," Clara said, frowning down at Bruce. "Usually, he's like this later in the day. Did they change his meds?"

"They raised the dosage on his antipsychotic; I meant to tell you. He blocked his door with a chair. He thinks some-one's taking his stuff."

"Maybe something else is scaring him." Clara patted her father's shoulder. He grabbed her hand and held it. "Time to set up that camera, Frankie," she said.

"Okay." She tugged at her turtleneck; the room was too warm. "I guess you're right."

"Of course, I'm right." Clara unhooked her tote from the chair. "I'll go talk to the director. If they're overmedicating Dad to make him easier to handle, I'm raising hell."

After Clara left, Frankie moved the empty chair closer to Bruce. She took his large hand in hers. No doubt her step-daughter would get some straight answers. While she admired Clara's initiative, she sometimes feared her questions and demands would provoke the staff into taking out their resent-ment on Bruce. On the other hand, Frankie was probably too accommodating, too understanding; after months of managing her husband's care at home she knew how challenging the job could be. Bruce plucked one earbud from his ear and offered it to her.

The gentle, melancholy strains of a Mozart clarinet adagio loosened the tight knot in her chest, and she breathed more deeply. The rain had become a misty drizzle and a weak light filled the solarium. This moment was as good as it would ever get. She remembered her mother's warning: "If you marry him, you'll end up being his caretaker." Anyone could have predicted that. What Frankie hadn't anticipated was how much it would hurt her heart to say goodbye to Bruce after every visit. Or the particular pain of imagining one of the night orderlies reacting with indiscretion or unkindness to Bruce's occasional incontinence. Or how she'd seethe when visitors or staff spoke to her brilliant husband as though he were a child. When Bruce was still begging her to take him home, she'd asked the director about weekend visits, but his doctor had advised against it. Frankie had been secretly relieved, remembering his wakeful nights, his belligerence when confused, and that terrifying fire in their kitchen.

Bruce's hand loosened its grip on hers. He'd fallen asleep.

Clara returned, looking agitated. Frankie removed the earbud. "Is something wrong?"

"Everything's fine. Well, not really. Dad *was* hallucinating. And the medication *is* helping, but it's making him sleepier." She glanced at her father, slumped in his chair, snoring. "I left a message for his doctor to call us."

"Oh, good. Thank you. Let's get someone to—" she began, but Clara talked over her.

"The thing is—oh my god, Frankie. I looked her up, that Suzy Whitacre. You are not going to believe what I found."

IN THE CAR, BEFORE they left the nursing home parking lot, Clara pulled up the newspaper account on her phone and read it aloud: "On June 15, 2004, in Bloomsburg, Pennsylvania, Thomas McCrae (42) threatened his wife, Susan Whitacre McCrae (39), with a butcher knife before kidnapping their two-year-old daughter, Tracey. After a weeklong manhunt, authorities found the father and daughter dead in a motel room 281 miles away in Fredonia, New York. Police labeled the deaths a murder-suicide. The child had been suffocated, and Thomas McCrae had slashed his own wrists."

On the short drive to the Princeton Café, Frankie silently read the newspaper account. She didn't want it to be true, but when she proposed that the woman in the article wasn't the same woman baking cookies in her kitchen, Clara shot her a pitying glance. "It all lines up: the dates, the name, your Suzy's weirdness."

Once they were seated inside the crowded café, Frankie and Clara forced themselves to read the menu and order lunch. Frankie selected a good bottle of sauvignon blanc. Their quiches grew cold as they both kept putting down their forks to pick up their iPhones. On the realty site, Clara found Suzy's professional bio, which featured the same headshot that was on all her local ads. A list of her credentials revealed a BA from Rutgers, an MBA from Wharton, and an earlier successful career on Wall Street. "No dates," Clara pointed out. "Looks like she's hiding something, doesn't it? There are dates for her awards though. See?" Clara held out her phone.

Frankie googled the most recent award. The newspaper announcement mentioned that Suzy Whitacre and her real estate lawyer husband, Bradley Clark, had resided in Princeton, New Jersey, for ten years.

"Seems like a miracle she could trust another man." Clara poured herself a second glass of wine and topped off Frankie's glass. "Does it say how long she and Clark Kent have been married?"

"It's Bradley Clark. No, it doesn't." She put her phone down and pushed it away. "Let's talk about something else," she said. "How are you and Jason doing?"

Clara had moved in with the thirty-eight-year-old, never-been-married orthopedist four months ago. Initially, Frankie had chalked up Clara's complaints about Jason's rigidity and brooding silences to the normal adjustment of living with another person. But after a few dinners with the couple, she wondered if they were a bad match. The alteration in Clara's personality on those occasions had been surprising. Her stepdaughter seemed subdued, her natural frankness and exuberance repressed in Jason's presence.

Clara blew out her breath. "You know how he was always dropping hints I might be able to change his mind about not wanting kids? Well, he told me he's made up his mind. No kids."

Frankie grimaced with sympathy. "I'm afraid you have to take his word for it this time." She had not taken Bruce's no-kids decision seriously. In the early days of their relationship, she'd managed to change his mind about so many things, including beach vacations, house cats, and Greek food. Yet, he'd held disappointingly firm on the issue of children. If he had relented, she would be raising a teenager now. Not an easy or affordable thing to do on her own.

Clara pulled her braid over her shoulder and held onto it with both hands. "To tell you the truth, things have been sort of shitty with him. This might be the off-ramp I've been looking for." She tossed her braid behind her. "Hey, did that Clark-Whitacre union produce any offspring?"

Frankie picked up her phone and skimmed the announcement. "Nope. Nothing on the realty site either." It made sense now why Suzy had cut her off earlier when she'd brought up her stepdaughters. Perhaps, Suzy could not bear to bring another child into the world after her daughter's murder. Or maybe by the time she'd met Bradley Clark, she had been too old to conceive—another kind of sorrow, one Frankie hoped Clara could avoid.

After they'd ordered dessert, Clara excused herself to go to the restroom. Frankie looked around the crowded restaurant. Most of the tables had big groups of professional people, men and women on their lunch breaks. Suzy had been a stockbroker, which Frankie imagined as a boys' club. Not an easy field to advance in unless you played the boys' game. When Clara returned, Frankie wondered aloud whether an affair had been the motive for the murder suicide. "You know Wall Street. Suzy's an attractive woman, working long hours, entertaining clients—"

"What are you saying?" Clara looked disappointed. "It's Suzy's fault her husband killed her kid? Really, Frankie? Check yourself."

She opened her mouth to speak, but closed it when the chubby young waiter appeared to set down their desserts: chocolate cake for Clara and for her, crème brûlée, which the waiter set aflame with a small propane torch he'd kept tucked beneath his arm. Frankie gasped. Clara clapped her hands. Heads turned at the nearby tables.

"I'm not saying it's her fault," she said, after the waiter had moved off, taking some of their dirty dishes and silverware with him. "I just want to know the story behind—"

"You want someone to blame," Clara said. "It's not that simple. If Suzy was fooling around, she probably had her reasons. Her husband was clearly unstable. Plus, who knows what their sex life was like." She scraped her fork through the chocolate frosting on her plate. "People in good marriages don't have affairs, do they? I mean, yeah, sure, it's a fucked-up way to deal with marital problems but not as bad as murder."

Their eyes met for a brief, uncomfortable moment. Bruce may have been oblivious to his wife's affair, but a teenage girl, roiling with hormones, would've been tuned in. Frankie had managed to meet Kip Jones at least four times a week, partly by making sure the household ran smoothly: regular meals, bills paid, clean laundry. If Clara had caught on, she'd kept it to herself. Having lost one mother, she wouldn't want to risk losing another. What an awful secret to keep, Frankie thought now.

She put down her spoon. The heavy sweetness of the crème brûlée unsettled her stomach. The waiter placed the check folder on the table next to Frankie, correctly assuming that she was the responsible party. She skimmed the charges. Clara offered to pay half, but Frankie pretended not to hear and reached into her pocketbook for her wallet.

"What I want to know," she said, sliding her credit card into the little plastic holder, "is how you recover from something like that? How do you keep getting up in the morning?"

"You become a realtor, that's how," Clara said.

Frankie looked to see if Clara was being sarcastic, but she was serious.

"You take over strangers' houses," Clara continued. "You *stage* the rooms to look like some idealized domestic space. You bake cookies in their pretty kitchens. You borrow someone else's life for a weekend. You become"—she made air quotes—"the *perfect mom.*"

Frankie smiled wanly at that impossible phrase. In a sense, she had borrowed Annaliese's life. She had been a good enough mother to the dead woman's grieving little girls. She'd done her best through Clara and Jean's rebellious teenage years. She'd handled it all—meeting with their teachers, meeting their friends, finding them therapists, raiding their bedrooms when necessary. Their stickier offenses, like truancy, sex, and drugs, she'd kept from Bruce, sensing he'd overreact, make things worse for everyone. In those instances, she'd behaved more like an empathetic and responsible older sibling. But it had all worked out. Everyone had survived, including Frankie, who had managed to keep a part of herself separate and safe, like a roped-off room in an otherwise open house.

After lunch, as they walked across the parking lot to the car, she asked Clara how she felt about selling the house. "I should've checked with you sooner," she said. "It's your childhood home. All those memories."

Clara didn't answer until they were both inside, seatbelts fastened. "It's your decision to make, Frankie. Your future. It's sad to think about, but he's not going to get better."

They drove in silence. The rain had ended, and the streets were busy with cyclists and runners. Frankie asked Clara to drop her off a mile from home. The open house still had an hour to go. Clara pulled over to the curb, and with the car running, she searched the internet for Wi-Fi nanny cameras. Frankie agreed: they couldn't wait for her son-in-law Wendell's suggestions. They settled on one model that was disguised as a small phone charger; it would allow them to watch videos, both live and recorded, on their phones or laptops. "Buy two," Frankie told her. "I'll pay you back." Clara sent her a questioning look. "One for the house," Frankie said.

FRANKIE WALKED HOME, BUZZED from the wine. She had the floaty sensation that she was outside her body, watching herself, attentive to what came next. The sky had cleared, and the late afternoon sun lit up the gold and green leaves arching over the street. Everywhere, the thunderous roar of leaf blowers and lawn mowers, the landscapers making up for lost time. The bright air shimmered with leaf dust. Her street, with its older houses, deep landscaped properties, and tall shade trees, had not changed much in sixteen years, though strangers lived in most of these houses now. Only a few people knew her as Bruce's wife and Clara and Jean's stepmother. Older people, Bruce's age, some his Princeton colleagues. She'd see them out strolling with spouses or dogs, and they'd wave to each other like survivors on adjacent life rafts, drifting toward the falls that were, for now, only a faint roar in the distance.

She slowed her pace as she approached her house. The old place had never looked better with its fresh coat of gray paint, new roof, and the yellow chrysanthemums dolloped along the walkway. Suzy's red Mini Cooper was still parked at the curb, a blue Audi station wagon and a black Lincoln SUV behind it. Through the open front door, Frankie spied shadowy figures moving about her living room. She checked the time on her phone: a half hour to go until the house was hers again.

She sat beneath the old tulip tree at the edge of her property to wait. The ground was uncomfortably hard, bumpy with roots. Dampness seeped through her jeans. Overhead, migrating Canada geese filled the sky with cacophonous honking. She tilted her head back to look through the yellow leaves, and spotted the frayed gray rope dangling from one thick branch—all that remained of the tire swing Bruce had hung years ago, back when Annaliese was alive. How could Frankie have forgotten the swing? Every time she'd visited Bruce, his girls would drag her outside, begging her to push them. Although she was younger then, it had taken all her strength to lift that heavy tire into the sky. That heart-stop-ping instant when she had to let go. Once, she'd ducked too slowly, or maybe in the wrong direction, and the hurtling tire had landed a glancing blow. Clara and Jean covered her throbbing shoulder with little kisses. Where was Bruce in this memory? Somewhere inside the house—in his study, proba-bly—already receding into the background.

IN JANUARY, SOON AFTER the house had been sold, Frankie put a deposit down on a two-bedroom condo, but the clos-ings were still a month off. She found solace in watching the nanny cam videos. Bruce, alone in his room, listening to mu-sic, napping, or serenely gazing out his window. By this time, he was calling her Anneliese and sometimes Doris, his beloved deceased sister's name. She minded less than she'd expected. On days when Frankie needed cheering up, she'd watch the video of Suzy recorded on the day she'd sold the farmhouse for twenty thousand over the asking price. The realtor entered Frankie's kitchen like a boxing champ, chin lifted, punching the air with two fists. She plucked one of the wooden spoons from the ceramic holder and spoke into it like a microphone. "I'd like to thank everyone who believed in me," she said. "My gorgeous husband, Brad, and all the kind, talented people I work with who probably thought I was a hot mess, but gave me a chance anyway—" she broke off, doubled over with laughter. Frankie could watch this video over and over again. It never grew old.

PLEASE SEE ME

TWO WEEKS AFTER GINGER buried her mother-in-law, she felt listless and blue. But she wouldn't call it grief. Definitely not grief. Eileen's death, following a year of mental and physical decline, had been—in so many ways—a relief. She stood over the kitchen sink dressed in a neon-pink cycling jersey and shorts, eating burnt toast. Tawny autumn light poured through the window, warming her face. If she hustled, she could catch her cycling group before they rolled out of town at nine. But only if she hustled. It stupefied her, this thing that wasn't grief. Her cell phone buzzed on the countertop. She picked it up.

"I did what you told me," her mother said. "I saw my doctor, and he sent me for tests." Ginger heard irritation in her mother's voice and worried she was somehow to blame. "And now they're saying I have leukemia."

"Are you sure?" she said, aware of how idiotic that sounded, but she hoped her mother was mistaken. All those vague maladies last summer: the fatigue and canker sores, the cold that lingered through June and reappeared in August. She must have tuned her mother out at some point while she was dealing with her mother-in-law's crises.

Joe came whistling into the kitchen. He stood before her, his face slack and questioning. A silver-haired man in his mid-fifties, her husband had gained weight this past year

176

in his face and neck. His shirt pulled tight across his belly, which embarrassed her for some reason.

"Hold on, Mom. Sorry." She covered the mouthpiece. "What is it?"

"Meet me at my mother's after your bike ride," he said. "Two o'clock?"

"Closer to three."

"Should be done by three," he said. "Come earlier." He left before she could respond.

"Mom? Sorry. Joe was just—"

"I'll let you go, Ginger. You're busy."

"No, it's just—so, what happens next? Did they mention treatment?"

"They want a biopsy on my lymph node," her mother said, exhaustion leaking into her voice. "Your father can tell you more, but he's at the Stop & Shop."

Ginger took some comfort from this. No caring husband would leave his wife alone the day after a terminal cancer diagnosis. Unless he wanted to shield her from his own distress. She choked up at the image of her eighty-four-year-old father pushing a shopping cart and blinking back tears. "You shouldn't leave it all up to Dad," she said, wondering why it was easier to feel sympathy for her healthy father. "Wouldn't you like to know what's going on?" she said. "If it were me, I'd be taking lots of notes."

"Okay, Ginger. I have to go."

"Come on, Mom. You're not mad at me, are you?"

"I'm tired. I've been sick since June, remember? I'm eighty-three. What've I got left?" her mother said. "My looks are gone. My children don't need me. Your sister lives halfway around the world and never calls. And you, forty-five minutes away. I never see you—"

"Work's crazy, and we've got Eileen's house to clean out."

"—but you have your own life. I won't keep you."

"Wait," she said.

"Bye, Ginger."

Her mother was gone.

ON WEEKENDS, GINGER'S CYCLING group met in front of the senior center, a restored nineteenth-century train station. The women often lingered, hashing out their route or waiting for stragglers. It was no surprise they hadn't waited for her. She rarely responded to the group texts, even though her part-time land surveyor's job at Joe's engineering firm left her with plenty of time for riding. In truth, she was losing her cycling mojo at fifty-five. She hated that everyone had to wait for her after a difficult climb. Not long ago, she had been the one waiting for slowpokes, and she'd be lying if she said she hadn't felt annoyed.

She pedaled through town and headed north on busy Piermont Road, holding her line and her breath whenever the landscaping trucks, with their clattering trailers, sped past. Last summer, a cyclist had been knocked off his bike and killed when one of those trailer doors came unlatched. That was life: you were rolling along, minding your own business, when your mother phoned to say she had leukemia. It was somewhat reassuring to know Ginger's father, a retired EPA chemical engineer, would read up on medical advances and ask all the right questions. Maybe now wasn't the best time to criticize her mother's overdependence on him.

Eight miles later, she crossed over into New York State and navigated the narrow winding, potholed streets to reach Clausland Mountain County Park. The main road meandered through woods ablaze with scarlet sumac, golden maple, and birch. Two weeks ago, the leaves were green when she and Frances, her only child, hiked on the marked trails after Eileen's funeral. At twenty-eight, Frances had a wholesome, effortless beauty. Tall and athletic, she had been a competitive pole vaulter in high school and college. For their spur-of-the-moment hike, Frances wore her mother's baggy track shorts and her father's neon-orange running shoes. Fashion never interested Frances. She had a PhD in biomedical engineering, specializing in heart devices like pacemakers and implantable cardioverter defibrillators. She worked long hours at Boston's Mass General dressed in shapeless scrubs and surgical masks. "A waste of your beauty," her mother had told Frances at Eileen's wake. Eavesdropping on their conversation, Ginger was stunned, but Frances had laughed—thought it was a joke.

GINGER'S MOTHER HAD WORKED as a model in the early '60s—catwalks and photo shoots, catalog contracts, and auto shows. Her stories were repeated like family lore: the French photographer who begged her to return with him to Avignon; the car dealership owner who dangled a new Cadillac in exchange for a weekend together at his Sagaponack beach house (which she'd refused like a good girl). After Ginger had taken a women's studies class her freshman year in high school, her mother's stories had made her uneasy—angry even. It became clear Ginger, age thirteen, would never enjoy the kind of male attention her mother valued. She took after her father: pale and plain, sturdily-built, a Bavarian milkmaid talented in math.

It was her sister, Kim, older by ten years, who had the Paris modeling career. Kim's father, a freelance photographer, "wooed" Diana with dinners at the 21 Club and promises of a *Vogue* fashion shoot before "luring" her into the Plaza Hotel.

Twenty and pregnant, Ginger's mother moved back home to sleepy New Milford, New Jersey, where she had been forced to work in a high-end dress shop after Kim's father disappeared. But the story had a happy ending, her mother always insisted. She married Ginger's father, little Ralphie Osterhaus, the boy next door who'd worshipped Diana since the seventh grade.

HALFWAY UP CLAUSLAND MOUNTAIN, the road leveled out briefly. Ginger caught her breath and unclenched her death grip on the handlebars. The air was unusually warm and close, but the good weather couldn't last. November would bring an end to the long light-filled days and cool morning rides. She looked up, sensing someone watching her. A white pickup, parked on the shoulder, seven hundred feet in the distance. She saw sunlight flash on his wristwatch before she saw the man standing outside the truck, naked from the waist up. The lower half of his body, hidden behind the truck bed, she imagined as furry goat legs. But he was no satyr she discovered when he moved closer to the road on pale, scrawny legs under cutoff denim shorts. Should she make eye contact? Ignore him? As she grew closer, she noticed his opened fly, his erect penis poking out. She stood up out of the saddle, making herself look larger as if confronting a bear. The sound of women's voices behind her startled her back into her seat. She glanced over her shoulder and was relieved to see three women from her group—Freya, Peggy, and Vanessa. They surrounded her, panting hello, before pulling ahead. Ginger tried but failed to catch up, watching helplessly as they crested the hill and disappeared from view.

At the summit, she shifted gears and began the long, twisty descent. Trees passed in a blur of green and gold and red. The breeze dried the sweat on her skin. She leaned into the turns, feathering the brakes, looking ahead to where she wanted to go. The women waited for her at the crossroads, straddling their bikes, chatting. Peggy and Freya were in their mid-forties, and Vanessa, early thirties.

Freya and Peggy had propped their bikes against trees and were walking stiff-legged in their cleats toward the woods to pee. "Way to charge the hill, dude," Freya told Ginger. "Impressive stuff," Peggy added.

"Thanks!" She blushed with pleasure at their praise.

"Did you see that guy?" Ginger asked Vanessa. "That flasher?"

"Oh, him," Vanessa said, eyes on her phone screen. "He's here all the time. You don't have to worry, he's harmless." The young woman's fierce appearance—the eyebrow piercing, the gaudy tattoos covering her toned arms from wrists to shoulders—led Ginger to expect a more outraged response, not this insulting reassurance. What had given Vanessa the idea she needed it?

"He's breaking the law," Ginger said with more vehemence than she felt. "Someone needs to report him."

Vanessa looked up from her phone. A subtle shift in her expression suggested she was taking Ginger's measure for the first time. "Maybe if he tried something?" She tucked her phone into her jersey pocket. "He just wants you to look at him. Don't give him the satisfaction."

Vanessa's advice made sense: ignore him, defuse his power. Ginger knew firsthand—working in the engineering field and moving through the world as an older woman—how disorienting it felt to be made invisible.

Freya and Peggy emerged from the trees, adjusting their shorts, asking where they were headed next. Vanessa suggested they cycle north to Rockland Lakes. This would extend the ride at least another twenty miles. Ginger decided to join them, though it would mean she'd be late to help Joe clear out his mother's house. As they rolled out, she positioned herself behind Peggy and in front of Vanessa where it would be harder to get dropped. After a few leisurely miles, Peggy cranked up the speed to twenty-two miles an hour. Ginger strained to stay on her wheel, spinning her legs, gasping for air, and feeling euphoric. Not for one minute could she forget Vanessa, drafting behind her, inches from her wheel. Everything depended on Ginger holding the line, maintaining the pace. One wrong move and they'd all fall like dominoes.

"SHE KEPT EVERYTHING," JOE said, lifting and dropping papers on his mother's coffee table. "A&P receipts, canceled checks going back to the '90s, coupons, bank statements."

Old news, Eileen's hoarding. This was her least offensive quality when compared with her flashes of anger, her weepy self-pity, and her sharp, insulting tongue. As Eileen's dementia and heart condition had worsened over the past year, Ginger and Joe had commandeered her car and hired round-the-clock home care.

"Look, here's what we'll do," Ginger said, ripping a leaf bag from the box on the couch. "Official papers in one bag— personal stuff in the other. No reading today, okay? Just sorting."

She sat next to him on the couch; after hours of being in motion on the bike, she felt her eyelids grow heavy, her energy flag. The sagging cushions forced them to sit close. Heat radiated from his body. Their arms bumped and their thighs rubbed, but she didn't move away. The closeness felt nice. Slanted sunlight fell through the bow window and lit up the dust on the old TV console, the matching maple end tables, and the tall brass lamps. It showed the blotchy stains on the white carpet. What stubborn optimism—or recklessness—had inspired her mother-in-law to choose white? Tomorrow, the estate-sale people would tag Eileen's books, kitchenware, furniture. Whatever remained. After a one-day sale, the real estate agent would put the property on the market. All orderly and predictable, so unlike Eileen's life.

When the light dimmed, Ginger stood to switch on the lamp. Her fingers came away coated with dust. Eileen's sloughed-off skin? The thought made her queasy. *And unto dust thou shall return.* Eileen was gone, but she was everywhere. Joe had cried at her funeral, soft choking sounds that had frightened her. She was sorry to dump more bad news on top of his grief. "Why haven't you asked who was on the phone this morning?" she said.

"I figured your mother. You sounded aggravated."

"Why would you think I was aggravated?"

"Twenty-nine years of marriage. I know when you're aggravated."

"Well, I was upset, not aggravated." She opened a grimy folder and yellowed greeting cards spilled out onto the floor around her feet. "My mother has leukemia."

"Oh, no." Joe slumped back on the couch, pushing his reading glasses to the top of his head. "I'm sorry. It makes sense, I guess. She was sick all last summer."

"If only her doctor had taken it seriously."

"So—what now? Chemo?"

"Who knows? She hung up on me."

"Because you were aggravated," he muttered, leaning forward to pick up an insurance statement from the pile.

Ginger *had* been annoyed, but she couldn't remember why. She gathered up the greeting cards and shoved them into the folder; silver glitter came off on her hands. She glanced over at Joe, running his finger down a column of numbers, and it came back to her, how the conversation with her mother had gone wrong. "Actually, it was your fault she hung up on me. I couldn't focus with you standing over me. My mother was telling me really bad news, and I couldn't hear her."

"I'm sure that's how *you* see it."

"Because that's how it happened."

Joe stood and stretched his arms over his head. His T-shirt lifted to expose a slice of his belly. He ate his feelings, when he could be sharing them with her. "Let's get out of here," he said, bending to swipe the remaining papers into one bag.

"That's it? You're done?" she said, annoyed at the way he'd shut her down just when she was close to understanding something important about her mother, about herself.

In August, Ginger's parents had invited her and Joe to their house for brunch. Minutes after their arrival, her mother hustled Joe outside to inspect the spot along the property line where she wanted to build a garden shed. Ginger's father invited her into his study to look at the old topographical maps of coastal New Jersey he'd found at a yard sale. While he searched for the maps in the closet, she went to the window and pulled back the curtain. In the yard, Joe held her mother's hand as they painstakingly crossed the sloping grass. At times, Ginger envied their easy relationship, but she had never trusted it. The way Diana stroked Joe's ego, complimenting his appearance and his business acumen, seeking his advice on financial matters and home repairs, made Ginger feel as though she'd been pushed aside. But now, watching them alone together in the yard, she realized their relationship—whatever it was—had nothing to do with her.

"Thanks for coming today," her father said. "Your visits cheer your mother up. She hasn't been feeling well."

Her father walked with cautious, measured steps to his desk, where he unrolled a brittle-looking map. He wore those orthopedic sneakers that looked like moon shoes. Her parents' old age felt like another planet: a frightening and faraway place she waited for them to return from.

WHEN GINGER WAS OUT in the field, directing her two-man surveying crew, she often thought about her mother. This life Ginger had chosen was so far removed from anything in her mother's experience. She'd given up trying to make her mother understand or appreciate it. So much separated them, it seemed.

This day Ginger was staking out a kitchen addition on a client's property. It had rained overnight, leaving the ground muddy and porous. When she discovered runoff flowing toward the house, she felt energized. Another problem to be solved. The straightforward jobs bored her.

She returned to the firm with drainage questions for Joe, but he had someone in his office. She stopped in the hallway to listen. Her face heated up when she realized it was Ben Ciardi, the real estate lawyer in his late forties who had a sideline flipping houses. Ben flustered her—made her feel unsure of herself. He had the sort of craggy good looks she liked—strong jaw and brow, broad crooked nose—but he lacked a sense of humor. At least he'd never responded to any of her biting rejoinders. He certainly had none of Joe's warmth, humor, or intelligence. She hurried past the door, feeling self-conscious in her baggy gray McCabe Engineering sweatshirt, cargo pants, and muddy steel-toe work boots, but Joe called out to her. The men looked up when she entered the office. In Joe's eyes, there was sly amusement. In

Ben's, nothing. He sat across from Joe at the desk, imposing in a well-cut dark-gray suit, an open-collared blue shirt, no tie. His legs were spread, of course.

"Ben's got a problem with the extra surveying charges on his bill," Joe said in a subtly mocking tone only she would've picked up on. Clients haggling over their bills was the most aggravating part of their job. "He says he didn't agree to the setting of the property corners."

Without a word, Ginger rounded the desk. Joe leaned out of her way so she could reach his keyboard. She felt his warm hand grab her calf as she pulled up the contract on his PC. She tossed her hair over her shoulder and turned the screen to face Ben. "Your signature," she said, presenting the evidence with an upturned palm.

Ben leaned forward to peer at the screen, his mouth slightly open, which, unfortunately, only emphasized his animal appeal.

"What did I tell you, Ben?" Joe said. "Ginger's on top of her game."

Ben threw himself back in the chair. "Okay, all right," he said, addressing Joe. "Let's talk about the load-bearing wall."

Feeling dismissed, Ginger went into her office and sat at her drafting table. Why had she tossed her hair? Mortified, she replayed the scene in Joe's office. Maybe she could've toned down the gloating a bit? *Nah.* The jerk tried to put one over on her. She'd let him off too easy. Ginger found an elastic band in her drawer and pulled her hair back into a tight ponytail and got back to work.

GINGER AND JOE WERE reading in bed together. Joe closed his book and turned to her. "I've been looking through those bags of my mother's stuff. The personal stuff," he said.

"Find something?" She saved her place in her book, Anne Sexton's *45 Mercy Street*, which she'd found on her mother-in-law's bookshelf among celebrity biographies and British mysteries.

"An envelope with some letters and CDs. It was returned to her by some guy."

"When was this?" she said. His parents had been divorced since he was fifteen. In all the time Ginger knew her, Eileen had never been with another man.

"From what I can make out, they had something going on twenty years ago," he said, avoiding her eyes. "She tried to start up with him again maybe four years ago, but he sent everything back, asked her to stop contacting him."

"What were the CDs?" She sat up, propping her pillows on the headboard. "Nothing disturbing, I hope."

"If you think Celine Dion is disturbing, yes," he said, and she laughed. "They went to a concert in 2000."

"How did we not know about this?" she said. "So, who was he?"

"Doesn't matter." He closed his book, a James Patterson thriller he'd been reading for months, and put it on his night table.

"What do you mean? Of course, it matters." Then she understood. "You know him, don't you?" she teased, poking his shoulder.

"Stop." He jerked away from her.

She felt ashamed for making fun of him. Neither spoke.

"Nick's father," he said.

She was stunned. Nick Galanis had been Joe's best friend since the third grade. In August, they'd gone to Nick's son's wedding. She vaguely remembered the squat, bald father, but Nick's mother was unforgettable, a striking woman in her mid-seventies—tall and rangy, like a rock climber, with a mane of silver hair. "What happened?" she said. "Did his wife find out?"

"No idea." He reached to turn off his lamp, and slid under the covers. "I don't want to talk about it."

"All right," she said, knowing he would eventually. She shut off her own lamp and snuggled up behind him, resting her hand on his thumping heart. This revelation about his mother's life reminded her of Escher's staircase drawing: ascending or descending? One Christmas day many years ago, she had glimpsed her mother and Eileen whispering on her staircase landing before dinner. At the time, Ginger assumed they were commenting on her soggy store-bought canapés or what her mother-in-law called her "loosey goosey" approach to childrearing.

She rolled onto her back and stared at the ceiling, trying to remember the startling line from Muriel Rukeyser's poem: "What would happen if one woman told the truth about her life?" She tossed and turned, trying to remember the poet's answer.

Eleven-thirty, Friday morning. All the lights on in the kitchen. The sky outside the windows darkened a purplish, bruised color. Ginger canceled her morning jobs. Low air pressure from the gathering storm made her head ache behind her eyes when she bent to unload the dishwasher. She held a warm drinking glass to her cheek before placing it on the shelf. Her mother had promised to phone after her nine-a.m. oncologist appointment to discuss the results of her recent bone marrow biopsy, but when Ginger's cell rang, it was the estate sale agent calling.

"Good news," Natty reported. "All the clothes, jewelry, china, and silver got sold. The furniture too, except for the upholstered pieces. Bedbugs freak people out." The woman sounded happy with the day's profit, but discussing the figures made Ginger uncomfortable for reasons she didn't have the energy to examine. After she hung up, Ginger paced from the dining room to the living room to her upstairs office, looking out the windows at the darkening sky. The quiet unsettled her. No roaring leaf blowers and lawnmowers. Only the lonely sound of cars passing on the road below her window. Her phone rang and she rushed downstairs to the kitchen. Too late. A voicemail notification popped up on the phone screen.

"Guess you're working," her mother said on the message. "It's raining cats and dogs here. So, I met the new oncologist this morning. Dr. Handsome." She giggled. "Your father's name for him. He looks like Cary Grant. And what a flirt! He told me I have lovely eyes."

"You do!" her father said loud and clear. He must've been sitting right on top of his wife.

"The treatment will give me four or five good years," her mother continued. "I'll be eighty-eight. Who wants to live longer than that?"

"Not me," her father said, and they both laughed heartily.

They sounded drunk. At eleven-thirty in the morning! Her parents were practically teetotalers.

"Anyway," her mother said, sounding sober now, "chemo starts next week. Your father has the details. You can ask him later."

Ginger called back and got a busy signal. Her mother was probably calling Kim in Paris. A recovering addict with thirty-five years' sobriety, Ginger's sister would not be spooked by dark or uncertain territory. Ginger left the kitchen and climbed the stairs to her home office. She had clients to call, drawings to complete. She sat at her drafting table and tried her parents' phone again. It rang three times before the answering machine clicked on.

Ten minutes later, she was driving west on Route 80 under the gloomy, threatening sky. All the cars and trucks in the eastbound lanes had their headlights on.

HER PARENTS' CARS WERE in the driveway. The yellow Dutch Colonial, Ginger's childhood home, showed its age: the foundation crumbled, mold and moss patched the roof, and the front steps were missing a few bricks. She rang the bell to give them time. Her mother despised drop-ins. "I want to be ready for you," Diana would say, and Ginger imagined her mother hiding behind a door, brandishing a pistol, defending her privacy. The mailbox was stuffed—store circulars, a few bills, and the November *Vogue*, thick as a dictionary. She yanked it all out and clutched the bundle to her chest as she bent to deadhead a few brown chrysanthemums in the clay pot.

She straightened to face a closed door. She tried the knob. Unlocked, as she knew it would be. She entered the shadowy living room, vibrating with Vivaldi on the CD player. A library book was butterflied on the couch where she'd expected to see her parents sprawled out, tipsy, celebrating their good news.

"Hello?" she called out. "Mom? Dad?"

In the kitchen, breakfast dishes sat on the table: hardened egg yolk, smears of jam, and dregs of coffee and congealed cream; sticky jam on the floor; the newspaper, still in its blue plastic sleeve. She took all of this in, feeling more and more alarmed. Vivaldi's frantic strings playing in the next room did not help. She dropped her parents' mail beside the dirty breakfast dishes before heading to the screened porch. She stopped outside the doorway.

On the wicker loveseat, her mother lay face up across her husband's lap, silently weeping. Her rumpled blouse was pulled out of her slacks, and her red flats had been kicked off onto the floor. Tenderly, her father stroked his wife's tousled hair, singing in a low, tuneful voice, "Red River Valley," the same song he'd sung to Ginger when she was a girl. She felt like a child, helpless and lost. Her mother was seriously ill. She backed into the hallway and leaned against the wall, her arms wrapped across her middle. She longed for someone to hold and comfort her. She longed, she realized, for her mother. Overcome, she headed for the front door.

The heavy rain thrummed the roof of her car, swept across the highway in sheets, and slapped at her windshield. The wipers could not keep up. For miles, Ginger followed the blurry red taillights on the SUV in front of her. Crawling along at twenty-five miles an hour, she switched lanes when the other driver did. A tractor trailer, rumbling past in the next lane, sent a spray of water across the windshield, temporarily blinding her. What she knew about her mother—the thrilling modeling career, the satyr's seduction, the unwanted pregnancy, her return to her childhood home, and her marriage to the homebody neighbor—were fragments, vague and disconnected, out of reach. She never had the whole picture. Muriel Rukeyser had asked the wrong question. Instead, it should have been: what would happen if one woman knew the truth about her mother's life?

She pumped the brakes. The SUV in front of her slowed at the exit and left the highway. She felt unmoored, set adrift. She pulled onto the shoulder and turned off the wipers. Rain slid down her windshield in silver rivulets. She reached for her phone in the cupholder to call Joe. But how could she describe what she witnessed—her parents' love story, the ordinary tenderness of a long and loving marriage—without somehow diminishing it? She couldn't. She would keep the memory close to her heart, an image to return to in the ebb and flow of her life with Joe. Outside, the traffic continued without her, the whooshing tires sounding like the pulse of blood in her own ears.

BE HERE NOW

WHEN I PULL INTO my mother-in-law's driveway, there to take Viva's dog to the vet, Manuela, the latest home health aide, is loitering on the porch. She hunches down the steps and approaches my car, looking worried, but probably not about Viva's sick terrier; dogs frighten her. A neighbor's pit bull attacked her when she was a child in Ecuador, leaving a bracelet of scars on her left wrist. Of all the aides Adela's Angels have sent in the last six months, this twenty-four-year-old is the least equipped to deal with Viva's quicksilver moods. I motion for her to get in. It's February. Too cold to be outside in a thin cardigan. I crank up the BMW's heat.

"Now what did you do?" I regret my jokey tone when her round face crumples.

"I did nothing! Viva says I took her pills, but she loses everything."

"Don't they all do that, though? The old people, I mean." I lower the heat blasting through the vents: I'm sweating inside my dead husband's oversized leather bomber jacket.

"She calls me stupid and lazy."

"Ignore her. Viva's loca, half demented." She's also as bigoted as the Grand Imperial Wizard, but Manuela doesn't need me to tell her that: her job puts her in close contact with old white people. "Try seeing it this way—Viva needs you more than you need her."

She sighs, looks down at her clasped hands. I imagine what she's thinking: Another clueless white lady, lecturing her in a luxury car. It's true I have no idea how the agency works. If this gig ends, will they give Manuela a new client or just a skimpier paycheck? She's mentioned a young son, a disabled mother.

"Okay, I'll talk to your boss," I say, trying to sound supportive. After all, Manuela is close to the age of my son and daughter. "Between us, I took Viva's Percocet. Months ago, before you got here. She was still driving. I found it in the back of her linen closet, rolled up in a towel."

Placated, Manuela follows me into the overheated ranch-style house but hangs back at the door. The odor is intense and unpleasant: an aggressive floral perfume layered over sweet dog puke and the intimate odors of a less-than-hygienic octogenarian. I breathe through my mouth and approach the couch where Viva reclines, watching *Fox & Friends* at a loud volume. The dog snores at her feet. Poor old Lucy, plagued with kidney disease and arthritis. The terrier is comatose most of the day, doped up on doggie painkillers, but she needs more care than my mother-in-law can manage or afford.

"How's Lucy?" I say. "She looks okay."

"Stella! Listen, hon, I need you to stop at the market first." Viva sits up and aims the remote to turn off the TV. She's traded her usual pink quilted housecoat for a gray cable-knit sweater and a pair of black wool slacks snowy with dog hair. "Run in for that yummy olive and rosemary bread, some coffee beans, and what else? A teensy bit of prosciutto."

It occurs to me—how could I not have considered this—that she invented the dog crisis to rope me in for a day of service.

Her son spoiled her. Easier to do what she wanted, he'd say. Bobby learned that at fourteen after his father's heart gave out in the VFW lounge.

"And I have a few bills for the post office—" she breaks off, points at Manuela. "What is *she* still doing here? That *thief*! I told her to leave!"

"I didn't take your pills," Manuela cries out. "Ask Stella."

I'm too stunned to speak.

"You lie!" Viva says, her voice shrill. Lucy climbs to her feet, barking in distress. Viva shouts at her: "Quiet! Enough!" The terrier whines, flattens out on the cushion.

"Tell her," Manuela begs me, her eyes defiant.

I've underestimated this aide: she's perfectly capable of taking care of herself.

"Let's all calm down," I say. "Maybe I can help. Which pills are you missing?" It comes out sounding snide, not obliging.

"What difference does it make?" Viva says. "None of your damn business."

I expected her to react in the same cowed, evasive way her son had when I accused him of using, but Viva loves a fight. Rage animates her. Her cheeks flush a youthful pink. She forgets her rheumatoid arthritis, her bad hip—her excuses for painkillers—and springs from the couch.

"I'll walk. I don't need you," she says, brushing past me to pick up her coat from the chair. "How dare you interrogate me. The two of you should be ashamed."

"Don't be ridiculous," I say. "You can't walk; it's two miles." If she expects an apology, she'll be disappointed. There's a new sheriff in town.

"Come, Lucy!" Viva claps twice. "Lucy! Come!"

The dog trembles at the edge of the couch, poised to jump. We all wait—for what? A miracle? Not going to happen. I lower Lucy to the floor. Manuela hands me the leash, and I bend down to attach it to Lucy's collar. Viva opens the door for us.

WHEN THE VET ENTERS the tiny examining room, the change in Viva would impress Dr. Jekyll. One minute she's shouting at Manuela: "I will not sit down! *You* sit down! Go back where you came from!"—and in the next instant she's entreating Dr. Goldsmith in a wispy voice to please keep her little doggie alive. Dr. Goldsmith, a pudgy, forty-something redhead—my favorite in the group practice—promises to do his best. I hoist Lucy onto the table, and he offers her a treat from his lab jacket pocket. Lucy sniffs and rejects it.

"She has no appetite, doctor," Viva says, hovering at the vet's elbow.

"Wouldn't you be more comfortable on the stool, Mrs. Celona?" he asks. She allows him to guide her to the corner. I try to catch Manuela's eye, but she's staring at the door the vet came through a few minutes ago. Dogs bark, howl, and whine behind it. I feel simultaneously protective and annoyed with her. The other aides allied themselves with me against Viva, but this young woman has staked out some neutral territory and I don't like it.

Dr. Goldsmith returns to the examining table. Eyes closed, he hums absently as his fingers travel Lucy's undercarriage.

"Don't tell me if it's bad," Viva says. "I can't take any more bad news. I just lost my son, my only child." Perched on the stool, hands folded primly on her lap, she's the epitome of a sweet old lady. Her "dog and pony" show, Bobby called it. I call it emotional blackmail. I call it bullshit. I call it— The vet touches my arm, startling me. In a lowered voice, he says, "I want to hold Lucy overnight and run some tests."

THE NEXT DAY I keep my cell switched on and within reach, waiting for the vet's call. In addition to bloodwork, he'll do a CT scan and excisional biopsies on four lumps. "Money's no object," I told him. *Live for the day* may have been Bobby's modus operandi, but as a hedge fund manager he had the foresight and financial acumen to set up his family with trusts and stock portfolios and various other safety nets for all our future days.

In my morning yoga class, I tuck my cell under my mat. My new screensaver is a photo of my son Charlie posed in front of cherry blossoms in Japan where he teaches English to executives. My friends Nadine and Annie have unrolled their mats on either side of me. Weak winter sunlight streams through the bay window, making me feel heavy and sleepy. I resist the drift, clench my gut, hold my breath. The yoga membership had been a gift. Weeks after Bobby's funeral, Nadine and Annie grew concerned when I refused their invitations to dinner and the movies and avoided the weekend cycling group. They predicted, correctly, that I'd be loath to waste their money.

"Be here now," Kaylee, the twenty-something instructor, says. She roams between the mats, talking in a hushed voice. I lower into plank position and transition into the cobra pose. The recorded sitar music, like a whining dog, gets under my skin. I peek at my phone. Nothing from the vet. A text from Andrea, my twenty-four-year-old daughter who lives in Manhattan and works as a program manager for the Gracie Mansion Conservancy. Pushing me to join her grief support group again. A few months before Bobby's death, she told me about her Al-Anon meetings, how they were helping her understand her father's problem. I pretended to be interested, but inside I seethed. Been there, I thought, done with that. Done with shaping my life around his addictions. Done with turning down social invitations. Done with tallying his drinks—

"Move gently into child's pose," the yoga instructor says, passing my mat. "Go deep within yourself. Nurture your soul with loving kindness."

Did I bail on Bobby too soon? Two rehab stints in five years. Two spectacular relapses. After his second stay in a private Upstate rehab facility, I figured out he was lying to me about using. I abandoned my searches for his drug stash, stopped draining his vodka bottles. I dove back into my novel revision, set off on fifty-mile bike rides with Nadine and Annie, re-engaged with my teaching. Life was easier when Bobby, a high-functioning addict, was using. Sober, he was moody and erratic; his ego needed constant stroking.

The yoga class ends with *savasana*, the corpse pose. While the others float on blissful waves of nothingness, I plan the best way to flee the studio to avoid my friends' concerned questions, their invitations for coffee.

TWO AFTERNOONS A WEEK, I teach an undergraduate fiction writing workshop at Saint Mary's, a small New York State college that's always on the brink of bankruptcy. Today, our class of eight women and four men will critique Pierson's story. Privately, I refer to him as Alpha Male. In every class, he sits directly across from me, legs thrust out, sleeves rolled back on baroque tattoos, sucking up all the oxygen in the room. His twenty-page story features a man who falls in love with a nurse/sex worker who castrates men who displease her. *Who hurt you?* I want to ask. I say, "Interesting choice of conflict."

My phone buzzes in my blazer pocket. I leap up, mumble "oncologist," and run into the hallway. Doctor Goldsmith informs me that Lucy has advanced metastasized cancer. The CT scan shows tumors on her liver and lungs. Bloodwork and biopsy results aren't in yet, but he's certain it won't be good news. I drift toward the exit sign, passing empty classrooms, my boot heels echoing. "You can take her home in the morning," he says. "I'll give you painkillers, but the kindest thing would be to put her down. Your mother-in-law doesn't want to hear this, but she has to decide. Soon." He pauses. "Do you want to tell her, or shall I?"

NINE MONTHS AGO, ON the twenty-third of May, my cell rang at one a.m. I groped on the nightstand and read the screen: *NewYork-Presbyterian*. Bobby had a serious head injury, a physician told me. He'd fallen on Broadway; a bystander called 911 and waited with Bobby until paramedics arrived. I was the emergency contact on his cell. As the doctor asked me about Bobby's medical history, I headed down the hallway into the master bedroom and switched on the lamp, half expecting to see him tangled up in the white sheets, smelling like a distillery. Most nights, he crept in long after I'd gone to sleep. Months ago, I'd moved to the twin bed in Andrea's old bedroom, claiming he disturbed my sleep, but it was easier to ignore his substance abuse if I didn't have my nose rubbed in the stink night after night.

I raced over the George Washington Bridge with a numbed detachment, my default self-protection, considering the horror that awaited me: Bobby on life support or fucked up and arguing with the doctors to let him go. I didn't know which would be worse. I left my car at a twenty-four-hour parking lot on Fort Washington Avenue. Bobby's office was in midtown. What was he doing in this neighborhood? A lover? A dealer? Maybe he was entertaining clients at that Ethiopian place where we celebrated Andrea's Barnard graduation a year ago. On 168th Street, the hospital was lit up like a stadium.

I entered the emergency department through the revolving door, scoping out the lobby. The chairs were filled. People, dozing, sniffling, murmuring into cell phones, their faces mottled in the sickly artificial light. A small boy spun in circles, arms akimbo, and then, dizzy, collapsed on the floor. Heads turned as I approached the receptionist's desk. The elderly man in a blue blazer took my name and Bobby's name. He picked up the phone. If he asked me to wait, I would go out to the sidewalk: I could hold it together as long as I didn't have to look into anyone's sad, hopeless eyes.

"Miss?" he said, putting down the phone. "Follow me, please." He led me through gray double doors, manned by a hefty security guard. We went down a long hallway to a room with four folding chairs pushed up against a blank white wall. Someone would come to talk to me very soon, he said. His voice betrayed no emotion, only exhaustion. I chose the chair closest to the door and stared at the furry grime on the baseboard, remembering that night at the Ethiopian restaurant. Bobby ordered for our table: kitfo, tibs wat, and lamb awaze tibs. He fed Andrea and Charlie from the communal plates with his hands, Ethiopian-style, he told us. "Gursha," he urged, pushing the sourdough flatbread, dripping with stews into their open, laughing mouths. He'd finished his third vodka, the fourth was on its way. When the check arrived, I breathed easier, another disaster averted, but then Bobby climbed up on his chair, commanding the room to toast his brilliant daughter. Andrea looked down into her lap. I tugged on his pants leg, but he ignored me. Applause burst out in the restaurant. Glasses were raised. "Brava," the waiter shouted. Andrea looked up, her face glowing with bashful pride. I wanted to join in, to celebrate my daughter, but I was holding my breath, steadying Bobby's chair.

A knock sounded on the doorframe. A woman wearing a pink hijab stood before me, and gave me a sad, pitying smile. I didn't need her to tell me. The lights had dimmed. The party was over. Bobby was gone.

IN THE MORNING, I pick up Lucy from the vet's office, along with more Tramadol. When I carry the limp, drugged dog into Viva's house, Manuela starts to tell me something about Viva and the dog's pills. "Can't do this now, Manuela," I say, cutting her off.

The living room is sunk into a funereal darkness, drapes closed, TV muted. Viva lies on the couch, wearing her quilted pink housecoat. When I set the dog down at her side, she looks up at me with glazed eyes. "My poor doggie," she says, slurring her words.

"Lucy shouldn't have to suffer," I tell her. "It's selfish to keep her alive."

"I'm not putting her down! Absolutely not."

"She's in pain. Look at her! Dr. Goldsmith said—"

"Dr. Goldsmith doesn't know what he's talking about. I'll get a second opinion." She sits up. "Manuela! Where are you? I need you!"

The dog lifts her head, sees Viva, then lowers it as if to say, *Not this again.*

Manuela enters the living room with two mugs of steaming tea and sets them down on the coffee table.

"I don't want that! I didn't ask for that!" Viva says. "Make yourself useful for a change and get me the phone book."

With a smirk, Manuela leaves the room, moving at an unhurried pace. Something has changed. While we wait, Viva tells me the *dog's* medicine, the Tramadol, is missing. I say nothing, find it hard to care. Manuela returns with the

Yellow Pages, drops it on the coffee table, and returns to the kitchen. Viva pulls the book onto her lap and flips through the pages, licking her index finger before each turn. She runs one gnarled finger down a column.

"Call this one, Stella." She's pointing to the twenty-four-hour animal hospital where we took Lucy last week at ten p.m. "I can't trust *her* to do it," she says. "Have you ever seen such an uncooperative person? It's the hot climate in their country. Makes them all lazy."

"Enough, Viva! Don't you realize how ignorant you sound?"

"Why are you picking on me? My dog is sick. My son died."

"No one's picking on you." I move away from her, dialing my cell. I make an appointment for Friday. Three days from now. When I go into the kitchen with the vague idea of apologizing, Manuela's talking on her phone. "Mami te ama," she says in a caressing tone. I recognize the words *mommy* and *love*. Her face hardens when she sees me. She lowers the phone to her side. "Sorry," she says, curtly. "What do you need?"

"It's okay." I hand her the pill vial. "Is that your son? On the phone?"

She takes the vial without answering, waits for me to leave.

LATER, IN MY WRITING workshop, a few students are angry with Pierson's depiction of women. "That Madonna/whore shit makes me sick," Shavonne says. Her last story was set in Afghanistan where she did two tours with the Army. Clare, who writes morally neat stories reminiscent of old *Twilight Zone* episodes, suggests that the story be told from the woman's point of view. "Maybe then she wouldn't be so cartoonish," she says. "Nothing she does makes sense."

Alpha shifts in his seat, his face red. I need to bring the discussion back around to fiction technique. I suggest to Alpha that he make his female character more dimensional, give her more agency.

"Zinnia has tons of agency!" he says. "She's a nurse and a sex worker, *by choice*—" A groan comes from the back; he swivels his head to locate it. "And she castrates men! Another choice."

"Are those really choices? Choices you'd want for your mother or sister?" I say, hearing the edge in my voice. I drop into a more soothing maternal register. "Okay, look, what if the man and woman in your story have a more emotionally complicated relationship? What if, despite caring deeply for each other, they consistently disappoint and betray each other?"

"Boring!" He throws himself back in his chair, crosses his arms over his chest. "Who wants to read about my parents?"

"BREATHE," KAYLEE, MY YOGA instructor, reminds me. *Breathe. Breathe. Breathe.*

"I am breathing!" I shout from the downward facing dog position. Nadine turns her upside-down head to look at me. I try for a joke. "I'd be dead if I weren't. Right?"

"Breathe more deeply," Kaylee corrects herself.

After class, I accept my friends' invitation for coffee. Otherwise, they'll call and text all day to check up on me. In the noisy café next door to the yoga studio, we choose a table near the window. A grizzled rain falls, darkening Pine Street. Cars pass the coffee shop with wipers swishing, headlights on. I catch Nadine looking at me when I take off Bobby's leather jacket.

"I know, I've lost weight," I say, sitting down. My ribs and hip bones bump through my yoga clothes like landforms on a relief map.

"Did I say anything?" Nadine says.

"You don't have to. I know what I look like. My clothes are hanging off me." I pour sugar into my cappuccino, smiling at her. "Happy?"

"Sorry," Nadine says. "I didn't mean to make you feel uncomfortable."

"You'll get your appetite back." Annie touches my arm, and I feel myself relax. I call her sometimes to vent about Viva. A good listener, she always takes my side even when I'm probably wrong. I like how she's furious on my behalf. Anger by proxy.

"Why don't you come for dinner Saturday?" Nadine says. "Nothing fancy. Just me and Matthew. I'm not going to let you say no again."

Dinner with two psychologists? No, thanks. "Can I say maybe? Only because I'm on call for Viva's dog."

Nadine and Annie exchange a private look. "Let's call it a soft yes," Nadine says.

I saw a therapist for three months after Bobby's first relapse, but in all that time, I was too ashamed to bring up the subject. It seems stupid now. I was in enough pain to seek help, but I couldn't say the words that would begin the process. The effort of holding in my dirty secret felt like all the times I stood, a skinny, shivering nine-year-old, on the high dive at the town pool, my mother shouting at me from below, "You climbed all the way up there, Stella. For god's sake, jump!" The humiliation when the other kids had to move off the ladder so I could descend.

Probably I didn't want to look too closely at the way Bobby was hurting me. I didn't want to make any big changes in our family's life. Andrea was a freshman at Barnard. Charlie was finishing up high school. I worked hard to hide Bobby's habit from my family and friends, but everyone knew. High-spirited, some people called him. Nuts, others said. Two weeks before he died, Bobby and I attended Nadine's fiftieth birthday party. He was manic that night, telling jokes and goosing the women. He set the deck on fire with a cherry bomb. I smiled along with everyone. *Such great fun. A barrel of laughs.* Close to midnight, when I dragged him home, he was falling into the furniture, opening and slamming the kitchen cabinets, looking for the vodka bottles I'd drained. When he threatened to drive to the all-night liquor store seven miles away, I dove for the car keys. He tried to pry them from my fingers, laughing like it was a game. *Such fun!* He gave up, told me he'd walk back to the party for a nightcap. He left the house barefoot, shouting that I was always spoiling his fun. The next morning, when Nadine went outside for the *Times*, she found him passed out under her weeping cherry tree.

"THE SHIT HIT THE fan. Literally." Manuela is propping open the storm door, airing the house, when I arrive at my mother-in-law's on Thursday morning. Viva vomited on the couch and the dog pissed and shit on the rug, she tells me. "I tried to clean, but—" She holds her nose as we enter the living room. The sharp smell of disinfectant stings my nostrils. Viva and Lucy are asleep on the couch. I tell Manuela that I'll come back in the afternoon.

In my car, engine running, I phone Dr. Goldsmith and ask if we can override Viva. "Legally, no," he tells me. "I agree with you, it's cruel. Mrs. Celona is stubborn. Keep trying," he says before hanging up. A loud bang outside startles me. The wind knocked over the neighbor's garbage can; a bread wrapper and crumpled pink tissues skid across Viva's lawn.

Manuela appears in the car window. I lower it. "Forgot to tell you," she says. "I have to leave early today."

I look at her blankly. Shouldn't she tell her agency?

"My sister's graduation." She meets my eyes. "From cooking school."

"Oh! Really? Cooking school?" I wait for her to tell me more, but she backs away from the car. I realize, too late, she may have misinterpreted my interest for skepticism. I want to make myself clear, but she's chasing the bread wrapper up the walkway.

In the afternoon when I return, Manuela comes out of the kitchen, drying her hands on a dirty white dish towel, and tells me Viva has been too nauseated to eat. From the couch, Viva adds, "I haven't been able to get down more than a teensy piece of toast. Manuela made my favorite chocolate pudding, but I couldn't. I just couldn't."

Her neediness disgusts me.

"What would I do without my angel?" Viva says, meaning, apparently, Manuela.

I follow Manuela into the kitchen. Bobby's faded high-school photo has slipped from the Garfield magnet on the refrigerator. I straighten it, staring at Bobby's opened mouth, his upper lip pulled back over his overlapping front teeth. The photographer must have cracked a joke.

His laugh. I've forgotten the sound.

"Is that her son?" Manuela says behind me.

She's clutching a bundle of butter knives, and the dishwasher door hangs open. "You're Viva's angel?" I say. "What's that about?"

"What else? She wants something from me."

LATER THAT NIGHT, I Skype with Charlie while eating a bowl of stale bran flakes. It's eight p.m. in the States, nine a.m. in Tokyo. Unnerving how much he looks like Bobby with the dark skin beneath his heavy gray eyes and his scoundrel's smile. But he has none of his father's frantic, impulsive energy. He asks again when I'll come for a visit, and I tell him soon.

He scoffs. "I don't understand why this is so hard for you. You need a break."

"Sorry. I've been busy with grandma's dog. She's sick."

"Lucy's still alive?"

"Barely."

"Poor dog. Grandma treated it like shit. But she treats everyone like shit. Especially Dad."

"What do you mean?" He's right, but I'm surprised he noticed.

"I don't know. Never mind." He mentions a new girl-friend, another English teacher from Iowa, the trip they took to Kamakura to see the Big Buddha. He trails off, and I won-der if he feels guilty about having someone to love. "You have to meet her, Ma," he says. "You'd get along great. She's got a big heart. Takes care of everyone. We call her our den mother."

"After the semester. I'll make arrangements," I say. This time it doesn't feel like a lie.

When I arrive at Viva's for Lucy's appointment, I can't bring myself to go into her house. I sit in my idling car, chewing the dead skin around my thumbnail, replaying her four-a.m. voicemail on speakerphone. Her voice sounds foggy and far-away. "Help me, Stella. Bobby's crying and shaking all over. I'm afraid he's going to die." Obviously, she's on something, but it occurs to me that maybe we're both confusing the dog with Bobby. The taste of blood in my mouth. My cuticle stings.

I let myself into the house with my key when no one an-swers the doorbell. Lucy dozes on the couch. Her ear twitches when I say her name, but she doesn't open her eyes or lift her head. I walk down the hallway, calling for Viva and Manuela, and find them in the small bathroom off Viva's bedroom. Viva is on her knees, retching into the toilet. Manuela holds her head. The sour smell makes me gag.

"I called an ambulance," Manuela says.

"I want to go with Lucy," Viva wails, her mouth flecked with vomit.

"No," Manuela says with authority. "Stella will take good care of Lucy. Understand?"

"Yes. All right." Viva lays her cheek on the toilet seat.

A siren bleats outside. I send Manuela a look: *What's going on?* She thrusts her chin toward the empty Tramadol vial on the tiled floor. Voices and heavy footsteps in the hallway. I can't do this again. I back out of the room and push past the two paramedics coming down the narrow hallway. The dog growls when I lift her too vigorously from the couch, but she slackens in my arms as I carry her outside to my car. The ambulance blocks the driveway. I throw the car in reverse and drive across the lawn.

At the animal hospital, the vet is running late. I wait in the examining room with Lucy asleep on my lap. She's as light as a stack of folded towels. How could Viva take this poor animal's pain medication? And how did she get her hands on those pills? The door swings open. A different vet enters, an older woman with flyaway white hair and ruddy, fleshy cheeks. She introduces herself as Dr. Mathias. She bends her knees and comes nose to nose with Lucy. "You don't look so good, sweetie." She looks up at me. "Neither do you, honey."

"Actually, I'm a wreck. I can't stand to see her suffer."

"Give me your names again." She steps to the computer.

A solution presents itself. A solution so obvious, I can't believe I didn't think of it sooner. "I'm Viva Celona," I say. "We were here a little over a week ago."

She squints at the computer screen, lips pursed. "Lucy is Dr. Goldsmith's patient?"

"He wants me to put her down. I said no; I regret it."

"Give me a few minutes to make a call."

After she leaves, I panic. What if she asks for ID? I dig through my pocketbook, looking for my wallet. I have Viva's old CVS discount card from the last time I picked up her prescription. I won't be able to use my own credit card. I'll have to pay with cash.

Dr. Mathias returns as I'm counting the money in my billfold. In her eyes, only kindness and sorrow. She lays her hand on the terrier's head. "You've had a rough time, haven't you, little westie?"

Lucy releases a long sigh as though she knows her misery will soon end.

THE DAY IS HALF over when I pull into Viva's driveway. I let myself inside, bracing for an ugly scene, but Viva's not on the couch. Manuela comes out of the kitchen, wearing her coat. "My sister's on her way." She sounds nervous for some reason. "I took a taxi from the hospital—" She breaks off. "What's wrong?"

"She's dead," I say, my voice cracking.

"No, no, not dead," Manuela stiffly pats my arm. "They're keeping her a few days to check her out, mentally. That's all."

"I meant Lucy. Sorry, I don't know what's wrong with me." I widen my eyes to hold in the tears. "*I'm* the one who told the vet to kill her."

"You did the right thing," she says, impatiently. "That dog was very sick."

Sick like Viva.

"I have to ask, Manuela, did you give Viva the Tramadol?" I try for a sympathetic tone. "I know she was pressuring you."

A car horn honks outside. Manuela glances at the picture window, but the drapes are closed. She sighs. "I would never give her those pills," she says wearily. "I hid them from her."

"You hid them? Where?"

"In *your* hiding place. The linen closet."

I search her unblinking eyes, but it's clear she's already gone. When the horn honks again, I tell her to go. "Don't keep your sister waiting," I say. "I should go, too."

A heavy darkness gathers behind the closed drapes. The day can still be salvaged. I have quizzes to grade, an overseas trip to plan, a daughter's call to return. No one, not even Bobby would blame me for walking away.

AFTER THE PARTY

As the Woods Hole ferry departs for Martha's Vineyard with a blast of the warning horn, Wendy stands at the rail watching the terminal recede from view. It feels like someone else's life now, all those summers they drove their Jeep, jam-packed with kids and sports gear, onto this ferry. Why had she bothered to book this season's passage and choose an Edgartown rental house when everything has changed? Beside her, Hank keeps his back to the rail, eyeing the other passengers. Women turn their heads. With little effort, he's kept his good looks into his early fifties. Gray threads his coarse, dark hair elegantly, and his stomach appears flat under his Eric Clapton T-shirt. After the five-hour drive from New Jersey, her cotton dress is rumpled and damp with sweat, and although she's as fit as her competition—she's a champion golfer—she's not exactly on her game.

"You're not going to freak out if I go look for the bar, are you?" he says.

"Don't do that. Don't turn me into the warden." It comes out harsher than she intended. "I'll be fine," she tries, more lightly. "If I get lonely, I'll make new friends."

He follows her gaze to the four men in golf shirts and khakis, sitting a few yards off in the rows of benches. "Your clan. Let me help with introductions."

Before she can object, he sets off with a swagger meant to amuse her, she's sure, but she has the sick feeling she's about to be humiliated. Serves her right for trying to make him jealous. The men draw Hank into their circle. One gestures with his cup toward the lounge. When Hank gives her the thumbs-up, the others turn too. Their scrutiny makes her queasy. A few days ago, she lost her assistant golf pro's position at Red Oaks. She's waiting for the right time to tell Hank.

She heads in the other direction. Inside the restroom, the droning engines insulate her from the commotion outside. One week on the Vineyard always seemed too short, but now she worries it'll be too long. She dampens a paper towel and reaches inside her collar to swipe her vinegary armpits.

What did those golfers see? Her face in the murky mirror seems to peer at her from under water: her shoulder-length blond hair, narrow gray eyes, and whitened teeth glowing. She recognizes the hunted, wild-eyed look she's seen on the older women who come to her—*used to* come to her—for golf lessons. A last resort in their quests for their husbands' attention. She tosses the paper towel into the trash. The boat rolls, and she lurches for the door.

She checks the gloomy lounge—no sign of Hank—and reenters the bright, dousing sunlight on the upper deck. Bodies are packed in tight like bowling pins, faces lurid with drink and sunburn. A restless anxiety prickles her skin. The decision to stay with Hank after his affair was easier to make than the one to trust him. She heads toward the stern, scanning the faces. She smiles with relief when she sees him down on his knees stroking a black lab. They have two golden retrievers and are in negotiations for a third. Dogs need a pack, Hank maintains, and two does not a pack make. When she draws closer, she notices the

woman—a waif in her twenties with cropped blond hair—
hovering over him. She hesitates.

"Wendy!" Hank stands and flashes his charming smile. "This
is Maxine and"—he bends to rub the dog's snout—"Maggie."

"Another black lab!" Wendy tries to modulate the manic
brightness in her voice. "They're everywhere. Is it a coinci-
dence or a massive lack of imagination?"

"It's because of the Black Dog Tavern in Vineyard Haven,"
the girl says. "The T-shirts, anyways."

"Of course it is." She touches the girl's silky arm. *Youth.*
Is that what attracts Hank? No doubt he wants to relive every exquisite minute, while Wendy only wants to erase hers.
"Isn't it weird though, that such a beautiful place gets associated with the symbol for depression and death?"

"Death?" The girl looks at Hank.

"Don't pay any attention," he tells her. "Sometimes a dog
is just a dog."

"You remind me of our daughter," Wendy says. "She's
about your age. Never knows when I'm joking. Right?"

Hank doesn't answer. He squats to scratch Maggie's
glossy head. "Who's the pretty dog?" he coos. "Are you the
pretty dog?" In the girl's fond smile, Wendy sees his demo-
tion from possible sugar daddy to awesome dad. After the
girl walks off, Wendy says, "What'd I tell you about talking
to strange dogs?"

THE CEDAR-SHINGLED HOUSE LOOKS large, looming at the
end of a deep stretch of emerald lawn. Inside, the deception is
revealed. The living room is the size of a foyer. The bedrooms
are stunted beneath the barn-style roof. The kitchen is too small
for a table. Last summer's rental had a long kitchen counter
where Olivia and Grace, their twenty-something daughters,

congregated with magazines, nail polishes, and the salads they carried back from the market in bicycle baskets. She keeps this comparison to herself. Complaining, she senses, would be hazardous, an admission of—what exactly?—their crummy judgment and what they lost out on.

Hank unloads the car, while she stays behind in the kitchen to pack the cooler for the beach. Earlier, they picked up sandwiches (lobster roll for Hank, BLT for her) from the café next to the real estate office. Through the dusty window, she watches him pull suitcases from the Jeep, whistling a tune she can't hear. How simple he is—how uncomplicated. Why does she persist in seeing him as someone more calculating? The girl on the ferry meant nothing; the dog tugged harder on his heartstrings.

Ten months ago, she came close to losing him. He was flying to the west coast every weekend. Preoccupied with her disappointing amateur golf circuit and with moving Grace into Manhattan, she didn't question his trips until she overheard Hank's uncle describe the L.A. project engineer as looking like a "Bond girl." Then she noticed how distracted and touchy Hank had grown. When he was packing again in mid-September, she confronted him. She expected evasion, but he seemed relieved to confess. He and Valentina—of course, her name is Valentina—had resisted a mutual attraction for months, he'd told her. Did he expect congratulations? Cancel the trip, she said, or she'd file for divorce. She was bluffing: she'd never leave him. Later, when she caught him crying in his car, she figured he must have called his lover from the garage to end it, because he didn't go to Los Angeles and his involvement in the project ended.

She gave him a mulligan. They haven't mentioned Valentina again, though all their conversations seem to be about her.

After finding her rival's photo on the company website—a fortyish Russian beauty—Wendy may have retaliated with a few harmless flirtations. Which may partly account for her dismissal from Red Oaks. The golfers from the ferry. Has Hank has ever been jealous? In this cold war period of their marriage, he has all the advantage: he's the only man she's ever loved.

South Beach is a mile from the house, but he takes a detour so they can pass by last year's rental. "Humor me," he says when she protests.

"It's too sad. The girls were with us."

"Why can't you enjoy memories like other people? This is our life."

"Fine. Keep driving." She avoids the old houses because she loved their life. Last summer, she took a wrong turn and found herself in front of the yellow Cape they'd rented in their late thirties. The girls had raced their scooters up and down that long driveway. Hank's father had just handed him the company's reins, and she'd made it to the quarterfinals of the U.S. Women's Mid-Amateur the month before. They were invincible. Idling at the curb, she had the feeling then that she could walk through the Cape's green door and reenter that magic time.

Would she go back now if it means she has to face Hank's affair again, the girls leaving home, and her stillborn dreams for a pro career? When Hank pulls up to last summer's house, she pretends to look, but behind her sunglasses, her eyes are closed.

The lifeguards and families are packing up for the day when Wendy and Hank arrive. The sun, low in the cloud-streaked sky, turns the sand golden. She sinks into the beach chair with the *Times*. He strips to his trunks and races into the water. When he disappears inside a cresting wave, she imagines his spine snapping in the rough surf. The image persists long after he bobs to the surface and swims a vigorous crawl.

She pulls his phone from his pocket, enters his passcode (their daughters' combined birthdays, his code for everything). He waves to her from the water. She returns the phone to his pocket and pretends to read. Minutes later, drops fall from above, darkening the newsprint. He looms over her. "Didn't you hear me calling?"

"Why'd you get out?" She stands to remove her sarong. "I was just coming in."

"Maybe later." He smiles tightly.

She unpacks their dinner on the blue blanket. They eat separated by the cooler and a thick silence. Two terns hop in the surf's yellow foam. A large gull swoops and scatters them. When she looks over at him, Hank turns away. She drops her half-eaten sandwich into the cooler. The last time he was this tense Valentina was in the picture. She draws up her knees and rests her forehead on them. After a moment, his heavy arm drapes across her shoulders. "Truce?" he says.

"Why are you acting like such an asshole?"

He takes his arm away. "I don't know. Maybe I miss the girls."

"Christmas we'll all be together." She hopes they're not the kind of couple that can only thrive with the distraction of family. "If we spend it with *my* parents for a change, we can ski."

"Guess it'll be here before we know it." He makes Christmas sound like something he can't fully believe in, like his own death. He climbs to his feet, brushing crumbs from his chest. She waits for him to say he'll be in L.A. for the holidays. "Let's check with the girls," he says. It's not an answer, but she can breathe again.

He returns to the car with the cooler and comes back with their sand wedges and a bucket of range balls. They set up several yards back from the blue blanket. Except for the occasional shoreline stroller, they have the beach to themselves. She lands shot after shot on their makeshift green, but Hank consistently misses the mark. He swears and strikes his club on the sand. Was he always such a spoiled brat? When they first met at the Roaring Fork Golf Course in Aspen (she was a twenty-four-year-old mid-amateur, struggling to make ends meet with concession stand duties and golf lessons), Ulf Bruckheimer asked her to check his visiting nephew's setup. A minor adjustment was all it took for Hank to drive his ball two hundred and fifty yards. "Beginner's luck," he said, and she fell in love. It took longer for the Bruckheimers to fall in love with her. The golf instructor from the working-class family was not who they'd imagined for the heir to the family's multimillion-dollar construction firm.

"I used to be good at this," he says. "What happened?"

"Give yourself a better lie." She levels the sand with her foot. His failure makes her feel magnanimous. "Play it up in your stance." She moves to help him, but he drops the club and heads sulkily to the chair. She hesitates, but he tells her to continue.

"I like watching you," he says. "You're a natural."

Her skill is a result of hard work—nothing has ever come easy—but she lets his comment go. She wiggles her hips before taking her next shot. He wolf-whistles. To hell with Red Oaks. So, maybe she did flirt: the older men need their egos stroked. But she'd outgrown that idiotic game, and that's probably why they're replacing her with a member's twenty-four-year-old niece, a U.S. Girls' Junior Runner-Up. Poor girl. She'll learn the score soon enough. I'll find another club, Wendy thinks; it's not too late for me.

When the sun sets, they pack up the Jeep and drive back in the dark. They sail past the old airfield, a grassy meadow dotted with biplanes. She imagines their Jeep lifting into the starry sky. "What's the forecast for tomorrow?" she says.

"Hot, ninety degrees. It's the fiftieth anniversary of the Ted Kennedy Chappaquiddick thing."

"That's right," she says. "We were here the same time last year. Wasn't there something on TV?"

"We found that book," he says. *Whitewash at Chappaquiddick.* She remembers the 1975 mildewed paperback they came across on a shelf in their rental house. "Actually," Hank says, "the author's giving a bicycle tour at six o'clock. I saw an ad in the *Vineyard Gazette.* We should go."

"What for? We read the book." The author had laid out Kennedy's account of the accident alongside the facts to support his argument for privilege run amok. It made for a compelling read, but now the idea of a scandal tour makes her uneasy. "Besides," she says, "we'd have to rent bikes."

"That shouldn't be a problem."

He pulls into the driveway, cuts the ignition. The house is a hulking shadow against the grainy sky; they forgot the porch lights. He unlatches his seatbelt and reaches across the console to slide his hand under her sarong. He wriggles his finger inside her bathing suit bottoms. Aroused, she opens her legs for him. She is the seductive, irresistible mistress. He is another woman's husband.

The sounds of laughter and voices come from the street. The spell is broken. She is the wronged wife again. She pushes his hand away.

THAT NIGHT SHE DREAMS the girl from the ferry is down on her knees, giving Hank a blowjob. His moans arouse her.

She stands behind the girl, stroking her hair and whispering encouragement. The girl morphs into a black lab, growling and snapping its teeth. Wendy wakes with a gasp. Hank is gone. A moan comes from the hallway. She finds him in the bathroom on his knees, embracing the toilet. He looks up at her, eyes bloodshot. "Fucking lobster roll," he says.

HANK SLEEPS THROUGH THE morning. The bedroom is clammy with sea air and the sour smell of puke. She picks up his discarded clothes and finds his phone in his pocket. She plugs it into the charger on the night table without checking it. She starts to leave, but stops at the door. Lying on his side with his knees drawn up, Hank looks like a boy. Ted Kennedy, partying with Mary Jo, was convinced he'd get away with adultery and sail on through his charmed life. She removes Hank's phone from the charger and scans his call log and texts.

Downstairs in the kitchen she washes her hands again. It's no use: she can't get the smell of Hank's vomit out of her nose. In the yard, she lies down on the lounge chair in the shade of a maple. Two hours later, she wakes in the blazing sun, feeling restless and prickly, stranded without Hank. She heads for the garden shed to look for a bucket to use for putting practice. In the cool, gasoline darkness, among the rakes, hoes, and clay pots, she spots a green touring bike. She rolls it outside for inspection. The tires are a bit soft. The brakes work. She rides it over the bumpy lawn, ringing the rusted bell, and parks it in the driveway.

She showers and changes into blue culottes and a pink polo. She leans over Hank. "Mind if I go out?" He doesn't respond. She shakes his shoulder until he opens his eyes. "I'm going out," she says. "Want anything?"

"Sleep." He closes his eyes again.

"I found a bike in the shed. Thought I'd check out that tour."

He raises his hand as though giving his blessing.

AT SIX O'CLOCK, WENDY disembarks from the Chappy ferry. Three cyclists are gathered near the shingled ferry shack: two heavy-set middle-aged women in purple helmets and an elderly woman. Wendy walks her bike over and waits. Minutes later, a man pedals up and introduces himself as Mike Saldona, their guide. Of course he looks nothing like his groovy 1975 book jacket photo. With his gray beard and Greek fisherman's cap, he's more like the man on the Gorton's fish sticks box. He collects ten dollars from each of them and checks his watch.

"Let's wait for stragglers," he says, making her pity him. But isn't she more pitiful: a woman seeking answers from another's misfortune?

She walks off a few yards to call Hank. The small barge-like ferry has returned from Edgartown with three more cars and a few cyclists. While Hank's cell rings, she pictures him dead, choked to death on his vomit. "Wendy?" He clears his throat, but his voice is still raspy. "Don't worry. Have fun at your thing."

He has no idea where she is, and that makes her feel like she's nowhere. She stares out across the channel at the shingle-style houses dotting the Edgartown shoreline, at the American flag flapping on the tall mast over the fishing pier. Dazed, she returns to the group. Two sunburned teenage girls wearing heart-shaped sunglasses have joined them, their floral perfume overpowering even in the outdoors.

The girls elbow each other, giggling. One shoots up her hand. "Did Kennedy really swim across after he left Mary Jo to drown in his car?"

"Spoiler alert!" Mike says, and everyone laughs. "As a matter of fact, you're right; he *claimed* he swam across after missing the last ferry. It's one hundred and seventy-five yards."

Everyone turns to look at the channel. A strong current carries a Styrofoam cup southward toward the lighthouse. The ferry sails back to Edgartown, a five-iron shot away.

"Let's not get ahead of ourselves," Mike says. "We'll start with the post-regatta party where Kennedy and his friends and the so-called"—he makes air quotes—"Boiler Room Girls spent the early evening hours of July 18, 1969. Hop on your bikes, folks. It's three miles to the cottage where it all began."

The teenagers cut off the old lady in their rush to ride up front with Mike. He's explaining that the Boiler Room Girls worked on Bobby Kennedy's '68 campaign. One of the purple helmets comes to a dead stop, and Wendy swerves to avoid her. As they pass the striped cabanas at the private beach club—featured in *Jaws,* Mike informs them—Wendy deliberately falls back. She has the irrational thought that what she's about to see are not the sights connected to Kennedy's tragedy—the fork in the road, the narrow bridge, the murky pond—but, rather, scenes from Hank's affair. She soft-pedals past the marshy tidal pools, letting more distance grow between herself and the others. Cars slow behind her. A red pickup takes forever to pass. She waves it on.

The scrub pines offer no shade. Feeling woozy, she stops at the Chappy Store, a shack surrounded by junked cars and overgrown weeds. The interior is unfinished with plank flooring and exposed studs and beams. A man with good calf muscles blocks the refrigerator case, and she has to reach around him to grab a bottle of water. She pays the pretty teenage girl at the register.

"Didn't I see you on that Kennedy tour?" The man is behind her, cradling two bags of ice. In his early forties, he resembles a Kennedy with droopy eyelids, sandy hair, and a careless smile. She moves aside, and he drops the bags on the counter. "Yeah, I'm sure it was you," he says. "You're hard to miss in *that* crowd."

She flushes, pleased. "I had a change of heart."

"Shame on that guy, making money off of someone's bad luck."

She narrows her eyes. "Bad luck? Is that what you call it?"

"Mary Jo's, I mean." He tosses money on the counter. "I'm Rory Barrett." He extends his hand, and she goes forward to shake it. "Wendy." She likes his clean, soapy smell.

"You headed to the regatta party?" he says.

"I don't know anything about it."

"My cousin Ian's on the winning crew." The girl behind the register hoists herself up onto the counter, giving Wendy and Rory a full view of her tanned thighs. She seems aware of her own attractiveness. "Tell him to save me some beer. I get off in an hour."

"You're underage." Rory sounds rueful. "No drinking allowed."

Wendy starts for the door, feeling ignored. She pauses. "You don't happen to have a bike pump, do you?" Before the girl can answer, Rory says, "There's one at the house. I'll give you a lift. You can check out the party."

She imagines eating alone in that cramped kitchen. Hank will be awake soon, summoning her to his sickroom. "Maybe for a little while," she says.

"Throw your bike in my truck." He shoulders the bags of ice. She opens the door for him and follows him outside. She grabs her bike. When he opens the passenger door of the red pickup, a black lab springs out and makes a beeline for her crotch. She fends off the dog with her water bottle. "Tino! Get in!" Rory waits near the lowered tailgate. The lab lopes off, jumps in, and whumps its tail against the hard floor.

She walks her bike over. "Go on," Rory says. "Pitch her in."

The truck smells of sunbaked leather and damp dog. A warm breeze from the open window blows strands of hair loose from her clip. She takes a swig of water, rests her feet on the dashboard. She's in Aspen again, traveling the backcountry roads. She shouts over the wind and rattling chassis, "Are you a local or a summer person?"

"I live in Boston, but I've been coming since I was in diapers," he says. "I'd say that makes me a local."

"Sure, you are." Ted Kennedy probably thought so, too. She spent her adolescence learning the distinction. The rich boys that kept her interested with kisses and prodding fingers in the bag room, but showed up at parties with girls from their private schools. The concession girls called them "gingerbread boys"; they were indistinguishable.

He slows the truck. The tour group is gathered in front of a small white house she recognizes from the photos. Rory toots his horn in warning before pulling past them into the next driveway. He jumps out and rounds the back of the truck. She gets out too, and the dog darts inside of the house ahead of her. When her eyes adjust to the darkness, she notes the seventies décor: orange shag rug, pine paneling, macramé plant holders. Except for the whirring fan, the house is quiet. Worry overshadows her thrill at being next door to the Kennedy party house.

In the kitchen Rory dumps the ice with a clatter into the soapstone sink. Beer bottles are lined up on the countertop. He plunges them two at a time into the ice. She steps forward to help. On the other side of the window about forty people mill around and under a white tent. The sound of voices and faint strains of music carry. Witnesses. She's relieved. The dog nuzzles her crotch. She pushes it away, aware Rory is watching. "Come on," he says, opening the door. "Let's get you a cold one."

On the patchy lawn, the mood is celebratory. People have the unsteady gait and blurry expression that comes with an afternoon of drinking. While Rory talks to a lanky blond guy, she loads up a plate with baked beans and chicken. Rory ends his conversation without introducing her. She's annoyed but lets it go when he smiles at her. He hands her a beer, and she notices his gold insignia ring. Usually, she doesn't like jewelry on men. They take a seat on a bench in the shade, and she steadies herself with furtive swigs of the beer. "This your house?" she says.

"My buddy's, Miller." He points to the lanky guy. "His grandfather left it to him. My family's place is up island. In Chilmark."

"That's the Ted Kennedy party house next door, isn't it?" He nods and she asks, "Did Miller's grandfather get mixed up in any of that?"

He takes a second to register her question. "No idea." His voice sounds irritated. She tenses. Why does she care what he thinks? She has no intention of sleeping with him. She's not even sure she likes him. She drains her beer and places the bottle on the grass. He picks it up and heads to the tent.

She relaxes and takes in the scene. The guests, from the preteens to the octogenarians, look suntanned and healthy. Their easy manner makes her think that this is one more party in a long line of summer parties, stretching back for decades. She spots Rory talking to a woman near the bar. Wendy can't see her face but guesses she's in her twenties: only a younger woman can get away with that long, straight, center-parted hair. Her green silk halter dress and gold bangles broadcast good taste, old money. Wendy knows her type. Free spirits, people call them. How free would they be without the safety net of family wealth? On her own home turf, they made her feel like an outsider. She's at the ninth-hole concession stand again wearing her JCPenney golf clothes, feeling invisible.

Rory returns and hands her a red cup. She gulps, thinking it is water, and splutters. "Gin?"

He chuckles. "Want something else?"

"It's fine." Her head feels pleasantly warm. She takes another swig.

He makes a point of looking her up and down and asks what she does. "Gym teacher? Personal trainer?" His guesses insult her.

"Golf pro." She's pleased when his eyes light with interest.

"Should've known. You seem coolheaded. You need that with golf, right?"

"Absolutely. You can't let every little setback fluster you." She thinks about Valentina. Her lost job. The alcohol makes her maudlin. She needs to pace herself. "Can I tell you something I haven't told anyone?" He shrugs. "I was let go last week. Replaced by a member's niece. A child. No one who's serious about the game is going to ask that kid for instruction. That's what the pro's counting on, I bet. Between you and me, he couldn't handle the competition, and that's why he let me go." She doesn't know why she tells him this.

He reaches down for his cup on the grass, and his knee bumps hers. He doesn't move away and neither does she. "You must be good," he says.

"Better than good. Four handicap. I was runner-up in the U.S. Women's Amateur at twenty-four." He jerks back with apparent awe. That's the respect she deserves, not an out-of-the-blue firing. She drains her cup. "I'll be fine. A few places are fighting over me already," she says. "Like I tell my golfers: if you let yourself get discouraged after one bad shot, you're doomed."

"Yup." He looks off.

"How about you?" She touches his arm. "You play?"

"Not as often as I'd like, but I get to the range. Short game's pretty decent. Could use some help with my driver though." As he talks, he seems to be searching the crowd. Wendy follows his gaze to the young woman; she's talking to a blond surfer type, a guy closer to her own age. "Don't get me wrong." He puffs out his chest. "I can hit it wicked far: two hundred, maybe two hundred and fifty yards."

Wendy affects a look of admiration, but he doesn't see it; he's focused on the girl. She touches the surfer's cheek, and her bracelets slide up her tanned arm. Wendy senses Rory's distress. "If I could just keep it in the fairway," he says. "I'd be golden."

"That's the problem with you younger guys. You don't want to give up any of your amazing power for accuracy."

He gives her his full attention.

"It's a matter of control. You might have to sacrifice a little of that distance at first." She's in the zone, relying on instinct. "You have to harness all that power. Make it work for you, not against you."

He looks at her searchingly. She confidently holds his gaze. "Let's go inside," he says.

WENDY WAKES NAKED IN the dark, airless bedroom. She has cottonmouth and her shoulder is sore. Rory, with her encouragement, was a bit rough, pinning her arm back as he shoved himself into her from behind. She didn't want tenderness the first time she fucked someone who wasn't Hank. She hears raspy breathing: Tino, sprawled on the double bed beside her. She sits up and spots the half-empty gin bottle on the dresser. She's numb but knows she'll be sick with regret later. Don't think, she tells herself; get out before anyone sees you.

She gropes the night table for her phone. The battery's almost dead. It's 11:45. Four texts from Hank: *feeling better. where r u? r u ok?* And the last one: *worried. call me.* She starts to call, but if they argue, someone might hear: she'll call from the street. She leaves the bed and finds her clothes. Her head throbs as she bends for her sandals. The dog follows her into the hallway. Low, lazy voices float over the harmonizing notes of Crosby, Stills, & Nash. Tino pushes past, bounds into the living room, and leaps onto the couch.

"Sleeping Beauty wakes!" Miller smiles at her and hugs the dog.

The young woman with the Sharon Tate hair lounges on the couch beside him, wearing a white bikini, the gold bangles. Her long legs are propped on the coffee table. Rory kneels beside the table, rolling a joint. He keeps his eyes on his task.

"I have to go." She holds onto the doorframe to steady herself.

"You're welcome to stay. Plenty of room." Miller gets up to let the dog outside. "But if you're going, you'd better shake a leg. Last ferry's at midnight."

"I have to go. My husband's sick."

Rory and Miller exchange a glance. The woman says, "Go already. What's stopping you?" Rory lays a hand on her leg, and her lips tighten, as though holding something back.

Mortified, Wendy brushes past Miller at the door and stumbles down the steps. The air vibrates with insects. The darkness swallows her as she crosses the uneven lawn and heads for the street. She digs in her pocket for her phone.

"Hey, wait up. Hold on."

Rory comes down the steps and hobbles barefoot to the pickup. He opens the driver's door. Tino emerges from the darkness and leaps inside. "Don't be stupid, you can't walk; you'll miss the ferry." When she doesn't move, he softens his tone. "Come on. I'm a little buzzed, but it's a straight shot. Rent-a-cop's an old friend."

They drive in silence with the dog panting between them. If she keeps her eyes on the road, she can manage her vertigo. She wants to tell him that he's a shitty lover, but it's not true. She needs someone to blame for how lost she feels. "Look, I don't want you to think..." she begins, but he's pulling up to the water's edge.

"Ferry should be along any minute," he says as though she hasn't spoken. Fighting off a wave of nausea, she climbs out and slams the door. The lab whines to get out. Rory restrains him by the collar and says through the open window. "Hope your husband's okay."

She gives him a tight smile. He backs up the truck with Tino barking and makes a K-turn. The red taillights recede in the darkness. She remembers the bike.

She makes her way to the small dock, fighting back tears. No one's waiting for the ferry. She takes out her phone: the battery's dead. On the far shore, the lights blur and waver. The clock on the ferry shed reads 12:06. What now? Instead of sobering her, the long nap has fogged her brain. She looks beyond the parking lot to the shadowy road. Past the salt marshes, there's a scattering of houses. Even if she were able to phone Hank, how could he help her now?

All that separates her from everyone and everything she loves is a small expanse of water. She removes her sandals and stashes them along with her phone under the bush near the shack. If Ted could manage it, so can she. The sand is cool as she makes her way down to the shoreline. She wades in, gasping at the cold. The murky, oily water lifts her culottes, billowing them around her waist. Before she can change her mind, she plunges forward. She takes her first stroke then another, settling into a steady rhythm, one she can maintain for hours if she has to. But she won't have to. The Edgartown shore is a five-iron shot away.

She lifts her head. What's she looking at? Marsh grass and cattails. The back of a house. The current has dragged her off course. She churns her arms faster, kicks harder. I can do this, she thinks; I got this. When she looks up again, she's halfway across but farther south, closer to the marina and the lighthouse than the Edgartown ferry dock.

Exhausted, she flips onto her back to catch her breath. Ragged clouds erase the moon from the sky. Hank's text said he was worried. Worried about her. Remembering this elates her. The black pocket of the sky glitters with stars. She feels as light as a Styrofoam cup as the current pulls her farther from Chappaquiddick Point. She turns over again. No more drifting. She takes a deep breath and then plunges her face into the cold water to swim again.

ACKNOWLEDGMENTS

Thank you to the editors who first published these stories, sometimes in slightly different versions: "Alamo," *Green Mountains Review*; "Wild Quaker Parrot," *Cimarron Review*; "Escape Artist," *Bellingham Review*; "Fearless," *Colorado Review*; "Creature Comforts," *Michigan Quarterly Review*; "Tabor Lake, 1993," *Michigan Quarterly Review*; "Wilderness of Ghosts," *Glimmer Train*; "Coyote," *Southern Humanities Review*; "Please See Me," *Chautauqua Journal*; "Be Here Now," *West Branch*; "After the Party," *Southern Humanities Review*.

Special thanks to Peg Alford Pursell for dreaming up Betty Books and inviting me to be a part of her dream. Her warm encouragement and insightful edits are deeply appreciated. And thank you to my colleagues at Betty Books, the talented inaugural authors, who brought their vision and expertise to my book's publication: Leah Browning, Polly Buckingham, Haley Hach, Patricia Henley, Joanna Choi Kalbus, Marianne Villanueva, and Sharon White.

Thank you to my friends for generously reading multiple drafts or otherwise offering their friendship, inspiration, and support: Rob Jacklosky, Anastasia Rubis, Jim Nash, Karla Greenleaf-MacEwan, Colleen Morton Busch, Sarah Gauch, David Galef, Randy Breindel, Lisa Manser, and Susan Gurian.

Thank you to my father, Gene Newman, for his humor, support, and love, and for being the first to show me the writing ropes. To my mother, Barbara Newman, for revealing the magic of storytelling and for her loving encouragement. And to my brother, Steven Newman, and sisters, Carolyn Duffy and Denise Newman, for their intelligent writing advice and for their kindness and friendship.

Many of the stories in this collection were developed in workshops led by generous writers and teachers, including Tessa Hadley, Antonya Nelson, and Robert Boswell—and for this, I am thankful. Additional thanks for support from the Vermont Studio Center and the Virginia Center for the Creative Arts where a few of these stories were written. And to Beth McCabe, Executive Director of the Rona Jaffe Foundation.

And finally, I am forever grateful to Michael and to our daughters, Caroline and Sarah, for making my life sweeter and more complete.

photo credit: Joey Pedras

ABOUT THE AUTHOR

Janis Hubschman has published over two dozen short stories in literary magazines that include *Cimarron Review, Chautauqua Journal, Southern Humanities Review, Colorado Review,* and *Green Mountains Review*. Her stories have won *Bellingham Review's* Tobias Wolff Award and a first-place award from *Glimmer Train*. She has published essays in *The New York Times, Glimmer Train Bulletin,* and *New York Runner*. She was the recipient of a Bread Loaf-Rona Jaffe Fiction Scholarship and a fellowship from the Virginia Center for the Creative Arts. She lives with her husband in New Jersey where she was born and raised and where many of her stories take place. She currently teaches fiction writing at Montclair State University. *Take Me With You Next Time* is her first book.

ABOUT BETTY

Founded in 2023, Betty is an imprint of WTAW Press, with a mission to publish books of prose by women for everyone. Betty aims to showcase and celebrate the diversity of women's voices.

By focusing on women's voices, Betty Books can contribute to a more nuanced understanding of women's experiences and foster empathy, understanding, and dialogue on important issues.

WTAW Press is a 501(c)(3) nonprofit publisher devoted to discovering and publishing enduring literary works of prose. WTAW publishes and champions a carefully curated list of titles across a range of genres (literary fiction, creative nonfiction, and prose that falls somewhere in between), subject matter, and perspectives. WTAW welcomes submissions from writers of all backgrounds and aims to support authors throughout their careers.

As a nonprofit literary press, WTAW depends on the support of donors. We are grateful for the assistance we receive from organizations, foundations, and individuals. To find out more about our mission and publishing program, or to make a donation, please visit wtawpress.org.